D1154071

Acclaim for

FOR WHOM THE SUN SINGS

"*For Whom the Sun Sings* presents a unique perspective on the world with an unexpected twist. One of the best stories I've read all year!"

—MORGAN L. BUSSE, award-winning author of The Ravenwood Saga

"*For Whom the Sun Sings* is a finely written and well-paced narrative that tells us that seeing the truth is one thing, but doing something about it is quite something else. A great read."

—DAVID D. ESSELSTROM, PH.D., Professor Emeritus, Dept. of English, Azusa Pacific University

FOR WHOM THE SUN SINGS

W.A. FULKERSON

Published by Enclave Publishing, an imprint of Third Day Books, LLC

Phoenix, Arizona, USA.
www.enclavepublishing.com

ISBN: 978-1-62184-117-3 (printed hardback)
ISBN: 978-1-62184-119-7 (printed softcover)
ISBN: 978-1-62184-118-0 (ebook)

Cover design by LoriAnn Weldon, www.Magpie-Designs.Weebly.com
Typesetting by Jamie Foley, www.JamieSFoley.com

Printed in the United States of America.

For everyone who has ever felt like
they are alone in knowing the truth.

ANDRIUS STARTED THE DAY LIKE HE STARTED EVERY other day: he opened his eyes.

It was still early and his song rang freshly inside his head. He remained under the woolen covers a moment and whispered the lyrics to himself.

"Who can make a world for us?
Zydrunas, Zydrunas
The strongest heart he turned to dust,
Zydrunas, Zydrunas
He made a place for us to be
Fought back the disease–"

Andrius stopped. That part didn't rhyme exactly, and the rhythm wasn't too good either. It hadn't stuck out to him when he was making it up yesterday, but now it sounded wrong. He would have to fix it before he arrived at lessons. Andrius wasn't very good at music. It seemed like he was the only one who struggled with it.

Take-home assignments were not his strong suit.

Andrius snuggled deeper into the warm, scratchy blankets. It was hard to hear this early in the day because the sun wasn't singing yet. The cows, however, were singing. They lowed softly from across the barn, asking to be milked. He hoped Daiva wouldn't hear them from the house.

"Andrius!" a husky voice called out, making him wince. "Are you deaf?"

He was out of the covers in an instant, trying not to topple the pile of hay that made up his bed.

"The cows need to be milked and you're sleeping in," the same voice shrilled. "Lazy cad!"

Of course she had heard the cows lowing. Father said that Daiva had ears as sharp as her tongue. Of course, even as Daiva chastised Andrius for lying in bed, he knew that doubtlessly she was doing the same, but Andrius didn't think about that. Instead, blinking sleep from his eyes, he walked to the milking pail and took it in his hands. He took a sip of water from his wooden pitcher, then he picked up the milking stool and made his way to the cows.

Teats felt uncomfortable in his hands. He hated milking. He hoped the sun would sing soon so that he could at least hear.

"ANDRIUS? IS THAT YOU?"

Andrius smiled as he entered the house, looking for something to eat. There was a plate on the table with five boiled eggs and a pile of bacon on top of a bowl of swelled grain.

"Yes, Father."

"Have you finished your chores?"

Andrius reached into his pockets and delicately placed each egg he withdrew into the basket hanging on the wall. The chickens were laying well recently. Spring was good for eggs.

"Yes, Father."

"Good, good. You're a good boy, Andrius."

His father took a bite of one of the eggs on his own plate, which was more reasonably portioned: two eggs, one piece of bacon, and a spoonful of grain. He was a thin man and his wispy hair betrayed his age.

Andrius kissed his whiskery cheek and sat down next to him, stomach growling.

Suddenly the door slammed and Andrius jolted, dropping a piece of bacon.

"Andrius!"

The shrill sound took the slouch right out of him. He turned his head toward Daiva.

"Hello, dear," his father greeted her gently.

"Aleksandras, is your name Andrius? Am I speaking to you?"

"No, dear."

"Then keep your 'dears' to yourself." Daiva slammed a meaty hand on the table and slid it to the teeming plates in front of Andrius. She pushed them away. "How many eggs did you collect today, Andrius?"

"Seven."

"Liar."

"You can check. They're in the basket."

Daiva frowned, then lumbered her way over to the wall. She had ratty hair that she rarely bothered to brush and speckles on her arms just like the eggs. She was much younger than her husband, but that did not make her pleasant. She had a quick temper and she never let anyone touch her. Hugs were out of the question, not that Andrius particularly wanted to hug her.

"And I know you aren't sitting in my seat," she said as she touched the fresh eggs in the basket, counting them.

There were only two stools, so of course he was in her seat. He stood up.

"Let the boy have a seat," Aleksandras said. "He's been on his feet all morning."

"And I haven't?" Daiva challenged as she counted the freshly collected eggs once more. "Certainly, put the boy in a seat but let your darling wife who slaves away all day long stand on her feet. Yes, I understand your point, Aleksandras."

His father leaned over. "You better stand up, Andrius," he said in an undertone. Andrius was standing already.

The floor shook as Daiva lumbered over to the table, felt for her seat, then collapsed into it. She was breathing from her mouth like she usually did. Andrius wasn't overly fond of the noise, but he stayed quiet. Daiva reached forward and pulled the mountain of eggs, bacon, and grain toward her and she began to eat.

She was a loud chewer, not bothering to close her mouth much of the time. Andrius's stomach grumbled.

"Are you still standing there?" Daiva asked halfway through her fourth egg. "Go to your lessons."

"I haven't had any breakfast yet."

"You're doing a poor job with the chickens."

"But you just counted the eggs! There were seven this morning and six yesterday."

"You're flustering them when you collect. That will make them lay less often, so I'm making up for it by saving eggs this morning. Now go to your lessons."

Andrius's shoulders slumped. This was so unfair. He

grumbled inwardly along with his stomach as he picked up his water pitcher and walked out the door.

He muttered to himself once he was far enough away that no one would hear him. "I need to eat something."

The door clamored shut and he turned around. His father was approaching, bumbling along as fast as he was able.

"Andrius!" he called. "Andrius, wait a moment!"

The old man caught up to him and let go of the rope that led from the main road to where they lived on Twenty-fifth Stone.

"Andrius," he said again.

"Yes, Father?"

Aleksandras held out a hand with two long, narrow sticks.

"You forgot your cane."

"Thanks, Papa."

Andrius took the walking stick and Aleksandras tussled his hair.

"Did you finish your song for your lessons today?"

"Not yet. I have something but it isn't right. I'll finish it as I walk."

His father, bent over, nodded in agreement.

"Yes, yes you will. You're a smart boy. You'll figure it out." He smiled. "How are your magic ears? Ready for tonight?"

Andrius stood his four-and-a-half-foot body a little straighter.

"They're sharp as ever."

"Herkus says he has a set of stones so smooth he'll finally crack your winning streak.

"The only thing he will hear crack is his heart when he realizes how much he has lost to us."

They laughed together then. The sun was now singing loudly overhead. He could feel its rays on his skin.

"That's my Andrius. You're a smart boy. Do well at lessons. You're always forgetting your cane."

Andrius held the stick in front of his face. He didn't know what the big deal was.

Aleksandras lowered his voice and reached into his pocket.

"Also," he said, "you forgot this." A beautiful boiled egg appeared in Aleksandras's hand, wrapped in cloth. Andrius practically leaped for joy. He took the food and kissed Aleksandras on his whiskered cheek.

"Thank you, Papa."

"Shh," Aleksandras whispered. He tilted his head up to listen for a moment. Hearing nothing, he patted Andrius on the shoulder. "Enjoy your lessons," he said louder. He chuckled to himself. "Is that your water pitcher sloshing around? Why do you always carry it with you?"

"I get thirsty a lot. Thanks, Father."

Aleksandras grunted in assent and made his way back to the house holding onto the rope with one hand and his cane with the other.

Andrius took a bite out of the warm egg and sighed in satisfaction. He skipped every few steps as he went on his way along Stone Road.

The village was divided into three main sections, each with its own road snaking out from the town center. Andrius lived on Twenty-fifth Stone, which is to say that he lived twenty-five roadstones from the town center. The roadstones were conveniently placed by the side of the road at regular intervals so a person walking along might keep track of his place. The other sections were Brick, where Andrius was currently headed, and Wood, which he had no real business going to, but he was a curious boy so he explored there whenever he got the chance. No one else in his age group seemed to much like exploring, so Andrius went alone. He did most things alone.

Andrius peeled away the last segment of shell and finished off his egg. He could feel strength coming into his bones again from the nourishment. He was uncommonly skinny, but he didn't always notice that sort of thing about himself.

He was a bit old for skipping, but his father's smuggled breakfast put a spring in his step and he continued to do it anyway, humming his song to himself, trying to fix the broken lyric. The end was good, but those few lines were terrible. He hated music.

A lark swooped across Stone Road in front of him and he started, then laughed.

"You're brave," he said after the bird, who was already flying away. It whistled like nothing had happened, and Andrius listened with delight. "That's the sort of music I like," he said aloud. "Not all this business with words and rhyme. The birds have it right. I'm awful with words." He had a bad habit of speaking to himself.

The lark held his attention as he traveled on, passing Tenth Stone and Ninth Stone, until it flew across the sun. Andrius blinked and turned away. He stopped to raise his wooden pitcher to his mouth, and then he dipped a hand in the water and wiped his eyes. His cane remained tucked into the back of his pants. He was already carrying his pitcher and he did not want to have his hands full.

It was beautiful where he lived. The huts and barns were nothing spectacular though the roads were nice enough. What really captivated Andrius was the mountains, the thick forests, and the rushing stream that cut through Stone and Wood. The village was situated in the valley below a crown of mountains:

tall, sheer, and majestic. They were as bare of trees as the road he walked on, and they never ceased to amaze him.

No one else seemed interested in the mountains. He would tell the others to listen, to stop and pay attention to their glorious song, but they only laughed and said they couldn't hear it. They said no one else had Andrius's "magic" ears. Only his father would humor him, sitting beside him, trying to hear the sound of the far-off mountains.

As Andrius approached Third Stone, there were more people on the road, so the going was slower. He thought they were overly cautious as they dragged their loads, buying and selling, planting and growing and going. Andrius dodged through some villagers carrying chickens and he stepped out of the path of an old nag. The road was clearer after that. He was halfway to Second Stone when he saw it, and his heart caught in his throat.

Gimdymo Namai: the most sacred site in all of the world.

None of the modest buildings were terribly interesting in the three sections of the village, but Gimdymo Namai was different. It was wonderful.

It was built from stone, for one thing–something that no other structure could claim. It was bigger, having a set of stairs, a second level, and supposedly rooms below it, beneath the ground. It was smooth all around, as if it had been carved from a single stone instead of masoned together. Its curved walls had large wooden shutters that could open or close to let in the air, which was pleasant during the summer and a vexation during the winter. Supposedly when their ancestors had built it, Zydrunas had decreed that all the windows would be made not of wood but of a smooth material that let in heat and kept out cold. Over the years, the first-floor windows must have been broken, but on the second floor, smaller windows were still present with this material. Andrius had heard that it was called "glass," but he wasn't sure.

Today, the large shutters were open. A delivery must have lasted through the night. Andrius wanted so badly to listen to what went on inside those smooth walls. He heid his pitcher in front of him and ran as best as he could while carrying the heavy thing and ignoring the stick that poked his backside every time he took a step.

Why did his parents always want him to bring his cane? It was stupid.

Though, to be fair, Andrius seemed to be just about the only one who felt this way. It was just another of his many unpopular opinions.

"Push, Ona, push. Take your breaths regularly now. Push, Ona."

A rich, soothing voice carried from inside the building as Andrius ran past First Stone. The delivery was still in progress! He could hardly contain his excitement. He'd never been around when a delivery was happening before. A woman's tired scream rang out from the sacred site.

"That's it, Ona. You're almost there. Keep pushing."

Andrius stopped running, and he stilled the sloshing liquid in his pitcher. He took a drink, then ran his eyes over the area. No one was paying attention to him. He tiptoed closer to the action until he was next to the wide-open window. He could hardly believe it.

"There we are. I have his head in my hands. One more good push, Ona, and we're through."

The woman screamed again. She was facing away from the window where Andrius stood. It smelled funny inside. The woman was drenched in sweat and there were bloody rags on the floor.

"Wow," Andrius whispered. He set his pitcher on the window ledge and leaned in.

The man in front of the woman was none other than the Prophet himself. Of course it would be him–he was the one who brought life into the world, but Andrius was struck by his focus, his heroism, his dedication.

There was the sound of crying suddenly, but it wasn't the mother. The Prophet stood up cradling a newborn infant in his arms.

"Can I hold him?"

There was no rejoicing yet. The Prophet kept his demeanor, acting decisively in the face of crisis.

"Ona," he replied to her, "you know how many the disease has taken. We must give him the cure quickly. Solveiga," he ordered the midwife, "tie off the cord."

The baby was wailing loudly, squirming its tiny fingers and toes. Solveiga took him in her arms and set him on a table where she quickly and expertly tied off the cord.

Then, already having wiped his hands clean, the Prophet took a pitcher into his hands and began to pour its contents onto the child's head. Solveiga prevented the viscous liquid from entering its mouth. It continued to scream.

"Shh, baby," Ona urged her newborn. "You won't be like the lost ones. The medicine will save you in time."

"The eyes are full of mystery," the Prophet declared as he smeared the cure across the baby's brow and into the eyes, anointing them. "The disease attacks them, rendering the whole body unto death, but you will be spared, child, for you have received the cure."

The baby stopped crying then, and the Prophet smiled. Relief washed over the room.

"Hold your child, Ona."

Forgetting that he wasn't invited, Andrius leaned forward further and muttered to himself.

"That was amazing!"

"Andrius?"

A sudden panic gripped him. He ducked down and tried his best to be silent.

"Andrius, is that you? What are you doing over there?"

A precocious little girl Andrius's age stopped a few feet away awaiting a response. Andrius's eyes went up to his pitcher, then back to the girl.

"Milda, stop saying my name!" he hissed. In one quick, deft motion, Andrius reached up and snatched his pitcher from the window's ledge and bounded away as fast as he could manage.

"Who's there?" he heard the midwife call from the window, but Andrius wasn't slowing down. His water sloshed around in his pitcher as he ran. His cane continued to scratch his backside.

He hated the cane.

THE CHILDREN OF ANDRIUS'S AGE GROUP MET FOR lessons at Eighteenth Brick, which was a long way from his home. It was at the end of Brick so that the children might not disturb the adults who were busy working for the village in the afternoon. Brick was the shortest of the three roads, and there were rumors of building a new house soon: Nineteenth Brick.

But for the moment, Nineteenth Brick was nothing more than open sky, full of the sun's song and the mountain's rejoicing.

There wasn't even a brick yet.

Milda finally caught up with Andrius at Sixteenth Brick. Children were already gathered around the spreading fir tree that served as their shelter for lessons. He could hear them clearly.

"Andrius, I know you can hear me," Milda challenged from behind.

"I can," he replied as she came up alongside. She walked straight and with confidence unusual for an eleven-year-old girl. Her hair was loose around her neck and onto her back.

"You have those magic ears," she said.

"I don't have magic ears. I just hear better than everybody else."

"Sometimes."

"Always."

"What were you doing at Gimdymo Namai? We aren't supposed to hang around there. It's sacred."

"No one knew I was there until you opened your big mouth."

Milda scoffed.

"You're mean, Andrius. It's no wonder why you don't have any friends. And you're the one who opened his big mouth, if you remember."

"I have friends," Andrius returned defensively. Milda tapped her cane rhythmically, childishly in front of her as she walked. She smacked it against Seventeenth Brick as they passed it.

"Oh yeah? Like who?"

"People you don't know about."

Milda giggled. "I don't think so, Andrius. You don't have any friends because you're mean and you're weird and you talk about weird things that nobody cares about. Maybe I'll tell on you for creeping around Gimdymo Namai."

Andrius's eyes went wide.

"No! Don't do that, please."

"We'll see," she sang.

"Milda?" came a voice from up ahead. "Milda, come sit with us."

Milda obliged her friends and passed Andrius without so much as a goodbye. He kept his eyes on her as she went. He lifted his pitcher to his lips, taking a long drink of water. He felt sick to his stomach.

The instructor clapped his hands ahead, underneath the fir tree.

"Come along, children, come along. One at a time now, say your names so I know who's here, and we'll begin."

The grass crunched under Andrius's bare feet as he reached the group of children speaking their names.

"Berena."

"Viktoras."

"Ugna."

"Milda."

Andrius set his pitcher on the ground at the back of the group and removed his cane from the back of his pants. He sat down and said his name.

"Andrius."

The other children piped up until all nine of them had spoken. No one was missing today, not that anyone usually was. That would have been unthinkable, unless they were really, really sick.

The instructor, met with respectful silence, began.

"In preparation for the Day of Remembrance, we have been spending more time than usual on the subject of our beloved founder's life. We have discussed his childhood, early inspirations, his education, his training, and of course his philosophy, statesmanship, and his victory over the sudden onslaught of the disease. Today–" The instructor broke off and held up a hand.

"Viktoras, I can hear you whispering. Perhaps you would like to teach lessons today."

Viktoras halted mid-whisper and bowed his head. "I apologize for misconduct, Teacher."

"Would you like to run our lessons today?"

"No, Teacher."

"Then you must despise your village and disregard our First Prophet who founded it."

"No, Teacher. Zydrunas has my allegiance. I apologize."

The instructor frowned.

"Then mind your tongue. As I was saying, today we will cover the First Prophet's final days and death, but first, we will hear your songs. Is everyone prepared?"

The instructor was met with enthusiastic agreement. The children loved music. Andrius's response was less enthusiastic.

"Viktoras, you seem so eager to speak today," the instructor said as he took a seat. "Why don't you begin?"

"Thank you, Teacher," Viktoras replied, and he stood up and sang for the class. His lyrics were clever and skillfully arranged, using rhymes that Andrius never would have thought of.

Milda was next and her song was, of course, perfect. Much to his annoyance, Andrius knew that the melody would stick in his head. He would probably find himself humming it later.

The best song was Berena's. She had the high, clear-ringing voice of a summer sparrow. Her lyrics danced with the melody seamlessly, becoming one inseparable, emotional entity. She sang with passion, with delight, laughter, then pain and sorrow at a world that did not understand. The triumph and hope in her last lines reduced all of the girls and several of the boys to silent tears. The boys thought no one would notice their crying, but Andrius did. He noticed everything.

This was the song he had to follow, being the only child left.

As he stood and the students turned their ears toward him, he got lost in the sky. It captured his attention often, so vast and beautiful. It made him forget his worries, even if for only a moment.

"Andrius," the instructor began. "You do have a song, don't you?"

Andrius shook himself. "Yes, Teacher."

"Well do you plan to sing it any time soon?"

He cleared his throat. "Yes, Teacher."

"Then please."

Andrius fidgeted. Why was it always that people only paid attention to him when he didn't want them to? He wasn't sure about what he had written.

It was too late to worry over now, however. A bad song was better than none at all.

"Who can make a world for us?
Zydrunas, Zydrunas
The strongest heart he turned to dust,
Zydrunas, Zydrunas
Friend to even bugs and bees
He saved us from the disease–"

Some of the kids were snickering.

"Is that all you have?" the instructor asked, irked. "Six lines?"

"No, Teacher."

"Then why did you stop?"

"I don't know."

"Are you able to go on?"

"Yes, Teacher."

The instructor waited. The snickering began again.

"Friend to even bugs and bees,
He saved us from the disease
He taught us his philosophies
To make us each revolutionaries–"

He had to say "revolutionaries" really fast in order to fit it in time. Several children were openly laughing now. Andrius blushed and stopped singing.

The instructor sighed.

"Andrius, save the rest of your discordant song for later. You can sing it to me after lessons. I don't find it necessary to waste any more of your peers' time."

"Yes, Teacher."

Andrius slinked back down, burning with embarrassment. He hated singing–the type of singing he had to do. He preferred the song of the ferns swaying in the wind and the sun's cheerful lilt.

The children continued to giggle. One of them hit him, but the instructor didn't notice.

"Alright, children, well done. Most of you. Don't forget, if you are still searching for an offering to submit for the Day of Remembrance, you can always use this or another song you've composed for class. Especially you, Berena."

Andrius raised his drooping head long enough to catch Berena beaming.

"Only one person is chosen to share their offering from each age group, as you know. I've been hearing of rumors spreading among you that two will be chosen this year. It isn't true. It's been this way forever and no one is changing it now, so be certain to pick your best work."

Some of the children seemed disappointed, but not Andrius. He wasn't getting picked anyway. No one ever liked his offerings.

"Now, we'll set aside our writing lessons to finish up on the death of the First Prophet. It is a history you all know well, but it bears constant repeating, lest we forget to honor and revere our great founder Zydrunas."

Andrius let his eyes move in Berena's direction again. She still had a smile stretched from one ear to the other.

"Must be nice," Andrius muttered.

The instructor's ears perked up and he stopped speaking.

"Who was that? Who's whispering?"

The children were silent. The instructor scowled.

"I thought we dealt with this already. This is not the introduction to lessons any longer, we were speaking of the First Prophet. Who was whispering?"

"It was Andrius," Milda tattled. She was sitting immediately to his left. Andrius jerked toward her.

"And I'm the mean one?"

"Oh Andrius, that's surprising," the instructor chastised. "Usually you have the good sense to at least stay quiet, which is the minimum that is required of you."

"I wish he had been quiet instead of singing his song!" one of the other kids interrupted, only to be met with a chorus of laughter. It was Viktoras.

Andrius narrowed his eyes at him.

"I agree with you," the instructor sighed in frustration. He picked at his hair, growing agitated. "Let me put this in perspective for you, Andrius. You think that flapping your lips in the wind is all right when I am speaking of the First Prophet?"

"No, Teacher."

"Was I speaking of the First Prophet?"

"Yes, Teacher."

Andrius hated how the instructor made him answer simple questions. He didn't mean to speak, it's just that he had a bad habit of talking to himself. Andrius never succeeded in explaining this to his teacher, however. It was a frightening prospect, saying anything to his instructor other than "Yes, Teacher," and "No, Teacher." It probably would not have gone well anyway.

"The disease wiped out the world, Andrius," the instructor whispered. He was worked up now, shaking with passion. "Wiped it out!" he suddenly shouted. The children stopped snickering. Andrius let his head fall, ashamed, as the instructor quieted down, but continued speaking. "The whole planet–a place unimaginably bigger than anything you have ever experienced–was once full of people and now they're dead. The disease killed all of them. Except for us. Because of Zydrunas. Echoing words of holiness and the Book of Emptiness! Child, don't you think it deserves your respect and attention when someone speaks of Zydrunas?"

A tear ran down Andrius's cheek, and no one made a sound. He nodded, ashamed.

"Well?"

Andrius swiped at his tear and tried to level his voice to hide that he had cried.

"Yes, Teacher."

"Particularly after such an embarrassing song. The least you could do is show respect by listening with those 'magic' ears of yours."

Andrius felt like he was two inches tall. His response was barely audible.

"Yes, Teacher."

The instructor let the phrase hang in the air. Finally, he cleared his throat and went on teaching as before.

Andrius pulled his knees into his chest and tried as hard as he could to keep from crying again.

ONE OF THE OLD MEN WAS PLAYING THE PIPES, and the bonfire popped and hissed every time Andrius dipped his fingers in his pitcher and flicked droplets of water into the flame. He smiled.

"Papa, why does it do that?"

His father was wrapped in a wool blanket, leaning close to the fire for warmth.

"What's that, Andrius?"

"Why does the fire pop when I put water in it?"

The old man raised his bushy eyebrows and leaned back. Some of the others around listened in, others ignored them, content to sip on their daily allotment of ale.

"Hm," Aleksandras said to himself. "That is a wonderful question."

Andrius kept his eyes on his father as he pondered, then he turned and listened to the four corners of the amphitheater.

Each district had an amphitheater for gathering together, and Stone's was the closest to Andrius's house, though it wasn't the biggest. Half of the village could fit in Wood's amphitheater. Valdas, the Prophet, said that neighbors ought to spend time together at the end of the day, keeping one another company and warm.

"A wonderful question," Aleksandras repeated. "I've never heard anyone ask that before, Andrius. Why do you think it is?"

"Fire is water's enemy." Andrius shrugged. "Maybe the fire is angry when the water mixes with it."

"Ha!" Aleksandras slapped his knee. "My boy is a poet! Did you hear that, Herkus? Is your boy a poet?"

Andrius couldn't keep back a bashful smile. He returned his eyes to his offering, which he had been working on before the fire distracted him.

"Ha!" Aleksandras laughed again. "My boy is a bard! A poet! The fire is angry at the water because they're enemies. Wonderful."

"Put a log in your mouth, Aleksandras, and spare us your sound. If your boy is a poet then mine is a mountain. Have you heard his songs?"

"He's a poet if he has a poet's ear, and he does. Your boy is the one who falls over constantly, if I'm not mistaken."

Some of the men nearby chuckled. Andrius noticed Herkus's cheeks flush, and it was not from the fire.

"If only you had so much courage when speaking to your wife, Aleksandras."

Andrius had turned back to his work, but now he listened intently to await how his father would defend himself.

"Well, Herkus, understand that–"

"Do not play pretend that you have a spine when you are at the Stone Gathering, Aleksandras. We know your wife had it removed years ago. She probably made you do it yourself."

The men roared with laughter. Andrius's stomach knotted. He wanted badly for his father to bite back, to leave Herkus with a retort that stopped their stupid laughter, but Aleksandras only pulled the blanket around his shoulders and stammered.

"I didn't mean that your son wasn't a fine boy, Herkus. He's bright and strong just like his father. That's–that's a good jest about my spine. Haha, you . . ."

The other men scoffed at Aleksandras's feckless response. Andrius set his offering to the side and pulled his knees to his chest.

"Enough of this," Herkus declared, still chuckling. He rose from his seat. "Is your boy ready to lose you all of your chickens in our wager?"

The corner of Aleksandras's lips curled into a smile.

"He hasn't lost yet."

"You're crazy, Herkus!" A hairy, bearded man shouted nearby. There was a chorus of agreement.

"Ah, ah!" Herkus raised his hands. "His magic ears fail him tonight."

Andrius kept his eyes on Herkus, who pulled a fist out of his pouch. He opened his hand to reveal nine rocks, smooth as the windows high up on Gimdymo Namai.

"I've polished these rocks for a fortnight. They are smoother than the skin of your backside when you were born."

The group of men booed and laughed at him.

"Wait," Herkus loudly interjected. "I have one more piece of strategy yet."

Andrius continued to follow Herkus with his eyes even as the man came around the fire and crouched just short of him. Herkus called to Adomas to serve as judge, and the young, beardless man came around the fire and stood between them. Everyone trusted Adomas, so he was a good choice. Herkus was confident.

The older gentleman playing the pipes laid down his instrument, listening in.

"River sand," Herkus vaunted. He put his hand back into his pouch and began to scoop a pile of it onto the ground. "Maybe I should call it silt. It makes no sound when a man steps on it. Should a tiny rock be any different?"

The men started to murmur, and a few began placing bets against the champion. Aleksandras's confidence, however, was unwavering.

"Do your worst, Herkus. My boy will hear."

Herkus smirked as he smoothed out the river silt, forming it into a rectangular bar.

"No one can hear this. Now be quiet. I don't want it said that the contest was unfair."

The amphitheater was instantly silent. Only the crackling fire scratched the surface of the crystalline silence.

Herkus gently spread his fingers so as to hold the rocks apart from each other.

"I'll know if you try and cheat, boy," Herkus muttered. "So take your defeat like a man."

"I think I'll just take your chickens," Andrius replied.

The crowd of men hooted at the boy's response. Harkus shouted them down, then shushed them, irritated.

"We're starting."

Then, silently and with extreme caution, Herkus took a stone with two fingers of his right hand and moved it from the palm of his left hand to the pile of sand. He breathed tentatively, reaching for another stone and gingerly pressing it into the sand. The fire continued to pop until he was done, and he leaned back in satisfaction.

"How many stones?"

The crowd waited with bated breath. Andrius had never lost

at this game, but Herkus had done well. None of the men had heard the slightest noise when he set his stones into the sand.

A grin spread across Andrius's face.

"I can hear your stones just as easy as anyone's. Five stones."

"What?" Herkus exclaimed. Adomas reached down and counted off the stones for all present.

"One, two, three, four, five. The boy's right."

Aleksandras beamed, and those who had bet on Andrius cheered.

"That is impossible!" Herkus growled. He stood up sharply and pushed past Adomas's arm. "You cheated!"

"How could he have cheated, Herkus?" Aleksandras said. "You were right in front of him the entire time. The boy has magic ears."

Herkus spit. "Magic ears or not, he cheated somehow. Those stones were silent."

The men who had bet against him laughed and teased him. Aleksandras also joined in the fun.

"He is unbeatable, Herkus, you fool! Your confidence isn't so helpful now, is it?" He chuckled. Andrius kept his eyes on Herkus's increasingly bitter scowl as the large man marched around to where Aleksandras sat and gloated. "Now when will I be receiving your chickens, Herkus the Brash? I have so many now, but two more will be wonderful."

Herkus grabbed Aleksandras by the front of his clothes and shook him. He pulled him violently to his feet.

"Close your trap, you old fool; you'll get nothing from me!"

Andrius stood up and cried out. "Let go of him!"

Herkus ignored him. No one else intervened.

"Why would I give my chickens to a spineless woman like

you, Aleksandras? Your boy may have won this stupid game, but you are still a useless excuse for a man."

"Stop that!" Andrius shouted. "Hit him, Papa!"

The other men froze, waiting for the outcome of the exchange.

It was Herkus who spoke next. "Remember, old man. My boy Viktor is strong, a talented musician, and he has the memory of an elephant. Your boy will never be anything more than a cheap trick."

He shoved Aleksandras back into his seat and spit on him. To Andrius's great shame, Aleksandras's only response was to cower.

"Come along, Viktoras," Herkus said.

Andrius shook as they left. In short order all of the others shuffled on as well, their canes creating a discordant symphony as they slid and tapped along the ground.

Finally they faded in the distance down the road, and Andrius and his father were left alone.

The fire was dying upon its embers, but Aleksandras remained where he was, curled up and cowering. Andrius held his eyes on him a long time.

With a sigh and a shake of his head, Andrius went to his father and helped him sit upright. He scratched at Aleksandras's whiskers with his hand.

"Magic ears," Aleksandras whispered. He smiled. "Well done, my boy."

"Let's go, Papa. It's cold."

Aleksandras nodded.

"Yes, yes, it's cold. You did it, my boy. Magic ears."

Andrius quietly collected his things, taking a sip of his

water and putting his offering under his arm. He walked back to his father and they began to make their way home along Stone Road.

"Yes," Aleksandras said, "you're a special boy, Andrius."

"Let's go home, Papa."

"All right. Let's go home."

"PAY ATTENTION NOW. PAY ATTENTION. YOUR BREAK is past and we have to resume."

Andrius sighed from where he sat in the branches of the spreading tree. He had not played with the other children during their recess. No one had invited him. Milda had talked with him briefly, but they only ended up arguing.

"Settle down," the instructor spoke again, clapping his hands. "Take a seat, fun time is through. Settle down and call out for roll again so I know you've all returned."

Andrius did not want to go back down. Viktoras might hit him again and no one ever seemed to notice. Besides, his mind was another place. The wind gently tousled his fine hair and he listened to the music of the crown of mountains, guarding him like sentinels in the place beyond the barrier. And the sun! It sang magnificently today. All he could do was listen in awe and let it warm his soul.

He definitely wasn't climbing down.

"Berena."

"Viktoras."

"Milda."

"Runas."

The other children faithfully called out their names as the instructor nodded. When there were no more names to be said, the instructor paused. Andrius was daydreaming and listening to the sun.

"I don't believe I heard Andrius's name. Did he wander off?"

"No, Teacher," Andrius replied from up above. He was bored with the class today. They would be learning reading skills again. It had been exciting when they first learned, but they stayed on the basics long after Andrius had picked it up. Reading was something that he was actually good at. All of the other kids had to run their finger across the page as they read, but Andrius didn't need to.

The instructor turned his head, piqued.

"Andrius, where are you?"

"I'm up here," he answered. "I can listen from up here."

Suddenly the instructor's face was aghast and the children began murmuring.

"You mean to tell me that you're . . . you're up in the tree?"

The children were really talking now. More than a few gasps were uttered. Andrius was confused. He swung his legs where they dangled off the large branch.

"What's wrong with that? I can hear you from here. I'm not up too high, only halfway."

The instructor stood up and approached the base of the old tree.

"Andrius," he said gravely. "I'm not mad at you, but you need to do as I say. Slowly, take your time, you need to feel your way down from that tree."

"I can't believe he'd climb a tree!" Berena whispered loud enough for the whole group to hear.

Andrius furrowed his brow as he shifted on the branch.

"But why, teacher? I won't cause any trouble up here."

"Blizzard and silence, Andrius! Are you so dull? It's dangerous, stupid, and reckless. Do you want to break your neck? Or an arm or a leg? Or your spine?"

They were reacting very strongly. Andrius did not understand why. He climbed trees all the time.

He turned back one last time at the meadow beyond him, the thick swath of woods on all sides, and the proud mountains in the distance. He began to climb down.

"I don't get why I have to come down," Andrius grumbled to himself.

With a little leap, Andrius left the tree and his feet thudded to the ground. The children gasped, making Andrius tilt his head up and scratch it self-consciously.

"He's crazy," Milda whispered.

"Idiot," Viktoras muttered.

"It isn't that big of a deal," Andrius protested, hesitantly walking to where he had set his things. His throat felt suddenly dry, so he picked up his wooden pitcher and took a long drink.

The instructor shook his head.

"Andrius, for better or for worse, you are one of a kind. Now do me a favor and never do something like that again. Let's not toy with death until we have a little more experience with life, hmm?"

Andrius sat down on the grass and twisted his cane absentmindedly in his hands.

"Yes, Teacher."

The instructor began droning on, and Andrius found his attention slipping away. He didn't see what the big deal was about climbing a tree during break. The instructor passed out reading sheets, but Andrius was more interested in the meadow and the forest and the mountains beyond. A cloud drifted lazily across the sky. The children laughed at a joke that Andrius had missed. He was in his own world. The tall grasses swayed gently in the wind, harmoniously to the sun's music.

Something caught Andrius's attention. Way off in the distance, did he hear something?

Forgetting about everyone around him, he stood up. His eye caught a flash of movement at the forest's edge.

"Andrius?" the instructor asked. "Andrius, I'm waiting for the answer. You are behaving most strangely today."

The boy's focus did not waver. There was definitely movement.

He ran to the tree suddenly, without thinking, and began to clamber up it.

"Andrius? Andrius! What are you doing?"

It might mean severe punishment, but Andrius couldn't think of that now. His hands reached up, one after the other, taking hold of alternating branches and pulling himself higher. If he was right, this was more important.

"Andrius!" the instructor shouted. Now he was angry.

"I heard something, Teacher."

Andrius's head emerged from the canopy of leaves and there it was. The meadow spread out before him in the dazzling song of the late afternoon sun. At its edge, just outside of the forest, was where Andrius had noticed movement. He knew for sure now that it was not just his imagination.

"There's a man out there! Past the barricade!"

The children reacted excitedly, chattering among themselves.

"How can you tell?" asked Runa, one of the duller students in his age group.

"I heard him!" Andrius replied.

The figure in the distance was in bad shape. His path was stumbling and erratic. Andrius was the only one to notice him stumble and fall.

"Where is he?" Berena asked while the instructor tried in vain to restore order.

"Past the barricade. He's probably a whole road away!"

"Andrius," the instructor huffed, turning his attention back to the impetus of the upheaval. "Get out of that tree this instant!"

Andrius was already in the air. His feet met the ground softly.

"He needs our help!"

"Andrius, this is so unlike you. Come back here and listen to me!"

But someone was hurt. Andrius was running toward the fallen man as fast as his legs could carry him. Usually he would shrink back at his teacher's instruction, but he knew that the man that he noticed, that nobody else did, needed help. Did not even the Prophet himself say that helping others was their primary occupation? For a better village.

"Follow me!" Andrius hollered. "I won't be able to carry him by myself."

Several of the children took up their canes and went shuffling after Andrius. The instructor, realizing that there was no stopping them, went along and urged caution.

"Andrius!" they shouted, but he was far ahead of them now. "Andrius! Where is he?"

"This way!" he cried. The grass whipped against his legs as he ran, and more than once he choked on pollen. He couldn't hear the man any longer, only what was right in front of him. Birds scattered as he sprinted.

Reaching the edge of the wood, Andrius stopped.

The man was right there in front of him, only a few body lengths away, but he was on the other side of the barrier.

"Andrius!" he heard his instructor call amidst the clamor of children. They were still hundreds of steps back. "Where are you?"

"Over here!" Andrius shouted. He cupped his hands around his mouth. "Follow the sound of my voice!" He waved in a grand motion, then turned back to the barrier and the strange man on the other side of it.

His skin was burned and his clothes were dusty. He had collapsed facedown, which was not a good sign. Andrius hoped desperately that the man could breathe. He wanted to help him.

A crazy thought came into Andrius's mind, but he dismissed it quickly.

"Andrius?"

"I'm just over here," he called to his instructor and his classmates as they parted the grass and tapped around with their canes.

Andrius had forgotten his cane. Again.

"He's on the other side," Andrius said simply.

"How did he get out there?"

"Is he a hunter?"

"Of course he's a hunter, stupid."

"Children, please!" The instructor was thinking.

"I don't think he's a hunter," Andrius mumbled, self-conscious again.

Viktoras hit the boy standing next to him.

"Of course he isn't a hunter if he's on the other side of the barricade. Stupid."

"He has a big pack," Andrius said, noting the large hump that covered most of the stranger.

"What do you think is in it, Andrius?" Milda asked, stepping forward and putting a hand on his shoulder. "Can you hear what's inside?"

Andrius frowned and took a step away. Milda tattled on him yesterday.

"I don't know. Food probably. And clothes."

The instructor was still thinking while the children gaped.

"I think he needs help," Andrius offered.

"I know, Andrius, hush. Now let's think . . . How far away would you say he is?"

Andrius considered.

"Three feet?"

"Too far to reach, then?"

The children nodded. The instructor tapped his lip.

"Problem-solving time, children. How are we to help this man?"

"Send someone for rope!" Berena's crystalline soprano rose above the chorus of mostly useless suggestions.

"Mm, I think we can do better than that, but perhaps. Someone needs to be informed, at any rate. Viktoras, can you find your way back? Get some rope and tell the Regent of Brick what's happened."

Viktoras hesitated and kicked at the dirt.

"There's no path."

"The wind was in our face the whole way here. Put it at your back and move. It isn't too far."

Still he hesitated. "I'm scared, Teacher."

With a sigh, the instructor asked for a volunteer to join Viktoras. A small boy named Paulius offered, and the two of them set out on their mission.

"Any other ideas?" the instructor asked.

Andrius couldn't take his eyes off of the man. A fly was buzzing around his head, then landed in his hair. The stranger still did not move.

"Teacher," Andrius said softly. "Do you think I might, I mean, since he is in trouble and all, just this one time . . . I mean, it wouldn't be hard. It's only a couple of big logs, and I wouldn't even need to climb, really. Could I–"

The instructor was horrified. The children were silent.

"Andrius," the instructor began gravely. "You aren't seriously suggesting that you would cross the barrier, are you?"

Shame filled Andrius, but he turned back to the helpless man again. The fly was crawling on his ear now.

"But . . . but he's only right there. He could be dying."

"And he could not. But if you pass this barrier, he'll still be dying and you could die too! Andrius, we are forbidden from the Regions of Death for a reason! I'm surprised at you."

A few birds tweeted nearby and insects clicked from their hiding places in the grass. Andrius hung his head, and all of the people there with him stood in helpless quiet, until finally Berena spoke up again.

"We could use a cane."

The instructor drew back the corners of his mouth thoughtfully.

"Hmm. That could work. Andrius, do you think we can reach his straps with a cane? His pack does have straps, doesn't it?"

"Yes, teacher." Andrius nodded vigorously as he borrowed Milda's cane and jumped up on the lowest tie that made up the barrier fence. It was about two feet above the dirt. The man should fit under it easily. They might have to get him on his side to accommodate for the pack.

"Andrius, here," the instructor said. "Use my cane; it's longer. Guide it into the straps and I will pull him in."

Andrius traded canes, and then he gently prodded the unconscious man. The fly buzzed away, but the man was still motionless. Andrius leaned over the barrier as far as he could and attempted to work the cane under the straps, trying to brace it somewhere.

"Did he do it?" one of the kids asked from the back of the small crowd.

"Not yet," the instructor patiently replied.

Andrius leaned over so far that he was balancing his torso on top of the barrier now. The cane kept slipping out, but an idea occurred to him. There was a little loop on the top of the pack. Andrius fitted the far end through, then dipped over just a little more and put the near end through the middle of the barrier. It seemed like it might work. They didn't have to move him far.

"Here you go, teacher," he said proudly. "Like a lever. Keep the far end up and pull him in."

The instructor took the cane wordlessly and began the laborious task.

It was rough going as the stranger was full grown and wearing a heavy pack. The cane slipped out of its hold several times and Andrius had to reposition it, but finally the instructor got the man close enough to the barricade that he could reach through and get a hand on his clothes. He and the children heaved him through to their side, to rescue, civilization, and life.

The instructor, who was not as strong as he liked to fancy himself, sat down in a heap after the man was through. Everyone who had helped was breathing heavily.

Andrius cautiously approached the man and pushed him onto one side.

He studied the man's face.

He was a young man, of marrying age no doubt, but perhaps he did not yet have many children. A bandana was tied around his forehead, soaked with sweat. His eyes were closed.

Andrius leaned in close. He was breathing.

"If I," the instructor began, pausing every few words for breath, "take him by the . . . arms. Can three of four . . . of you . . . carry him by . . . the legs?"

Andrius turned to the unconscious man again and patted his chest.

"You're going to be okay. We'll help you."

THE CHILDREN AND THEIR INSTRUCTOR BROUGHT the strange man to the house at Eighteenth Brick, falling down several times along the way. Andrius had never been around Zydra and Stephinius before—the people who lived in the house at Eighteenth Brick. He had heard of them, of course, being so close to where he attended lessons. They were a young couple with two small boys, making their living by raising cartwheel flower on the outskirts of the village and supplying Gimdymo Namai with ingredients for the cure.

The house was full of dust. Zydra cleared the wooden table with an arm, sending everything clattering to the floor, and they laid the strange man on the table. The instructor was going about the business of removing the man's sizeable and heavy pack when Stephinius chased all of the children out of the house.

As an afterthought, the instructor called out over his shoulder that lessons would be cancelled for the rest of the day.

Andrius didn't know what to do with himself. He had never heard of lessons being cancelled before. Even when he was in ninth-year lessons and his instructor had come down with brain fever they did not miss a single day. A replacement was simply sent. From earliest childhood until the Age of Attainment, afternoons were for lessons. Then after reaching the Age of Attainment, afternoons were for village work. An afternoon was never free.

Most of the children took to it well, delightfully shuffling away to play games among themselves or to gossip and make up stories about the stranger. Andrius didn't want to leave. He thought it only fair that he, as the man's discoverer, should at least get to stay and find out what happened to him.

He didn't bring this up, of course, lest someone tell him no. Instead, he surreptitiously eased the shutter windows open and monitored the proceedings inside. He reminded himself several times that he would have to keep from talking to himself. Once he nearly reminded himself aloud, so he ceased reminding himself and tried as best as he could to simply keep from thought altogether.

Zydra, Stephinius's wife, wasted no time in wetting a cloth to clean the man's skin. Stephinius busied himself with attempting to wake the man up and get him to drink some water, while the instructor tried to figure out how to remove the upper portion of the man's clothes.

They were strange clothes. They were similar to his own, in some ways, but nothing alike at the same time. The patterns . . .

There was a sudden movement of shutters in front of Andrius's face, and he yelped in surprise, falling to his backside. Zydra, not noticing Andrius, had absentmindedly swatted the shutters closed, and in such a way he was discovered. He was sent away again, explicitly this time and with a surfeit of threats of punishment. In such a wake, Andrius scampered off, just as four men came down the road.

It was the Prophet. Valdas himself and his three Regents were coming his way. Andrius gasped and froze. Then he feared the worst, that the Prophet might have heard his name when Milda caught him spying at Gimdymo Namai the other day.

Quickly, Andrius moved off of the road and faced away into the wilderness, pretending to mind his own business and hoping that they wouldn't stop. He could hear them already. The Regents' voices were harsh and deep, but the Prophet's was smooth as butter and sweet as honey.

"It isn't anything good. I'll tell you that much."

"We shall determine that if he wakes."

"There is only one action we can take, Valdas."

"I will be the judge of that, Aras."

They continued speaking with one another, taking no notice of the boy on the side of the road. They entered into the house that Andrius had just left, and he breathed a sigh of relief.

The relief renewed a spring in his step, and though still worried over the fate of the stranger, he wasn't about to let a free afternoon go to waste.

He ran off to retrieve the pattern he was working on as his offering. He still had a lot of work to do on it, and the stranger's odd clothes had inspired him.

Besides, it would be nice to work while the sun was singing. He paused for a moment to joy in the melody of it, to close his eyes and feel the warmth upon his face.

And then he was off again.

It was only a few moments until he realized that all of his things were back at the spreading tree where he did his lessons. He was really thirsty, and his pitcher was there.

He changed directions and set off at a run again. He gathered his belongings and took a breath, and then he was jogging again. The water sloshed around in his wooden pitcher with every step he took and he wondered what would become of the strange man.

THE SUN'S SONG WAS SUCH A THING OF BEAUTY TO Andrius. It sounded different depending on the time of day. In the first moments of dawn it was soft and simple, and then it crescendoed into a dramatic, fiery symphony. Every hour, every second, the song shifted, and no two days did the sun ever sing in exactly the same way.

It was a shame no one else heard it. Andrius took a drink of water then readjusted his offering under his arm. He wasn't certain if it was totally finished yet, but he had gotten to work on it quite a bit yesterday after the instructor had cancelled classes.

It was due today, at any rate. Remembrance was only two days away.

He knew no one would like his offering, but he liked it. It was better than his other attempts. It was difficult to be in poor spirits, anyway. Daiva had been in a yelling mood all morning, and his father's single, weak attempt at containing her was rolled over. It was nice to just be out of the house, even if he was heading to lessons.

A striking butterfly flitted by, but Andrius didn't pay it much attention. He was considering his offering. Maybe it would get picked this year.

No, it wouldn't get picked.

But suppose it did?

He had reached Fifth Stone when Milda emerged from her house and joined Andrius on the road. He debated with himself, but he decided to walk next to her.

"Hi, Milda."

"Andrius," she replied meekly.

It was quiet for a while. The water in Andrius's pitcher slapped against the sides as he walked.

"So?" he said after they reached Second Stone. He wasn't sure how to act. "Aren't you going to make fun of me or something?"

"Why would I make fun of you?"

Andrius was nonplussed. He squinted.

"You always do."

"I do not! You're just a friendless, creepy jerk, so I have to—"

Andrius sighed and sped up to avoid the girl's abuse. She stopped midsentence, then stumbled to catch up with him.

"Andrius, wait!"

He kept walking.

"Andrius . . ." she whined. Andrius turned his head around, and he frowned. It wouldn't be hard to run away from her, but somehow he couldn't get up the resolve. His stomach was tied in knots. He hated arguing with Milda.

"Andrius," she shouted, louder than necessary. "I'm sorry, okay? Slow down."

Andrius stopped and let out a sigh. "Why?"

"Because I didn't mean it. I wanted to say I was sorry for tattling on you the other day. Okay?"

Andrius furrowed his brow. He rested his eyes on her as she stopped, and he took a sip from his pitcher.

"Why?"

Milda scratched her head. "What do you mean, why? So you aren't mad at me anymore and we can talk again."

Andrius opened his mouth then closed it again. He wasn't sure what to say. Nothing like this had happened to him before. It was confusing.

"Why?" he asked again.

Milda huffed and stomped her foot. "Piles of snow, Andrius! Is 'why' the only word you know?"

"Well, no. It isn't."

"Okay?"

Milda was acting very strangely. She waited for an answer while Andrius leaned away, keeping a skeptical eye on her.

"Okay," he said at length. He was not perfectly certain what it was exactly that he had agreed to, but Milda looked satisfied. She smiled, then began walking again, tapping her cane the way she always did.

"So do you have your offering ready?" she asked politely. Andrius fell into step with her. They were almost to First Stone.

"Yes. Do you?"

"Of course I have mine, Andrius. What is yours? A poem or a speech? I know it isn't a song."

"It's a pattern."

"Again?"

Andrius nodded. "It's better this year."

"Andrius, you always do the weirdest things for offering." She held up a pacifying hand. "I'm not trying to be mean, but they are. Nobody really gets them."

Andrius knew she was right. He held his offering out in front of his face. He liked it.

"Well I don't get everybody," he said under his breath.

"The year you made that pitcher was okay. Not good enough to get picked, of course, but respectable. You carved all of those cool designs into it."

Andrius felt the weight of the water pitcher in his hand. He was proud of the work he had done to make it. He had only been eight.

"You should do something like that again," Milda offered.

There was a lull in the conversation as they grew closer to Gimdymo Namai, then began to angle around it to where Brick Road began. Andrius strained his ears, but there was no delivery happening today. The shutters were closed anyway.

"I'm reciting a poem I wrote," Milda declared.

"You aren't singing?" Andrius asked, surprised.

Milda laughed. "Not when Berena has a better song. I want to get picked again, so I'm doing poetry this year."

Andrius hadn't thought of that. "So you think a poem has a better chance?"

Milda grinned. "Well, think about it. If–"

"Milda! Listen!"

Milda stopped dead in her tracks. They were nearly to the beginning of Brick Road, and the building didn't hide him anymore: on a modest stump that served as a temporary seat, sat the stranger from beyond the barrier.

His eyes were closed and his head tilted back. He breathed in the cool afternoon air steadily in through his nose, then out through his mouth.

"It's him," Andrius whispered.

Milda crouched down instinctively and whispered back.

"Who is he?"

Before Andrius could answer, the man opened his eyes and lazily swiveled his head in their direction.

"What are you two gawking at?"

Andrius's heart seized in his chest and Milda gasped. He considered running, but Milda had grasped his hand tightly and he wasn't sure what to think about that. In short order, it was too late.

"What, are you gawkers and deaf? I asked what you two were marveling at in my general direction."

The strange man wasn't smiling, but there was a certain reassurance to his bearing. Andrius averted his eyes, but he was curious.

Milda put a hand on her hip and answered defiantly. "We were gawking at you." She then leaned in and whispered to Andrius, "What does 'gawking' mean?"

Andrius shrugged. He didn't know.

The stranger chuckled, surprising them both.

"I'm only having some fun with you. Come here if you want to talk. I could use some information anyway. You do have some information, don't you?"

Andrius shrugged again. Milda frowned but did not speak.

"What, can't you look at me? What are your names?"

"What does 'look' mean?" Milda asked Andrius. He didn't answer her; he spoke directly to the man.

"I'm Andrius. What does 'look' mean?"

"My name is Milda," she interjected.

The stranger tilted his head back and his eyes rolled along with the motion. Andrius was still facing the ground. He only perceived the stranger out of the corner of his eye.

"It means turn your head and face me. Don't you speak Lithuanian? It was starting to seem like everyone in this place does."

"Of course we speak Lithuanian," Milda replied matter-of-factly. She let go of Andrius's hand and crossed her arms. "What else would we speak?"

"Well," the stranger returned, "being as we are in Lower Tatras, I thought maybe you spoke Slovakian or Russian maybe.

Your town is very strange, but I will say that it was pleasant to wake up hearing my mother tongue. It was weird, though." The stranger stretched his legs out in front of him, yawned, and wiped his face. "Little boy–Andrius, was it? Why won't you look at me? It's rude."

Slowly Andrius lifted his eyes and rested them on the stranger. His clothes were ripped in a few places, and he had a raggedy beard, but he still looked like he was in the prime of his life. Twenty-eight, maybe. But none of this was what captured Andrius's attention.

"There, that's better," the stranger said, studying Andrius closely. "Thank you."

"What happened to you?" Milda asked. Andrius was still mesmerized. It was the strangest thing that he looked upon.

"Heat exhaustion, I think. Stupid, I know. I had plenty of supplies, but I got lost and spent an extra two days wandering around. All of the trails are overgrown. No one appreciates nature anymore. Did you know that a couple hundred years ago backpacking was a pretty common pastime? Outdoorsmanship, they called it. Now I couldn't even pull a partner away from his elon screen long enough to come on a weekend trip." He shook his head. "Well, it was supposed to be a weekend trip. Longer now, I guess."

Andrius was still examining and puzzling over this singularity in front of him, and Milda was quiet for several moments before responding.

"What?"

"What do you mean, what?"

Milda huffed and patted Andrius on the back.

"He's confusing, Andrius. I'm going to lessons. Bye."

"Goodbye, Milda." The stranger waved. He watched her go

for a moment, and then he looked back at Andrius and frowned. "What's the matter with you, kid? You look like you're staring at a zombie or something. An alien, maybe."

Andrius shook his head and tried to look away from it, but he couldn't. It was so bizarre, so fascinating.

"I'm sorry," he said.

"Eh, don't worry about it. I'm sure I've done my share of rude staring too. Who knew there was a village all the way out here. You guys been here long?"

Andrius set his pitcher on the ground. "What do you mean? We've been here since the Fallout and the end of the Hausen War."

The stranger raised his eyebrows. "Really? Wow. It's been a while then." He held out his hand. "The name's Daniel."

Andrius looked at the extended hand, then squinted up at Daniel.

"You shake it," the man said at length.

Confused but wanting to be polite, Andrius took Daniel's hand between both of his and shook it up and down and back and forth.

Daniel laughed.

"That's one way to do it, I guess. How old are you, kid?"

"Eleven." Andrius was still transfixed by that one thing. He continued to stare.

"Eleven." He stuck his lip out and nodded. "Eleven's a good age. Lots of climbing trees and running around, I bet."

"Your eyes are beautiful," Andrius stated in awe, suddenly, unable to contain it anymore. They were so deep and the patterns inside . . . They were like the sky and the sun all at once.

Daniel raised an eyebrow, then laughed again.

"Yeah, thanks. My baby blues. I get that a lot, actually. Just usually, you know, from women. Not so much from eleven-year-old boys. Man to man here, it's kind of a weird thing for you to say."

"Oh."

Andrius looked down as Viktoras wandered by suddenly. He kicked over Andrius's pitcher, spilling water everywhere.

"Oops," Viktoras said, continuing on.

"Hey!" Andrius yelled, but that was all he could muster. He picked up his much lighter water pitcher and set about dusting it off.

"Eh, I wouldn't sweat it. It was an accident," Daniel commented as Andrius fumed.

"You don't know Viktoras."

"No, I guess I don't. But anyway, that Milda–is she your little gal pal?"

Andrius felt the blood rush to his cheeks. "No!" he replied a little too vehemently.

"Uh-huh. Right. Well anyway, I don't know why you're freaking out about my eyes when yours look, like, exactly the same. I bet everybody tells you–well, maybe not."

Daniel seemed troubled for a moment. A strange feeling of pride welled up in Andrius's chest.

"You mean . . . my eyes are like yours? My eyes have patterns and . . . and . . . I don't know. They're like yours?"

"Are you serious? It's like a mirror image."

"A what?"

They stared at each other, confused. Daniel turned his hand over, gesturing.

"Haven't you ever seen your own face before?"

Andrius laughed.

Daniel persisted. "You're telling me that you've never looked at your own face?"

"How could I face my own face? That's funny."

Some more students passed on their way to lessons, but none of them acknowledged him.

Daniel seemed as if he was debating with himself whether or not he ought to continue the discussion. He pointed down at Andrius's offering.

"What is that?"

"Oh, it's my offering."

"Your what?"

"My offering."

"Oh."

Andrius picked it up, halted, then looked at Daniel guardedly. "Did you want to check it out?"

"Sure."

He gingerly handed it over, and Daniel ran his eyes over it. He stared for a while, then nodded. "This is actually really good. How old are you? Eleven?"

Andrius nodded excitedly. "You like it?"

Daniel had not taken his eyes off of the offering. He was transfixed. "I really do, actually. I'm impressed."

"No one else likes it."

"For obvious reasons."

Andrius's heart sank. Daniel didn't notice his reaction. He handed the offering back.

"Well," Andrius began, "I'm going to be late for lessons."

"Yeah," Daniel replied. "I'm just waiting out here while they talk about me in there. Maybe I'll see you around."

Andrius wrinkled his brow. He didn't know what was going on, exactly, but he didn't have time to talk any longer. It was inexcusable to be late for lessons.

"Okay. Bye."

"Say, Andrius," Daniel stopped him. Andrius looked over his shoulder, then came back a couple of steps. "Why doesn't anybody get . . . fixed around here? You know what I mean?"

Andrius stared blankly. Daniel sighed, then tried again.

"You know what I mean. Look, I work at a hospital. I don't do anything fancy, I'm just in residency. And yes, you can be in residency when you're thirty. But they do a lot of specialty surgeries, and we could fix all these people if they came down from here–down the mountain to Brezno. So why don't they? Do they know that it's an option?"

"I really shouldn't be late for lessons," Andrius replied, baffled by Daniel's nonsensical conversation.

"Here, just a second. Come in a little closer." Andrius cautiously obliged, and Daniel looked both ways before speaking. He lowered his voice. "Andrius, why is everyone here blind?"

Andrius heard the last of his classmates in the distance. He was going to be late.

He backed up toward the road. "I have to go."

Daniel kept talking anyway. "No, I mean it. It's kind of freaking me out. Why is every person in this village blind? You're the only one I've seen so far who's not."

"I have to go," Andrius said. He turned and ran, not having to worry about spilling his water pitcher, which was now empty. He was definitely going to be late.

"He was weird," Andrius said aloud.

He had a bad habit of talking to himself.

ANDRIUS'S OFFERING WAS NOT PICKED. NO ONE liked it or understood it, and his instructor even made him stay late to scold him for his lack of effort. Andrius tried to explain about his patterns, but once the instructor got annoyed, he stopped trying.

Berena's offering was picked. She would be singing on the Day of Remembrance as representative of the village's eleven-year-olds.

It wasn't surprising, really, but Andrius had let himself hope. One day he would come up with a pattern other people liked. Maybe.

Andrius walked alone down Brick Road, past Fifth Brick and then Fourth Brick, pondering. The sun sang its dying dirge, and it made Andrius solemn. He was glad he had his cane today. When the sun stopped singing, he might actually need it.

He was hoping to run into Daniel again when he came to Gimdymo Namai, but when he reached it, Daniel was gone. The shutters were closed and he couldn't hear anything from inside.

The stranger had talked funny and he didn't make a lot of sense, but still, Andrius was curious to talk with him some more. He didn't get to ask him why he had been on the other side of the barrier. That might have been the most curious part of all.

And his eyes.

Andrius walked pensively until Fourth Stone, where Milda

and Berena were talking outside of Berena's house. The sun's singing had stilled to a whisper.

"Hi, Milda," Andrius said, waving. "Berena." He meant to keep on walking, but the girls stopped him.

"Berena, listen to this – Andrius was there with me. Andrius, come here."

Andrius hesitated. No one ever called him over unless it was to give him a lecture, but they seemed innocent enough. He wandered over cautiously.

"What's going on?" he asked.

"You two talked with that man we saved?" Berena asked. Her clear, high voice sang through the air effortlessly. Still, Andrius preferred Milda's.

He nodded. "Yes. We talked with him on the way to lessons."

"What did he say?"

"Andrius?" Milda prompted him.

"Well," Andrius began, furrowing his brow. "A lot of things that didn't make sense. He liked my offering though. The pattern."

"He liked your pattern?"

"He kept using words we didn't know," Milda interrupted. She put a hand on her chest. "And I'm sorry, I know that we're only eleven, but I do have a great vocabulary. I think he was making things up."

"Is that true, Andrius?"

"I don't know. He did use a lot of strange words."

Berena leaned on her cane and twisted it into the dirt. "Well, guess what I heard him say?"

"You talked to him too?" Andrius asked, wide-eyed.

"She caught him for a little bit after lessons, in the same

spot," Milda explained. "What did he say, Berena?"

"Oh, normal things, mostly. But when I said something about the Day of Remembrance and I expressed my love for our heroic founder Zydrunas . . ." Milda and Andrius nodded, hanging onto Berena's every word. She stopped and pursed her lips, and then she dropped her voice to a whisper. "He got really weird, like he was disgusted or surprised or something. He asked if I meant *the* Zydrunas, and of course I meant *the* Zydrunas, and you know what he called him?"

The question hung in the air. Andrius held his breath.

"A murderer. He called our honored Zydrunas, the First Prophet, a mass murderer."

Milda gasped.

"Why would he say that?" Andrius demanded.

Berena shrugged. "I don't know, but he did. Then he got sort of angry and asked if we worship a bunch of other people's names I don't remember. Hitster and Jenkius Can, or something like that. I had never heard of them before."

"He's crazy!" Milda exclaimed. "I knew he was."

Berena was nodding. "I wanted to ask him why he'd say something so . . . so . . . disgusting, but then the Prophet and the Regent of Stone came out and took him into Gimdymo Namai."

"Wow," said Milda breathlessly.

"Wow," Andrius repeated.

"And he used a lot of words I didn't know. Like you said."

"Huh."

"But you can't tell any of the other kids, okay? Touch four walls and begin."

Milda's face scrunched in confusion. "Berena, village leaders only say that when they're discussing matters of life and death so they can make sure no one overhears, but there aren't any walls out here."

"And you already said what you don't want people to overhear," Andrius added.

Berena sighed. "It's just an expression."

A voice called out from the house suddenly. "Berena? Berena, are you out there?"

"Coming!" Berena shouted back. It was never very loud when Berena shouted, but she tried. "I have to go. Dinnertime, you know."

"Bye, Berena."

"Bye."

She groped for the guideline that led from Fourth Stone to her house. Once she gripped it, she followed it away and was quickly gone. It was getting harder to hear.

Milda walked with Andrius to the next stone, where she lived, but they did not speak much. Andrius was thinking.

He couldn't help a smile. Milda had called him over. Thoughts of his bizarre conversation with Daniel kept trying to creep to the forefront of his consciousness, but he pushed them away. For the moment, he wanted to think about Milda.

"HELLO?" ANDRIUS CALLED. THE OLD WOODEN door creaked as he opened it and stepped into the hut at Twenty-fifth Stone. It was impossible to hear inside. "I'm back," Andrius said. "Have you gone to the Stone Gathering already? Is there any dinner?" he added, mumbling to himself.

Daiva's harsh voice came out of the nothingness. "You come home late and you dare to ask about dinner?"

Andrius's stomach knotted up immediately. He didn't like to be wrong. "It's not my fault," he began. "My instructor made me–"

"All I hear are excuses for disrespect, tardiness, and . . . what else? Gluttony."

The chair Daiva must have been sitting in made a popping sound as she shifted her girth in it. It almost sounded like something had broken.

"No, I didn't mean any of that. I was just hungry and no one was around, and sometimes I talk to myself, so–"

"Quiet!" Daiva railed.

"Daiva," another voice soothed. "Let the boy slide. I'm sure he has a–"

"Daiva?" she cried. "Aleksandras, you can't even call me by a pet name or show me any sort of affection at all? I know you don't love me anymore, but at least be subtle about it."

"Daiva, that isn't–I mean, my dove, of course that isn't–"

"Don't touch me!"

Andrius heard Daiva strike Aleksandras's hand away with her meaty arm.

"Sorry, dear."

Andrius felt sick. He was still hungry, but the sick feeling was more powerful. He wanted to crawl in a hole somewhere and die.

He turned to leave, and the door creaked open once again.

"Andrius, I'm not done with you yet! Stay right there," Daiva ordered him. Andrius was suddenly rooted to the ground. The floor shook with Daiva's thundering footsteps, and she breathed heavily from the effort of shifting her mass. Andrius shivered.

"You've been slinking out of here an awful lot lately. Leeching off our food, leeching off our property, and thinking you can come and go as you please. Your sly little sarcastic comments . . ."

"Sarcastic comments?" Andrius asked, confused. His stomach was knotting tighter.

"Yes, sarcastic comments!" Daiva screamed. "You think I don't know what you think of me? Your own mother, and you treat me like garbage. You think I'm just a fat, useless monster."

"What? No–"

"Well you're wrong, Andrius! Do you have any idea how much work I do around here?"

She hit him. Andrius stumbled to the side and caught himself on a chair.

"I slave and I slave and I slave, and what thanks do I get from you?"

She kicked him in the shins over and over. Andrius tried to avoid her feet, but he was in the corner. He could feel hot tears escaping from his eyes.

"Daiva," came Aleksandras's voice. She ignored it.

"Nothing! I get nothing from you!" Her voice was raspy and her breaths were deep from exertion. She was getting frantic.

"Daiva," Aleksandras said again, a bit stronger this time.

"I hate you! I hate you, you worthless child! You can't sing or write like the other children. You're a greedy, gluttonous slob. I hate you!"

Daiva's twitching fingers curled around her thick wooden cane, and she brought it down hard, smashing across Andrius's face.

He squealed, crying out in pain like an animal's yelp. He crumpled to the ground.

"Daiva, stop that right now!"

Everyone stopped. It was silent but for the crickets chirping outside. Andrius had never heard his father raise his voice before. He tasted blood in his mouth and he covered his head, awaiting the next blow.

It didn't come. Daiva's breathing came in through her mouth in halting, labored gasps. Finally it slowed enough for her to speak.

"Go to the barn, Andrius. Mongrel."

In the nothingness surrounding him, Andrius raised his head, then clumsily lifted his body off the ground, holding his already-bruised face. It was throbbing fiercely, and it hurt to close his jaw. No one spoke as he slid up against the wall, then shuffled out, keeping an arm in front of him just in case. The door creaked as it eased open, then fell shut.

He stumbled through tears to the barn. He was shaking badly.

One of the cows had laid on the pile of hay that served as Andrius's bed, so he just sat against the wall and let himself sink down until he reached the ground. One hand held his face, the other held his ribs.

"It's been a while since she's hit me," Andrius whispered to himself. "I thought it was done."

He was wracked by sobs then, feeling the salt dry on his face, trying not to taste the iron flavor in his mouth. A calf wandered by and stood in front of him for a while and then moved on. The sun was deathly quiet, and Andrius was half a world away from its song.

He was finally bedding down on the hard-packed ground when he heard footsteps crunching on the hay.

"Andrius? Andrius, my boy? Are you here?"

It was Aleksandras. Andrius wiped his eye and stifled his sniffling. He sat up.

"Yes, Papa."

The footsteps halted for a moment, and then he heard them angling toward him.

Aleksandras reached out, and feeling the barn wall, he crouched down.

Andrius waited, resolutely looking away from his father. Outside, the night-sun had begun to sing her soft, mysterious song. The melody drifted in through the barn's open door.

Andrius felt a hand on his head then, rubbing the hairs between his fingers, then stroking him.

They sat like this a long time, Andrius trembling and Aleksandras stroking his hair. The animals were all long since slumbering. Andrius wanted it to stay like this forever—or part of him did. Another part of him desperately wanted his father to say something, to make sense of the world that suddenly seemed meaningless.

Still, he had raised his voice and the beating stopped. Andrius had never heard him do that before. Aleksandras was terrified of Daiva, and so was Andrius. He was thankful somewhere inside of his sadness and bewilderment.

Andrius was the first to speak. "I'm sorry I was home later than usual."

"Shh," Aleksandras hushed him. "I'm sure you had a good reason. Don't feel bad about that." He continued to stroke the boy's hair. "You didn't do anything wrong."

Andrius tried so hard to hold back the tears, but they came again anyway. "But then why did she hit me?"

Aleksandras felt his son's shaking body and he heard him weep. He stopped stroking his hair and sat down next to him, pulling him into a fragile embrace.

Andrius continued, screaming in a whisper. "It just isn't fair!

I know I messed up–I don't know how I could have done any different though. I didn't even know that coming home late was a rule." He was hyperventilating. "Why? It just . . ."

"Shh, Andrius, my special boy. You're all right."

"I'm not all right! She . . . she's my mother!"

Andrius spat the last word and was overpowered by sobs once more. Aleksandras hugged him tighter.

"Andrius!" came Daiva's muffled voice from inside of the house. "Is that you wailing? Some of us sleep at night."

Andrius made despairing, hopeless sounds. He had been beaten too many times to count in his short life, but tonight he couldn't take it anymore.

Aleksandras released his embrace and sat back. "She's not your mother."

Andrius sniffled and raised his eyes. The old man sighed heavily and let his head bump against the wall.

"What do you mean?"

"Daiva isn't your mother."

Andrius stared at Aleksandras, who only nodded solemnly. The gears inside Andrius's young mind turned steadily.

"You mean . . . you were married before Daiva?"

"No. I waited until I was almost old to marry. It was sort of a scandal, actually–me being single and having done so well with the farm. I had to marry someone. And Daiva wasn't always . . . Well, she was younger. She was different. We're actually very different ages, her and I."

"I know you're older than she is," Andrius replied quietly, wiping the last of the moisture from his eyes.

"You do?" Aleksandras asked, surprised. "How did you know that?"

"I've heard people talk about it, Papa. And I can hear your age. Hers too."

Aleksandras was silent for a moment, and then he chuckled. "I believe you can, my boy. Magic ears. You're a special one, Andrius. Hearing a person's age–ha!"

"What were you saying about Daiva?" Andrius urged him. "You said she's not my mother?"

"That's right. Yes."

Sadness came over Andrius. "Well, then who is?"

Aleksandras patted Andrius's shoulder. "I don't know exactly, my boy, but it was probably a young woman named . . . Oh, what was her name?"

Andrius held his breath as his father rubbed his forehead and wracked his memory.

"Janina. Her name was Janina."

"Janina," Andrius repeated. The name felt funny on his lips.

His father nodded. "Yes. A very troubled girl named Janina. This was only a year after I had married Daiva. But this girl Janina, she lived a few stone up the road. She was always getting into trouble. Getting caught where she shouldn't have been, missing lessons, speaking irreverently of the Regent a few times too, I think. She was on the wrong path. Only fourteen years old."

Andrius squeezed his father's hand tighter and listened intently.

"She disappeared one day," Aleksandras continued, "and no one ever saw her again." He paused to cough into his fist and clear his throat.

"I don't understand," Andrius said.

"You will, my boy. I took the pigs out that evening, after village work. I used to turn them loose to let them root and they would lead me to truffles. I followed them a while. I remember thinking to myself, there must be a treasure trove somewhere for these sows to walk so long. They led me all the way to the barrier that night, and I heard you.

"You were crying. I thought, what is a baby doing out here at this late hour? I couldn't remember any recent deliveries in Stone. The village was a little smaller then, not like today when we have almost a thousand people. But I heard you, and it was an infant's cry, a newborn child.

"The pigs led me to you, and I had to shoo them away. Your mother had set you right at the edge, thankfully on our side of the barrier. You were wrapped in a cloak, cold, and there was dried blood all over you." He paused, briefly. "You still had your umbilical cord attached. I picked you up and felt how cold you were, but still crying. Always a fighter you were, Andrius. My boy is a fighter."

He smiled weakly, but then it faded.

"I brought you home as fast as I could and cleaned you up. I bathed you in hot water, wrapped you in wool. I massaged your skin and held you to my chest, whatever I could do to keep you warm. I stayed up with you all night and you lived. I wasn't sure if you would. I fed you goat's milk and held you, and you lived through a second night, and you lived and you lived, and you kept on living."

Andrius noticed a tear slide out from the old man's eye and run down his cheek. He let go of Andrius for a moment to wipe it away.

"You always were a special boy," Aleksandras whispered. "A miracle."

Andrius let out his breath. Suddenly he didn't care about the hurt in his face, his ribs, or in his heart. He had so many questions.

"What about my mother?"

"I think she went over the barrier, into the Regions of Death. She must have given you the cure before she left you, thank goodness. You were so sticky all over that it was hard to tell, but I figured you had been exposed to the air for so many hours that if she hadn't given you the cure, then it was too late. She must have done it before she left you, so you have that to thank her for, at least." Aleksandras shook his head. "Fourteen years old . . . No one even knew she was pregnant, or at least no one spoke about it. Not to me anyway."

"And Daiva?" Andrius began slowly, hopefully. "She helped you raise me? She took me in."

Aleksandras bit his lip. He hovered his hand over Andrius's back for a moment, and then he began to gently rub it.

"I don't know what to say, my boy. Have I told you how special you are? You're different, Andrius, in a good way. I know your life is going to be a good one. An important one. I found you a wet nurse after the first few nights, and she loved you well. Came by a few times a day to help feed you. She's dead now, unfortunately."

"Papa," Andrius whispered. "You didn't answer my question."

He let out a long sigh. "You're old enough. I hate to say it, but you are." The old man scratched his head. "Do you want the truth or a good story?"

It wasn't even a question for Andrius. "The truth."

"Daiva . . . She didn't want you. She told me to put you back. She insisted that we would be outcasts, you would embarrass us—and she was already embarrassed that she couldn't have a child, understand. She said to kill you, bury you, leave you, forget about you. She screamed and cried." He laughed bitterly. "Oh how she threatened me. She said we were not going to take you in no matter what."

Andrius pulled his knees to his chest. The knots in his stomach were back. Aleksandras nodded his head once and sat up straighter.

"But I put my foot down. It's probably the only time I ever have. A man has to put his foot down sometimes, Andrius. I know

I'm a bad example for you, but it's true. I said, 'No. I'm keeping this boy.'" His lip began to quiver and he drew Andrius into a firm embrace. "'I'm keeping my special boy, even if the whole world judges me for it.' My son."

Andrius was short of breath. He didn't know how to think or how to respond. He only knew the scrawny old man who wouldn't let go of him.

"I didn't make you," Aleksandras whispered. "But I am your father. You are my son and I'm your father."

"I know, Papa," Andrius told him softly. He clenched his eyes shut as hard as he could. It was so much to take in.

The old man held him for a long time, and then he rose to his feet, wiped his eyes, and unceremoniously shuffled out of the barn, sliding his cane back and forth as he went.

ANDRIUS WAS WALKING ON EGGSHELLS ALL morning, trying his best to go about his chores without incurring the wrath of Daiva, the woman who was not his mother. The woman who had begged his father to leave him out in the cold to die when he was an infant.

Leaving the house was a relief when the time came. It was nice to hear the sun singing again after a long night. Andrius's jaw felt tender to the touch still and a little puffy, but he could close it now. It would hurt badly to chew, but he could do it when he had to.

So much of the world had changed for him in a single evening. Daiva was not his mother. He was grateful, in a way, but it raised all sorts of questions. He did not particularly want to think about the sorts of questions it raised.

It was slightly hot today, and Andrius felt a bead of sweat form on his back as he raised his pitcher to his lips. He left his cane at home, but that didn't bother him. He opened his eyes wide and listened to the crown of mountains in the Regions of Death, beyond the barrier.

He wondered momentarily what would happen to a person who crossed over.

It was a silly question, of course. That person would die. The village was a safe haven from the dangers lying outside.

It was odd that the stranger had come from across the barrier.

Daniel. He made it sound like there was civilization in the Regions of Death.

It couldn't be true, of course.

Andrius shivered. He had reasons for believing that there was nothing but death outside of the barrier. He wondered if there was a chance that his mother was alive, but no. He knew she was dead.

A rock spun off of Andrius's foot as he took a step and he followed its motion as it rolled. He kicked it again once he caught up to it. This little game of 'kick the rock' kept him amused until about Seventh Stone.

Maybe he would get to talk to Daniel again today. He was very odd, but he was interesting. Andrius had lots of questions for him buzzing in the back of his mind.

Despite everything, the hint of a grin appeared at the edge of his lips. He thought of Milda. Maybe he would run into her again, and they could walk to lessons together.

Sure, they had had their differences in the past, but she really was wonderful. She was smart and she always smelled nice, and she was good at writing songs.

He daydreamed of her until Fourth Stone, when he saw her walking up the road, tapping her cane in her own particular rhythm. Next to her was Berena, and they chatted as they went.

Andrius's hint of a grin grew to a smile.

"I think I'll join them," he said aloud. They were a ways off, but he would be able to catch up quickly.

He was excited. He never approached someone he knew just to talk and walk with them. He'd never had a friend before, let alone two.

As he drew closer and they passed Second Stone, he could

hear their voices with good clarity. They were still facing away from him and about thirty steps distant, but the sound carried well where they were. They hadn't noticed him yet. He was just another pair of feet on the road.

Andrius knew that eavesdropping was rude, so he tried not to listen, but then a thought occurred to him: how would he join their conversation if he didn't know what they were talking about? Other people made it seem so easy. He decided to listen so that he would be able to join in once he caught up to them.

"No, I don't think that man will be there again today. He was talking badly about the First Prophet, and they can't let *that* go on," Berena was saying.

"That's fine with me," Milda answered. "It was fun finding him and everything, but he was weird."

"So were you really with Andrius yesterday when you talked to him?"

Andrius beamed, hearing his name. The world was, after all, a beautiful place.

"I mean, on purpose?" Berena added with a laugh.

Milda scoffed. "Berena, please."

"I mean it, Milda. Are you his friend now?" She sounded disgusted.

"I'm not his friend," Milda replied, bored. "I just talk to him sometimes because I feel bad for him. He's annoying and nobody likes him. I don't know why I do it sometimes, but no. He's just a weird kid I feel bad for."

Andrius's steps slowed until he stopped completely. It was as if he was a tree and disappointment was the wind, beating against him again and again.

He stood there in the middle of the road, hearing the girls' laughter and conversation grow softer and softer until it was gone.

His arms hung limply at his sides. His pitcher of water was heavy in his hand.

It wasn't that surprising, really. It had been foolish to hope that things were different, like with his offering. Of course it wouldn't get chosen. It had been silly to think that it had a chance.

The familiar old weight was back on his chest, and Andrius took a sip of water from his wooden pitcher.

"I can't be late to lessons," he said after a while. He wanted to say that it didn't matter what Milda and Berena said, but he couldn't bring himself to do it. He would think about something else, or better yet, nothing at all.

He took a mechanical step forward, then another.

"ALL RIGHT, THANK YOU FOR CALLING OUT ROLL, children. Everyone is here, it seems, except for Andrius," the instructor said a little venomously. No one was late for lessons, ever. "We will deal with him later. Children, let me take a moment to once again remind you all of the importance of being on time. Our great founder once said that timeliness may well be the first among virtues. A few minutes early is on time, on time is late, and being late is unacceptable. Of course, the individual who needs this lecture isn't here."

"I'm here, Teacher," Andrius said fecklessly as he arrived. He had heard the whole thing.

The instructor crossed his arms.

"Nice of you to join us, Andrius. Now tell me, laggard, do you have a good reason for joining us late?"

Andrius considered lying and saying that he had been sitting there the whole time. It would probably work. Everyone was so oblivious to the things around them.

"No, Teacher."

"Very well," the instructor replied with a frown. "I do not need to tell you how inappropriate your tardiness is. We will discuss punishment after class."

Andrius was nervous, but typically he would have been hysterical, nearly inconsolable. Yet the pain in his heart dulled things. It was like a blanket of snow over the land, making everything seem farther away.

"Now," the instructor began again, shifting his tone, "we will be working on writing today and recitation of several wonderful odes to our Prophet and his predecessors, including some of your favorite poems, and after tomorrow's celebration–aren't you excited?–we will review the history of the disease, the cure, and the world that was. First, I would like you to each take a piece of parchment so you can–"

"What does 'blind' mean?"

All of the children perked up their ears. Some put their arms around themselves nervously. The instructor had frozen where he was, half bending down. His mouth hung open.

No one interrupted lessons. Not with a non sequitur, at least. Andrius noticed the discomfort around him, but he didn't care just then.

The instructor remembered himself at last, straightened, and cleared his throat.

"We don't go over vocabulary again for another week, Andrius. Now please try to keep your questions relevant and well-timed. As I was saying–"

"But what does it mean?" Andrius asked again. "Blind. What is it?"

The instructor wanted to be upset with Andrius, but he was more bewildered than anything. Andrius was usually very quiet in class. He was usually very quiet all of the time. The instructor decided he would just add to his punishment after class.

Andrius noticed the academic demeanor come over his instructor, briefly replacing the disciplinarian.

"It is an old word. Archaic, even. I heard my grandfather use it two or three times when I was a boy, which is the only reason I know it. No one uses it anymore."

"But what does it mean?" Andrius pleaded. The grass tickled his calves as he leaned forward. The other students didn't know what to think about the unorthodox exchange.

"I was getting to that. It means not being able to understand a concept, or when a person misses something obvious. 'I just explained that to you; are you blind?' or 'The pig is right beside you; are you blind?'"

Andrius leaned back, a little disappointed. He had been thinking about his conversation with Daniel during his whole walk down Brick Road. The stranger had not been outside of Gimdymo Namai, and he wanted to ask him about some of the unfamiliar words he used.

"Oh," Andrius replied hollowly. The sun sang cheerily

overhead. Bugs buzzed and jumped through the grass.

"Why?" the instructor asked. "Where did you hear that word?"

The way the instructor asked the question made Andrius afraid, but his numbness softened the blow. "From Daniel."

"Who?"

"From the strange man that we found. Yesterday. He said that everyone in the village was blind except for . . . Well, except for–"

"By the sacred Book of Emptiness, Andrius!" Viktoras exclaimed. "Just say it already."

"Except for him and me."

The instructor scoffed then grew serious. "How long did you speak to him?"

Andrius was looking off into the distance, listening to the majestic mountains that encircled their glen.

"Andrius?"

"Hm?" he said, coming back to attention.

"How long did you speak with him?" The instructor was stern. His eyes were shut.

"Not very long." Then, a surge of moxie struck him and he pointed. "Milda was there. Berena talked to him too."

The girls gasped.

"That isn't true!" Berena insisted.

"Andrius!" Milda hissed. "Why would you say that?"

"All right, all right," the instructor interrupted, waving his hands. "I was going to talk about this regardless, but here we are and now seems like the time. The Prophet and his Regents have examined the stranger and questioned him and they found him to be quite unstable. He believed that he was from some magical city in the Regions of Death when in fact, his name is Drunas, Benas and Ieva's runaway child. He left the village years ago and has been living in the outskirts of the meadow ever since. His parents, as well as all of us, thought he was dead."

Excited conversations erupted. The instructor's raised voice shushed them.

"They also discovered, as I said, that he was very unstable. Do not believe anything you heard him say. It was good of us to bring him home, but he is unfortunately mad from living in the meadow for so long."

Andrius wrestled with himself. He spoke, not intending to address the teacher, only to muse, but his thoughts came out loud.

"He couldn't have lived out in the meadow. I listen to it every single day, and the day we found him was the first time I had ever heard him."

"Even your magic ears are not perfect, Andrius. Now stop speaking up. Shall we continue with our writing, children?"

"We found him on the other side of the barrier . . ."

"Andrius, enough!" the instructor snapped as he threw his stack of parchment to the dirt. "That is quite enough out of you."

"I'm sorry," Andrius said, looking down. The other students were still as death.

"Sorry only goes so far, Andrius. You mock our traditions with your lack of effort, you expose yourself to reckless risks, you are disrespectful, disruptive, and late!" The instructor took a breath and shook his head. "Andrius, I'm sorry, but it's what must be done. I have to take you to the Prophet."

Fear gripped Andrius's heart. The other children gasped in unison.

"No, don't do that, Teacher," Andrius pleaded.

"Teacher, isn't there another way?" Milda added.

"He's just dumb, Teacher," Viktoras chimed in. "You don't need to take him to the Prophet for discipline."

"Silence!"

Everyone waited for the instructor to continue. Andrius was terrified. He hadn't the slightest clue what seeing the Prophet for discipline might be like, but he had heard rumors and he had some idea of what the punishment might be. The peace had to be kept and a severe peace must be kept severely, as the First Prophet had said.

"It is necessary," the instructor said evenly. "Andrius, we must wait until the proceedings are through for the Day of Remembrance before your case is heard. You will stand with me atop Gimdymo Namai so that the Prophet can receive you after it is over. Use this evening to reflect on your behavior of late and what it does to the community." The instructor took a deep breath, then bent over and felt around for the parchment until he had collected it all. "Now," he said in a too-quiet voice, "everyone take a sheet please. We will be practicing our letters."

The children did as they were told, but joylessly. They didn't even like Andrius, but still they were afraid.

Andrius was terrified. His stomach tied in knots worse than it ever had before.

The instructor continued speaking, but Andrius didn't hear him. He was afraid of shame. He hated being wrong. He wanted to be right for once. Just one time.

And he wanted to live.

6

ANDRIUS DIDN'T EVEN REMEMBER THE REST OF THE day. He was a ghost drifting through the land of the living. After lessons the other children avoided him more purposefully than usual, as if the cloud of doom that hung over his head might be catching.

Discipline was rare in the village. It was not lenient.

He had stumbled home in a haze, and his father had insisted that he come along to the Stone Gathering in the evening because the Prophet says to share company and warmth. The cane-makers and the apothecary and the farmers and the ranchers and the cartwheel flower growers all sat together in the evenings because the village was one.

As Andrius sat on the ground by the fire, he did not feel part of that blessed union. He rarely did, but at no other point in his young life had he ever felt so far removed.

There was music and the neighbors laughed, sang, and talked, but all Andrius had were his thoughts, his fears, and his pain.

He couldn't help feeling that this never would have happened if he had not found Daniel.

Where was he anyway?

It didn't matter. Nothing seemed to matter.

"Andrius, my boy. You are uncharacteristically silent this evening."

Andrius looked up from his daze. His father had a fragile smile on his lips and that reserved but earnest desire for approval that he perennially wore.

Andrius hadn't told him yet. How could he?

"I was just thinking, Papa."

Aleksandras clapped his hands and grinned.

"My boy the poet has a thought! Listen, all ye near him!" He chuckled good-naturedly. He was so sincere in everything. "Herkus," he said, leaning to the side. "My boy's been thinking. You better listen to what he has to say."

Herkus broke from his conversation just long enough to curse Aleksandras, and then he was deaf to them again. Andrius looked around. No one was listening to them or paying any sort of attention at all. It was like he and his father were a bubble in the midst of the river, but impenetrable.

"There you are, my boy," Aleksandras declared earnestly. "Now you have an audience."

Andrius hesitated. He couldn't tell his father what he had been thinking about. The old man's heart would break. And yet he had to tell him something.

He settled quite by accident on something he had been wondering about earlier.

"I was just thinking, why don't you open your eyes more, Papa? Everyone keeps them closed almost all of the time."

Aleksandras waited a minute for the punch line. When it didn't come, he lightly chuckled, then stifled himself for fear of offending the boy.

He scratched his chin.

"Well, the eyes are sensitive, I think. Dirt or sand can get in them, I suppose, and that would hurt. And the disease attacks through the eyes first, so keeping them open seems unwise. Besides," he added with a laugh, "it's hard to keep your eyes open for very long! Those little muscles are very weak."

Andrius pulled his knees to his chest, distracted finally from his impending doom.

"I keep mine open," he said quietly.

"You do?"

Andrius nodded.

"Except when I sleep. I keep them open all day."

"You are a special one, Andrius. You must know something I don't. A lot of things, I'm sure." The old man dug his cane into the soft earth around the fire.

"Papa," Andrius said timidly. "Would you open your eyes for me?"

Aleksandras cocked his head. "Why?"

"I want to . . . look at them and listen."

"Look? What does that mean?"

Andrius felt embarrassed. Maybe it wasn't a real word after all. His instructor had told him that Daniel was crazy. His name wasn't even Daniel, it was Drunas. It was hard not to believe him though. He had been so convincing, like he wasn't trying to convince Andrius of anything at all. He had just talked with him.

"I want to listen to them, I mean."

Aleksandras very obviously did not understand, but he wanted to please his son.

"Very well," he said.

His eyelids trembled. Then, amidst the twitching, his left eye opened halfway, then the other. He was concentrating quite a bit. His eyes opened to about two-thirds of their capacity and stayed there, continuing to tremble.

Andrius rose to his feet, transfixed by his father's eyes. They were like standing at the edge of a hole, and yet it was different somehow. They were like milk and clouds. They were emptiness and hollow. They were frightening.

"Your eyes . . ." Andrius began, struggling to find the words as he touched his father's face. "They sound different than mine."

He kept thinking back to Daniel. Crazy or not, his eyes were . . . alive. Patterns and sky lived inside of them. Circles within circles.

Daniel had said they were just like Andrius's eyes.

Aleksandras laughed.

"They sound different than yours? Here, let me check."

The old man tapped his eyes and made a funny sound with his tongue. Then he gently touched Andrius's eyelid and made another noise, from deep in his throat.

"Hm, you're right," he said. "They do sound different."

He laughed again thinking he had made a good joke and one that his son would like. Usually Andrius would have chuckled along, but not tonight. All he could manage was a sad smile as his father closed his lifeless eyes.

"Hey, Aleksandras!" came a voice from the other side of the amphitheater. "Is your boy going to be challenged again tonight?"

Aleksandras patted Andrius on the shoulder and raised a cupped hand beside his mouth. "Only if someone wants to lose his chickens!"

Several bystanders laughed.

"Herkus didn't lose any!"

"That's because Herkus is a lying oath-breaker!" a less jovial voice declared.

Andrius looked up, searching for the source of the conversation's sudden shift in tone.

It was Daumantas, Berena's father. He had wavy hair and the broadest shoulders in the village. He shaped the canes that they all used. Men were afraid of him, even though he was good-humored most of the time.

The fire popped and crackled. People listened.

Daumantas took a step forward and spoke in his low, resonant voice. "Aleksandras, did Herkus ever pay you for his bet?"

Herkus spat where he was sitting.

"Oh, die in a blizzard, Daumantas. It was no fair contest, so I'm keeping my chickens."

Aleksandras looked uncomfortable. His bony knees stuck out from under his wool blanket.

"Aleksandras," Daumantas demanded again. "Did Herkus settle his debt?"

"Well," Aleksandras stammered. "It's not that–I mean, what did we . . . Well, the agreement was that–"

Andrius closed his eyes and sighed. Herkus interrupted his father.

"Come down off your pedestal, Daumantas. I didn't pay him and I won't. The contest wasn't fair."

"Can you prove that?" he challenged.

Herkus spat again. "It wouldn't have been successful cheating if I knew how it was done, now would it? His boy has been cheating you all for years."

"Come around, Herkus," a woman shouted. "You're being a poor sport.

"Bah," Herkus replied, taking a sip of his ale. "I won't

let my property go to that fool. Say what you like. Two chickens is too much."

"So you willfully break your oath?" Daumantas asked gravely.

Herkus went back to his conversation. His friends seemed nervous, but they chatted with him nonetheless.

Daumantas shook his head. "Very well. Aleksandras may seek justice against you, or another may do so on his behalf."

Herkus burped grotesquely in defiance of Daumantas's posturing. He had consumed his own ale, as well as those of several other men who were willing to part with theirs.

Andrius returned to his place on the ground, rocking back and forth gently.

By and by the music started up again and the tension melted away. A dull roar of conversation filled the amphitheater once again.

Elze, the apothecary, came up to Andrius after a while and nudged him with her elbow.

"Andrius, is this you?"

"Yes, Elze," he answered listlessly.

The apothecary flashed a toothy grin and pulled a handful of rocks out of her pocket. "What do you say we play, eh? No betting, just sport. My rocks and your magic ears counting them as they lay down. What do you say?"

Andrius couldn't take it anymore. He felt something bubbling up inside of him that he tried to suppress.

"Why is this impressive to you?" Andrius snapped. The apothecary was shocked, and she took a step back, but the boy was unabated. "Honestly, I just don't understand why anyone even finds this game amusing. Someone sets down some rocks and there they are right in front of me. And people bet against me? That I'll forget how to count? The rocks are right there—anyone should be able to hear them! It's a stupid game," he concluded sullenly.

The apothecary stood in place with her mouth agape.

"Andrius," Aleksandras chided. "Did you mean to speak that way to Elze?"

Andrius was thinking about tomorrow and the Prophet's judgment. He was so afraid. He trembled.

"No," he said softly, his voice cracking.

"Well, I . . . I don't know what to say," the apothecary replied.

"He's very sorry, Elze," Aleksandras assured her. "He has been quiet all night. I think he is sick. I'll take him home. Please do not take offense. Come by my hut tomorrow and I will give you a gift to make up for the insult, which was certainly accidental. Right, Andrius?"

Andrius wiped his nose with his arm. His stomach was all twisted up.

"Yes," he said. "I'm so sorry, Elze. I didn't mean to be rude."

The apothecary tapped around her with her cane, and then she began to shuffle away. "Well, you were. Keep your gifts, Aleksandras. I'll accept the boy's apology. Teach him how to speak to his betters," she added, stopping to say one bit more. "Others in this village do not drop a slight so easily as I do."

Andrius felt awful, but what did it matter? He was already facing judgment tomorrow. Nothing could be worse than that.

Aleksandras came over to Andrius and felt around for his shoulders. Finding them, he wrapped the boy in a fragile hug.

"Come on," he said. "Let's go home."

ANDRIUS AWOKE BEFORE THE SUN HAD YET STARTED to sing, like he always did. He wondered if today was the last chance he would ever get to wake up.

He had to face the Prophet for judgment today. A severe peace must be kept severely.

Andrius jumped out of his bed of hay, as if propelled by the thought. He sank to one knee hard and exhaled into his hands. The cows were lowing already. They wanted to be milked.

Andrius's breathing came in fast, panicked gasps at first. Over time it slowed until it was almost regular. He removed his hands from his face, suddenly struck by the smell of the old barn again.

"If it's my last day, I'll live it well," Andrius softly declared. He rose unsteadily to his feet and stepped outside.

The chill of the dawn wrapped around him, making his hairs stand on end, and there was moisture in the air. It was pleasant. He listened to the pigs' occasional snorting. They hadn't woken up yet. He curled his toes and felt the soil beneath his feet. He tasted the dew on his tongue and inhaled the sweet, pungent smell of plants and animals thriving. Then he looked to the sky.

It reminded him of his father's eyes, but it wasn't like milk or clouds. It was like a squirrel's fur, or the ash that's left after a fire.

"Maybe that's what it is," Andrius mumbled aloud in response to his thoughts. "It's the ash leftover from yesterday's sun." It was lovely, whatever it was. Everything seemed more real to Andrius this morning: harsher, more beautiful, more tragic, and more exciting. His senses were alive and so was he.

For now.

With a deep sigh, Andrius returned his eyes to the world around him and got to work.

Today was the Day of Remembrance, so no unnecessary work was to be done. Unfortunately, most of his chores had to be done every day. That's the way it was with raising animals.

It was difficult not to despair.

By the time Andrius wandered into the hut for breakfast, he had lost that fleeting sensation of vibrancy. The world was dull now, and it remained to him for only a short time more.

The door creaked as he pushed it open.

"Andrius? Is that you, my boy?"

Aleksandras sat at the modest table, smiling. He held a knife to a loaf of bread that by the looks of it had just been made. Normally that would have excited Andrius.

"How did you know it was me?" Andrius asked lifelessly. He went through the motions of conversation for his father's sake.

"Your step is"–Aleksandras paused, catching himself–"different than Daiva's."

His step didn't shake the foundations of the house was what his father meant.

Andrius sighed as he lifted the pail of milk he had collected and set it on the table.

"Milk," he said simply, and then he reached into his pockets to retrieve the eggs he had collected. He set his water pitcher on the ground so that he would be able to use both hands.

"Splendid!" Aleksandras declared. "Oh, Andrius," he sang in a low voice. "In case your nose has failed you, and perhaps your magic ears too, would you like to know what I've got?"

Andrius placed the last of the eggs in the basket. "Bread."

"Bread! And freshly baked. I walked to Bronius's home just

a few minutes ago. It is a special occasion, after all."

Andrius was about to take a seat, but he noticed his father rising, so he remained standing. He placed his right hand over his heart like Aleksandras was doing, and he spoke in unison with the old man.

"Let us never forget, or may the earth swallow us up in punishment.

Let us never forget, or may the disease take us and send us the way of the whole world.

Let us never forget, lest we become like the unenlightened, the cowardly, and the perished.

We remember the Hausen War and its valiant heroes.

We remember the First Ones, who fathered this remnant in new life.

We remember the fires of purification, where they destroyed their possessions.

We remember reverence for our Prophet, and the legacy and wisdom he embodies.

We remember our duty to the village and its good.

We remember Zydrunas, his philosophy, and his great deeds.

He is our First Prophet, the embodiment of science, the slayer of the disease.

First among warriors, first among kings, our leader and our hope.

Zydrunas! We will not forget."

Aleksandras smiled widely and took his seat once more. Andrius wondered how many times they would all say the pledge today.

"It is the Day of Remembrance," Aleksandras declared. "Or had you forgotten?" He laughed as if he didn't tell this same joke every year. "May it be a happy one for you, my boy, my Andrius. Today we celebrate our beloved founder Zydrunas and Valdas who keeps his legacy."

"Yes, Papa," Andrius agreed. The Day of Remembrance was not the only holiday celebrating Zydrunas, of course. There was a celebration at least every month, in fact, but the Day of Remembrance was the greatest. It was a special day, and typically Andrius would have been bouncing up and down with excitement.

Aleksandras went back to happily cutting his bread, whistling. Daiva was probably still in bed, as usual.

"Papa," Andrius began, putting an arm around the old man.

Aleksandras seemed surprised but welcoming. He set the knife down straight away. "Andrius, my boy, what is it?"

"Thank you," was all that Andrius could manage. "Just . . . thank you."

The old man raised his bushy eyebrows.

"You're welcome, son. It's only some bread."

Andrius shook his head. The weight on his chest was unbearable, overwhelming.

"Will you give me a hug?" he asked quietly.

"Why of course," Aleksandras replied with a sweet chuckle.

Andrius closed his eyes as he felt the thin arms wrap around him. He treasured the moment until it was gone.

Andrius thought he would say more, but he was out of words. He backed toward the door and halted only long enough to pick up his water pitcher. He kept his eyes on his father.

"Goodbye, Papa."

"Wait! Don't you want any bread?"

Andrius stopped for a moment as his father scooped up a thick slab of the fresh bread, grabbed his cane, and tapped his way over to

Andrius. He pushed the morsel into Andrius's hands.

"There you are. Goodbye, my boy. Enjoy the festival!"

Andrius kept his eyes on his father walking back to the table, as Andrius backed out of the hut.

The door creaked as it shut.

THE WALK DOWN STONE ROAD FELT LIKE A WALK TO the gallows. It was like each roadstone counted down the last precious hours of Andrius's life: Fourth Stone, Third Stone, Second Stone . . . Everywhere he looked there were smiling faces and he like a ghost among them. No one heeded his frown or the mountains in the distance or the sun singing over them all. It was like they didn't notice. They couldn't.

Andrius's emotions came in swells. He no longer felt panic quickening his heart and making his eyes dart around him in paranoia. At this moment he felt only morbid realization as he shuffled one foot in front of the other. Gimdymo Namai was only a short distance ahead of him now, beyond the crowds that eagerly gathered for the day's celebration. Andrius couldn't bring himself to care. It was probably inside of that very same sleek building where he would be killed for his crimes.

Maybe they would only cut off an ear or something. That wasn't unheard of, though less common. True, he had been late for lessons and disruptive and he didn't fit in exactly, but it wasn't like he had spoken against the Prophet or something.

What was he thinking? It would be just like Egidijus, who got the ultimate punishment when Andrius was little. He had been a few years older than Andrius, but their crimes were not very different.

They were going to kill him. A severe peace must be kept severely.

He felt briefly like he understood his mother then–his real mother. If it was discovered that she had an illegitimate child, her life would have been put to an end for sure. It's no wonder she went over the barricade and into the Regions of Death.

Of course, there was even less promise there than with the Prophet's judgment.

Unless Daniel had been telling the truth. *We could fix all these people if they came down from here–down the mountain to Brezno.*

Andrius was no fool, but he did wonder. He never heard anything dangerous from the edge of the forest. He wished he could talk with Daniel some more. Maybe he would be at the festival. Of course he would be at the festival. Andrius would ask after him.

He saw Milda, Berena, and a few others of his age-peers as he neared Gimdymo Namai, but he did not bother with greeting them. They belonged to a different world, one that Andrius never quite seemed to fit into.

The people were not much for decoration, and the state of the village's center reflected this. They were, however, much for music. When Andrius began wading through the crowds, a mighty forty-piece pipe orchestra was playing a dirge in honor of Zydrunas. It was ethereal and sad, beautiful and yet with a feeling of inevitable and inescapable doom. The reed pipes rose and fell, then rushed all together like the violent river that bisected their village.

The proceedings would begin soon. Already the village had started organizing themselves by age group. From three years old and upward every villager stood with his own age-peers, regardless of marital status, health, desire, or wealth. Coming into the world is an important rite of passage, and it is the first rite that anyone ever has. They stood with their contemporaries.

The only exceptions to this very stringent rule were the Prophet, his Regents, and anyone awaiting judgment. They stood on the roof of Gimdymo Namai, facing the crowd of nearly a thousand.

Something sharp caught Andrius's attention from the top of Gimdymo Namai. A huge bronze gong swung on its ropes and rang out, low and powerful across the masses. Andrius squinted up at the figure beside the hanging cymbal, trying to discern his identity.

Barrel-chested and bowlegged, he couldn't be mistaken. It was the Regent of Stone. The Regent drew the mallet back and stuck the gong again and again, causing the milling crowds to break into a flurry of action.

Everyone knew that it was time to get where they were supposed to be. The proceedings would begin in a matter of minutes.

"Thirty-fives!" a gruff voice rang out amid the waves of people moving to their places.

"Eight-year-olds!" a much higher voice called.

"Fifty-threes!" came another.

"Jokubas!" an old man called out as loud as his weak voice could manage. Andrius recognized him as he passed. It was Pilypas, and he was seventy-one years old. He didn't need to call out his age because Jokubas was the only other person in his age group. There were a few people older than Pilypas, but none of them still had an age peer, and they stood alone. These were chosen to represent their age groups every year de facto.

As far as Andrius could tell, Jokubas and Pilypas just switched off every year.

"Jokubas!" he called again, hobbling around, both leaning on his cane and searching around with it.

Andrius felt oddly sorry for him as he hobbled past. He didn't know why.

"I'm the one who's going to die," Andrius muttered to himself.

"Andrius?"

Andrius turned around. It was his instructor. His hands were on his hips, like Daiva when she got mad.

Of course, his instructor was much slimmer than Daiva. It would take four of him to be Daiva.

"Yes, Teacher."

"It's almost time. Go up, go up!"

Andrius put his hand on the two-story ladder that leaned against the sleek building, placed there for the day's ceremonies so that the various representatives from each age group could ascend to the roof and deliver their offering on behalf of their age-peers.

The ladder was made from long, thick branches, stripped down and lashed together with leather thongs.

"I would think you would leap at the chance to climb this ladder, Andrius," his instructor called over the noise of the crowd. "After the way you were so eager to scurry up a tree." The instructor shuddered, and he was a human being for a moment, albeit an odd one to Andrius. "I can't stand it, personally. It frightens me. I've had to climb up four times to represent my age-peers." His bearing changed and he regained possession of himself. "It is an honor, of course."

Andrius put his foot on the first rung of the ladder and started up. A ladder wasn't as interesting as climbing a tree.

"Yes, Teacher," he said.

By the time Andrius reached the top of the building, which was surprisingly spacious and hard underfoot, the gong was sounding again. The Regent of Stone struck the bronze instrument only once.

Andrius's instructor followed him up, then quickly ushered him out of the way. The three Regents were on the roof with Andrius and his instructor, but no one else. Those picked to represent their age-peers would only ascend the ladder when it was their turn to present. There was no sign of the Prophet yet.

In one collective motion, every right hand in the village went over its respective heart. With one voice, the village chanted.

"Let us never forget, or may the earth swallow us up in punishment.

Let us never forget, or may the disease take us and send us the way of the whole world.

Let us never forget, lest we become like the unenlightened, the cowardly, and the perished.

We remember the Hausen War and its valiant heroes.

We remember the First Ones, who fathered this remnant in new life.

We remember the fires of purification, where they destroyed their possessions.

We remember reverence for our Prophet, and the legacy and wisdom he embodies.

We remember our duty to the village and its good.

We remember Zydrunas, his philosophy, and his great deeds.

He is our First Prophet, the embodiment of science, the slayer of the disease.

First among warriors, first among kings, our leader and our hope.

Zydrunas! We will not forget."

Andrius's lips moved without thinking. He had said the pledge so many times that it was automatic.

That was not what stirred him. The gathered crowd was interesting, but that wasn't it either. Where was the Prophet?

Andrius scanned back and forth, but he could not hear him. The crowd waited silently, patiently. There was not so much as a whisper.

The moments between the first pledge and the impartation by the Prophet were sacred silence. No one would ever think to break it.

Finally, there he was. The main doors of Gimdymo Namai burst open and the Prophet boldly strode forth. His flowing robes danced at his sides with each assured, self-possessed step that he took.

Then he did a curious thing. Instead of climbing up the ladder and joining them on the roof, he waded out into the crowd, deeper and deeper among the people. It was an incredible gesture. The Prophet, though rightfully above, sometimes graced the villagers with his presence.

Andrius almost spoke aloud, but he caught himself at the last moment. If his fate wasn't sealed already, it would be if he broke the sacred silence.

The Prophet moved further into the forest of people, who dipped their heads and stepped back as he passed. It was like a wedge had been driven into the formerly singular mass. The Prophet left a trail of open space behind him.

He reached the thirteen-year-olds and then he spoke for the first time. His voice was like sun and honey, the smell of cedar and the roar of a hearth fire. It could just as soon lull a man to sleep as it could call him to action. It was strong, solid, and pure.

It was with this voice that he spoke very simply.

"The sacred silence is broken!"

In accordance with tradition, the rest of the village placed their hands over their mouths, then removed them and spoke with one voice.

"Its purpose accomplished, our memories fresh. Zydrunas is great! So is his Prophet who continues his vision."

Andrius couldn't take his eyes away from the man. He was rapt.

"Children," the Prophet began, "what is your age group?"

"Thirteen years, Prophet."

The Prophet nodded, then held out his hand.

"Let the one called Jehena step forth."

The smaller group parted again, and a young girl with her smooth hair in a tight and complicated braid walked toward the Prophet, gently swaying her cane in front of her. Wood struck that strange substance called metal as Jehena's cane came against the Prophet's. She wore the biggest, most elated smile that Andrius had ever observed.

The Prophet reached a hand around her back and kissed her, and then he led her back along the path through the crowd, toward Gimdymo Namai.

Jehena bounced as she walked. Andrius realized that she was not much older than he himself was, and the Prophet had chosen her.

It was a tremendous honor. Andrius had never seen a Day of Remembrance begin this way.

The Prophet put Jehena up to the ladder first and he followed behind. As they climbed, Andrius's heart filled with eager expectation.

It didn't make sense; he knew that on some level. The coming of the Prophet almost certainly meant Andrius's doom, and yet . . . The man was so majestic. When he spoke, the whole village listened. When he sang, trees were said to weep. He was entrusted with the sacred Book of Emptiness, with continuing the visionary work of Zydrunas, and with administering the cure to every new child born in the village. In a very real way, he gave life to them all.

Andrius couldn't help but admire him. His fear was a separate issue entirely.

As the Prophet pulled himself up the last rung and stepped over onto the roof, Andrius's heart raced. It was the closest he had ever been to him.

He wore an amiable smile, and yet it was paternal as well. His beard was perfect, like a field of wheat stalks in the summer. He had a strong chin, broad shoulders, and a lean build.

He was the Prophet.

Andrius looked toward the others on the roof, wondering what their response to the great man would be.

The Regents of Stone and Brick seemed proud. They stood up straight as the Prophet passed and gave them his greeting. The Regent of Wood, a tall, wiry man who was younger than the other two, did not seem happy. He crossed his arms and tapped his fingers neurotically.

"The Regent of Wood is Jehena's father," Andrius's instructor whispered excitedly. "He must be so proud."

Reaching the fore, the Prophet raised his hand and spoke over the crowd, across generations and time itself.

"I wish the enlightenment of Zydrunas upon you all," he declared in his thick, buttery-rich tone.

"Gladly do we receive it and live it with our lives," the crowd responded.

"Today is an important day: the greatest and gravest of our celebrations. Today, as with each day, we commit ourselves to the memory and the philosophy, the hardships, the triumphs, and the ultimate vision of the greatest man who ever lived. I speak of the honorable Zydrunas, in whose stead I speak. Do you remember?"

The village recited the pledge again, and Andrius thought somewhere in the back of his mind that this was the third time he'd said it today. He was betting he'd break thirty by the day's end.

As he formed the words in unison with the others, Andrius could not help but turn toward the Regent of Wood. He seemed angry. He was breathing slowly but heavily, and he kept reaching down to his leg, then pulling his hand back.

The village finished the pledge and the Prophet spoke over them.

"Do you remember our founder, our First and Greatest?"

"Yes!"

"Have you brought tokens of offering: song, speech, poetry, and any other means of honoring him and passing truth to the village to come?"

"We have brought it, each from his age."

"Very good," the Prophet declared. "You have done well."

Andrius wondered why the Regent of Wood was acting so

strangely. Everyone else seemed content, and soon, Andrius was drawn in by the Prophet's charisma once more, listening intently. His own fate didn't matter in this moment. For the good of the village, by the Prophet's word.

"My children," the Prophet began once more, "I come to you today bearing good news. In honor of Zydrunas, I will add to my wives today. Tatjana, Solveiga, Vilte, Estera, Justina, and Ilona will be joined by Jehena!"

The village applauded.

"I have said it and it is good."

"The Prophet has said it," they replied.

Something sharp caught Andrius's attention suddenly, like the gong had earlier. He turned toward the Regent of Wood.

He had pulled a knife from his robe, and he was lunging for the Prophet.

"HE'S GOT A KNIFE!" ANDRIUS SHOUTED AT THE TOP of his lungs, over the Prophet, over the crowd.

The Regent of Wood had crossed the distance, grabbing the Prophet by the shoulder with his free hand.

"She's too young, you filth!" The Regent spat the words through gritted teeth as he reared back with his blade.

Andrius did not know what happened and he did not even remember moving, but before he knew it, he was crashing headfirst into the Regent's side, just as he stabbed at the Prophet.

Being hit so unexpectedly took the tall man down, and his knife, instead of plunging into the heart, sliced across the Prophet's leg.

The Prophet cried out. It was like the sky had fallen. Confusion broke over the crowd below, and Andrius found himself on top of the Regent of Wood, very close to the roof's edge. He tried to scramble back, but the enraged father clasped him by the shirt. Jehena was crying and stomping her feet.

"Daddy? No, Daddy, this is good! It was supposed to be good!"

The Regent of Wood restrained Andrius despite the boy's best attempts at escape. His fingers closed around the knife again.

"You fool!" the Regent of Wood hissed. "You've ruined me!"

The blade would end him, no doubt. The man cradled Andrius's head in a vise-like grip and his legs held Andrius's body. He watched the approaching knife, helpless.

There was tremendous pressure suddenly, as someone landed on him, also pinning the Regent of Wood's arm to the ground. An arm peeled away Andrius's attacker, and he squirmed away as the two men struggled, joined quickly by a third.

The Regent of Stone had intervened–Andrius's Regent. Andrius stumbled and fell onto his backside, astounded at the chaotic scene around him.

The instructor had rushed over to the Prophet and was holding his own shirt onto the wound to stop the bleeding. Jehena, in full tears, was leaning over the roof's edge and screaming for the medic, who was already on his way up the ladder.

The Regent of Stone was a large man, perhaps only surpassed by Daumantas. Yet still the Regent of Wood managed to wriggle his arm free and draw his knife in a long scrape along the bigger man's torso. The Regent of Wood rolled, jumped to his feet, and began swinging his knife wildly.

"Where are you? Come on. Come on!"

The Regents of Stone and Brick stood in front of him, waiting for the right moment. The Regent of Wood twirled around suddenly, and Andrius saw their chance.

"Now!" Andrius cried. "Rush him now!"

The Regents of Stone and Brick collided with their third counterpart at the same time, catching him from behind and much too close to the edge. They tumbled, but the Regent of Wood went farther, having been ahead of them. His screams were chilling in the brief moment that he went off the roof and hurtled to the ground. The Regent of Brick was too far out as well, but he caught the lip of the building as he fell and hung there by his fingertips.

There was a dull thud, and the Regent of Wood didn't scream anymore.

Andrius ran over to the edge just as the Regent of Brick called out to the Regent of Stone, who reached out a bloodied arm and pulled him to safety.

All Andrius could focus on was the mess on the ground. The man must have landed directly on his head, judging from the way he was crumpled over himself. His body was leaking.

The Regent of Wood was dead.

"Stop that," the Prophet was saying. His voice was calming, even in the midst of chaos. "It isn't so bad, just a slice across my leg. Now stop for just a moment."

There were several more people on the roof now. Panic and shock held every heart captive, including Andrius. Most people in the crowd had no idea what was happening.

"Wait for just a moment," the Prophet urged his attendants once again. He moved them away from his leg and amazingly he pulled himself up. "Silence," he said. The village went silent.

The Prophet gathered his thoughts and his breath, and the people waited anxiously. Andrius wanted to slink back to his corner, but he dared not to move for fear of the noise he would make.

Blood dripped from the bottom of the Prophet's robe, and it trickled down his leg. Andrius was sure that he was the bravest, toughest man who ever lived, second only to Zydrunas.

"A great evil was tried today," the Prophet began. "Betrayal from a trusted advisor and friend." Surprisingly, the Prophet shook with the most dignified tears Andrius had ever seen. It was as if he didn't cry for the pain or the hurt in his leg, he cried for humanity, for betrayal, and the worldly instinct in man that caused him to raise a weapon against his brother.

The Prophet's eyes dried as quickly as they had watered, and he inclined his head, speaking with authority.

"Who was the boy who foresaw this, who heard the danger and intervened?"

Andrius's voice caught in his throat. Luckily he did not have to speak.

"It was Andrius! Aleksandras and Daiva's boy–his name is Andrius," his instructor declared. "He's my student for this year's lessons. My name is Adomas, his is Andrius."

The Prophet nodded. When he spoke to Andrius, Andrius felt like everything and nothing all at once. It was sublime paralysis.

"Andrius, my child, is this true? Where are you?"

He cleared his throat with a purpose, trying to sound like the Prophet, but a timid eleven-year-old voice came out instead.

"I'm here, Exalted One. My instructor is telling the truth."

"You heard him cry out, didn't you?" the instructor added from behind. He was a funny spectacle, or would have been in another circumstance. He stood at attention behind the majestic Prophet. He was shirtless, having removed it to stop the Prophet's wound from bleeding. The garment in his hand was covered with bloodstains now.

A brief smile ran across the Prophet's face, and Andrius wondered why.

"Ah, Andrius. It isn't surprising. I know all about you."

This was too much. How did he know all about Andrius? There were a lot of things he would rather the Prophet didn't know, but that wasn't how it worked.

"You do?"

The Prophet nodded. "How did you do it, Andrius? How did you hear him and know of the danger?"

Andrius's chest tightened and he thought of Daniel. The things he had said . . .

"Magic ears!" someone shouted from the crowd. Another enthusiastically shouted the same, and soon the village was chanting his nickname.

He heard the Prophet shout "gong," and the Regent of Stone let go of his bleeding side to find the cymbal's mallet and strike the bronze cymbal. The crowd grew quiet.

The Prophet seemed genuinely interested. He took a step forward.

"Is that how you knew, Andrius? You hear so well that you understand better than your peers? Magic ears . . ."

For the first time, something about that phrase didn't sound right to Andrius. It was true–sort of. And yet he felt like his hearing was not always so special. People heard things before he ever did all the time. But still, there was something special. He closed his eyes, then opened them.

The crowd wanted to hear an explanation, and so did the Prophet.

Something rose up from deep inside of Andrius, or perhaps something came upon him from the outside. However it happened, he had a flash of understanding. Andrius knew.

"I don't think it has anything to do with magic ears, Prophet."

"Well, then how did you hear?"

Andrius closed his eyes and thought hard. He was reaching for something in the void. It was right at the edge of his grasp.

"It's . . . a different kind of hearing. Like when the sun sings or the mountains call their names. I . . . It's hard to describe."

The Prophet urged him on with such kindness and impartation, all in a word. "Try."

Andrius rubbed at his forehead. Then, it struck him.

"You know if you put your hands over your ears you can't hear? It is a different sort of hearing. When I put my hands over my eyes . . ." He did. "I can't do the other kind of hearing. It's another sense."

Not even the birds sang into the depths of the ensuing silence. They all waited, listening for what Andrius or the Prophet might say.

But the Prophet didn't say anything, and the stillness started to grate on Andrius. He had to speak. He had to do something. He was fairly sure that everyone else was missing out on something that he had. They were all . . . blind.

The words tumbled out of him.

"I'll teach you how to learn this new hearing!"

He had meant it to the Prophet, but he was so nervous that he nearly shouted it. The village erupted with applause, understanding that Andrius would instruct them all in the ways of this new sense.

The Prophet smiled. "Very good, Andrius." Then, to his attendants, "Bring me below."

There was a lot of tapping about with canes then, until they struck a hollow sound in the roof. A female attendant, the same one Andrius had seen assisting Ona's delivery, pulled up on a ring in the floor and a flat trapdoor opened up. The medic went down first, and then others began helping the Prophet down into the hole.

"Tadas," the Prophet said to the Regent of Brick, "take over the proceedings. We must not neglect the Day of Remembrance."

He nodded. "Yes, Valdas."

"Petras," he said to the Regent of Stone, "I heard you cry out. Are you injured?"

"Not more than I can abide, Valdas."

"Come with me and have your wounds taken care of."

Andrius was reaching down to retrieve his fallen pitcher just as the Prophet's head was about to disappear down the hidden stairway. The great man stopped to give one more order.

"Bring the boy."

IT FELT LIKE A DREAM STEPPING INTO GIMDYMO Namai. The air tasted different as he breathed it in. The atmosphere was cool and pleasant. Shelves lined the walls stacked with what was likely every book in the village. Andrius could just picture the Prophet sitting in this upper room, running his deft fingers over the lines and lines of upraised dots that made up the words of the books. The Prophet was very wise. Andrius was willing to bet that he spent much of his time reading.

The Prophet sat in an exquisite stuffed leather chair in the corner while several people attended to his leg. Solveiga, his assistant, was holding a towel against the bleeding, another was crushing a pile of herbs to make a poultice, and another had brought a wash basin and was shouting for water.

Andrius looked down at the pitcher in his hand. A lot of it had spilled out when he dropped it to run at the Regent of Wood, but there was still a good amount left.

Gingerly, he stepped through the frenzied group and tipped

his pitcher into the basin, and water splashed into it.

"Thank you," the woman with the washbasin said hurriedly. "Who is that?"

"Andrius," he said weakly.

The Prophet's rich, golden voice spoke out, riding atop of every other less important sound.

"He saves me again, Ilona," the Prophet said. "Are you being taken care of, Petras?"

The Regent of Stone was laid out on a plush leather sofa. Andrius had never seen such furniture. It looked amazingly comfortable.

"Yes, Valdas. He's sewing it now."

A woman came up the stairs from the lower level with a tray of chilled fruits from the spring house and salted meat. Jehena was in the corner biting her nails, but when another attendant came through with a skin of wine, she eagerly agreed to that rather than her fingers.

"The rest of your wives have been called, Prophet," someone said.

The Prophet laughed, a great booming guffaw that let everyone know it was going to be all right.

"Why? I don't want all my wives in here now. Jehena is here, Ilona and Solveiga are here. Aren't there enough people milling around?" He laughed again, and Andrius couldn't help but chuckle along with him.

There was a clatter of footsteps coming up the stairs, and another attendant entered to give his news.

"The former Regent of Wood has been carried away. The fall killed him, and his knife was found near his body."

"Really? It feels like it's still stuck in me," the Prophet joked. Everyone laughed lightly, their spirits raised at the Prophet's unflappability.

It wasn't so tense then. Andrius helped himself to a piece of salted meat as it went past. He did it without thinking, and he was horrified at himself when he looked at the morsel in his hand.

No one yelled at him, however, or even noticed. No one seemed to be counting the pieces, like Daiva always did, and other people took food from the platter as well. Maybe it was all right.

Andrius ate the meat and it was incredible. His lips smacked with salt and just a little bit of grease.

"All right," the Prophet declared, clapping his hands. "Thank you all very much for your attentiveness. Your village is honored by your diligence, but you are missing out on the ceremony! I know most of us, all of us, look forward to the Day of Remembrance the whole year. Go outside and join your age-peers. Remember Zydrunas and all that his legacy means to us. I require only one to attend to my wound. Solveiga, that is you, if you please."

Everyone thanked the Prophet profusely, including Andrius, who made his way toward the stairway. The Prophet held up a hand and stopped them.

"As long as I am here, however, there is the matter of judgment. Attend to it that I may make a ruling now, those of you leaving. Andrius, stay."

Andrius's heart sank, overwhelmed once more by the fears that were his constant companion.

He had forgotten about the judgment in all of the excitement. A good deed does not wipe out a bad one, as the villagers were fond of saying, and a severe peace must be kept severely.

His stomach tied in horrid knots. Whatever the Prophet decided, it was good. Andrius was not above the village's wellbeing.

"Prophet, should I stay as well or should I go?" came another voice. "I am sewing the Regent of Stone's wound."

"You may stay," he said benevolently. "Andrius, come and sit by me."

Andrius hung his head. His impending doom was finally drawing nearer. Resigned to his fate, he crossed the room to the padded stool next to the Prophet's grandiose chair. He didn't know that a stool could be padded, but it was very nice. Everything in this room was more luxurious than Andrius knew was possible.

There were footsteps on the stairs again. Solveiga continued cleaning and drying the Prophet's wound, a great gash across his thigh, but it must not have been as bad as it looked.

"My child," the Prophet began, leaning to his side. "Now I'm afraid you must experience judgment firsthand. I do not relish in it, but it is necessary. A severe peace must be kept severely, after all."

Andrius nodded. He was shaking and trying not to. "Yes, Exalted One."

"Very good. This is for the good of the village, you understand."

Andrius sighed, then agreed.

"And Andrius?" the Prophet asked. "Call me something more familiar than 'Exalted One.'"

Andrius wrinkled his brow. It seemed like an odd occasion to bestow such an honor upon him. He didn't have time to respond, however, for at that moment the footsteps from the stairwell grew louder such that they were about to be joined by the witnesses against him. His instructor would come into the room and tell the Prophet all of Andrius's shortcomings and anti-communal behavior. He did not need to look up. He could hear just fine.

"Who appears before me," the Prophet asked as the newcomers entered the room, "to accuse this man of wrong?"

"I do," one of the men replied. Andrius looked up, confused. It wasn't his instructor, it was Daumantas, Berena's father. With him was Herkus, looking disgruntled and enraged.

"And who stands accused?"

"Wrongfully," Herkus seethed. "I do."

The Prophet nodded wisely. Solveiga threaded a needle to sew his wound, and when she stuck him, he did not even flinch.

"State your names."

"Daumantas."

"Herkus."

"And what is the complaint or the nature of the crime? Daumantas, do you stand as accuser on your own behalf or on the behalf of another?"

Andrius could not take his eyes off of the needle dipping in and out of the Prophet's fresh wound. He was jabbed again and again and again by the needle, but still he did nothing to acknowledge the pain. Across the room, the Regent of Stone, who was by all accounts a sturdy and fearless man, winced each time the needle went across his own wound. Andrius was in awe of the Prophet.

And why was he not being interrogated instead of Herkus? Was his case to be heard next? Andrius did not know what to think.

"I stand on behalf of another, Aleksandras, who was afraid to come to judgment because Herkus, after committing his crime against the village, threatened him."

"Lies," Herkus spat. "Aleksandras's guilty conscience kept him from calling me to judgment, as well as his striking lack of a backbone. I've done no wrong."

Andrius stiffened, but the Prophet continued the proceedings.

"Daumantas, state your case."

"You are aware, Prophet, of a game called Akmenys that many in the village play. One player sets rocks upon the ground, the other tries to guess how many rocks he's placed. It is often bet on."

The Prophet nodded.

"I am aware."

"Herkus, in the presence of many witnesses at the Stone Gathering, bet two chickens against Aleksandras that he could best his son in the game. He lost. He then refused to pay his debt, threatened Aleksandras, and days have passed without remorse."

"Is this everything, Daumantas?"

The broad-shouldered man thought for a moment. "Yes, this is all."

"Herkus, state your case."

"He cheated!" Herkus practically shouted. "I prepared for weeks–smoothed the most delicate rocks and gathered the most delicate sand. It was impossible to hear. I refused to pay the debt because the boy cheated. You heard him today; he has another sense."

Solveiga tightened the sutures across the Prophet's leg and then tied off the thread and cut it. Andrius hardly noticed.

"Thank you, Solveiga," the Prophet said, dismissing her. "Daumantas, do any of the others agree that it was cheating?"

"No, Prophet. No one."

"Is this true, Herkus?"

"It doesn't matter! The boy used another sense. He *admits* to cheating!"

The Prophet fixed his robes over his exposed leg. He sat in thought for several moments, during which time the medic working on the Regent of Stone finished as well, and excused himself.

"Hearing by ears or by eyes, as the boy claims, is hearing in either case and was not forbidden by the rules. Furthermore, you did not have any knowledge of this additional sense at the time of your refusal to settle your bets. Herkus, I judge you guilty. Daumantas, I judge you vindicated on behalf of Aleksandras."

Herkus gnashed his teeth, resisting the urge to growl. He submitted, however, because the Prophet's word was good.

"Thank you, Prophet," Daumantas said.

"Thank you, Prophet," Herkus agreed, as he was required to do.

"Now as to punishment," the Prophet began. He smiled and opened his arms. "My life was saved today. I am filled with thankfulness and mercy."

It didn't seem like the Prophet was finished speaking, but Herkus sighed with relief. "Thank you, Prophet. Your mercy is good, and I thank you."

The Prophet frowned.

"I am sorry, Herkus, but I intend to spend my mercy and thankfulness elsewhere. My village has no room for an oath-breaker." Herkus's countenance fell sharply, dread descending upon him. "Petras, Daumantas, take Herkus behind Gimdymo Namai, so that his screams will not be heard. Snap his neck."

Herkus opened his eyes–something Andrius had never known him to do. They were like milk and clouds, and hollow, like his father's.

"What? I will pay the debt! This is not necessary; it was a misunderstanding! I will pay *four* chickens to Aleksandras. Wait!"

He was already in Petras's and Daumantas's strong hands.

"Petras," the Prophet began, "Herkus reminded me–ensure that Aleksandras receives two of Herkus's former chickens, plus one for the delay in payment. Ensure that Herkus's wife and children are taken care of from the communal stores, and look for a widower for her to marry. Goodbye, Herkus," the Prophet said in a softer tone. It was like love and acceptance met in the perfect timbre of his voice. "Thank you for your years of service to the village. Change your heart and go into oblivion unashamed."

Herkus began crying. It came in spurts and he sank to his knees. He did not bother to resist. His fate was a foregone conclusion.

His sobbing echoed up into the room just like the footsteps that carried him away to his death. Andrius was left alone with the Prophet in a room full of exquisite furniture.

Finally, the echoes died away.

Andrius trembled. The rumors were true. Judgment from the Prophet was rare, fast, and harsh.

"When–" Andrius's voice caught in his throat. He coughed and tried to speak again, but he was too tight with fear.

"What is it?" the Prophet asked, concerned. Andrius could feel his genuine care for him, but he could feel the Prophet's care for Herkus too, and he was still dead. Viktoras would be left without a father.

He realized that he would leave Aleksandras without a son.

"Go on," the Prophet crooned. "You can tell me."

"When do I receive my . . . judgment?" he asked. His leg was shaking and he couldn't seem to make it stop.

The Prophet laid a warm hand on Andrius's back.

"This is my judgment, Andrius."

"You know about my instructor?"

"I know about him."

"You know about everything?"

"I know everything, Andrius."

A chill went down his spine. "Oh."

"This is my judgment: you can ask me for whatever you wish, and it is yours."

Andrius clenched his eyes shut. He hated choosing his own punishment. You couldn't pick something too lenient, or else they would choose something worse for you, but you couldn't be too harsh on yourself either–because then they would do that–but Andrius wanted to live.

"Maybe . . ." he stuttered. "Maybe just cut off one of my ears?"

He held his breath. It was terrifying, but it was the most he could hope for. Perhaps the Prophet would be merciful.

Instead, he laughed. "Andrius, you're funny. You aren't under judgment today."

Andrius looked up, shocked. "I'm not?"

The Prophet's smile was contagious.

"Of course not! A man tried to kill me today and you stepped in. I want to reward you, not punish you."

Andrius was speechless. Relief washed over him, blooming through every stretch of his skin, and yet he was almost afraid to believe it.

"Tell you what," the Prophet suggested, "the offer stands, but for now why don't we start with giving you a forum to teach the village this eye-hearing of yours. I will push back lessons and village work an hour so that whoever wants to attend may do so. Does this sound agreeable to you?"

Andrius could not believe it. He nodded his head, then struggled to put his lips together long enough to form words.

"Yes. Yes, thank you."

"Thank you, Andrius. I'll be keeping an ear out for you."

THE REST OF THE DAY OF REMEMBRANCE PASSED without incident, except for the constant stream of praise that Andrius received whenever someone noticed that he was near. It was very strange, and he didn't know what to think of it. Usually people just ignored him or, failing at that, scolded him or laughed at him. But suddenly he was some kind of hero.

The ceremony went on. A representative from each age group climbed the ladder to the top of Gimdymo Namai and delivered their offering. Berena sang her crystalline song, piercing each villager to the heart. No one presented anything like the patterns Andrius spent so much time contemplating, but that wasn't unusual. When it was all over, the feast was brought out and the old men swapped stories while the old women shook their heads. The younger crowd was more interested in the feast and its accompanying songs. All the while, whenever Andrius spoke up, which was not often, he was heartily patted on the back and praised.

The day passed like a dream he had awoken from, only remembering details and pieces but not the whole and certainly not the meaning. He had spent hours meditating on this new conundrum, something he never really considered before. He was supposed to teach the village how to use their eyes to hear, but he hardly understood it himself.

Daniel had said that people in his village could fix broken eyes, but Daniel was crazy. Andrius would have to teach them himself.

Admittedly, he was still the slightest bit incredulous that he actually possessed a sense that others lacked. His “magic” ears were not magic at all.

He now stood on the top of a low rise, a verdant hill in the space between Stone and Brick. The grass tickled his feet as he fidgeted.

He had thought long and hard about what he would say here at the first session, but still he had no idea.

A massive crowd had gathered already, mostly out of curiosity. The Prophet had granted an hour of time between morning and afternoon work so that he might teach this new method of hearing that had saved the Prophet’s life. His father, Aleksandras, was front and center and smiling as wide as could be. Even Daiva was there, though she did not seem happy about it. Andrius could not imagine how long it had been since the sun had touched her skin on any but a Day of Remembrance.

It was nearly time for him to start, but he was nervous. There was a piece of him that was excited too, but for the moment all he felt was expectation, obligation, and fear.

He raised his wooden pitcher to his lips for a quick drink and then he walked to where Aleksandras sat.

“Papa,” he whispered. He didn’t want anyone else to hear. The light roar of chatter ensured that not even Aleksandras heard. “Aleksandras?” he said louder, putting a hand on his shoulder this time. The old man startled. “Papa, it’s me, Andrius.”

"Andrius, my boy!" the old man declared. He was bursting with pride.

Wind swept through the grass and rattled leaves on the trees nearby as Aleksandras waited for him to speak.

"Well," Aleksandras continued when his son said nothing. "Are you ready to teach us? This is a great honor. Everyone is here to hear you and learn from you."

Andrius looked off into the gathering of villagers. His eyes lighted on Milda, talking with her friends twenty yards distant.

"They're here because the Prophet said they should be," Andrius said morosely.

Aleksandras laughed and slapped his knee, drawing a snort from Daiva, who was apparently not talking.

"And that isn't an honor? A great honor?"

Andrius stopped. His father had a point.

Aleksandras carefully pushed off of his cane and stood. He felt around for Andrius's head, then tussled his hair.

"You'll do great, my boy. I always knew you were meant for special things. Speak from your heart."

Andrius nodded. He felt a little better, if not fully convinced. Aleksandras gave him a grin and a pat on the back before sitting down again. Daiva proceeded to chew him out in a harsh whisper. It saddened Andrius how his father cowered under her words.

He returned to his place at the top of the hill and looked over the crowds again. There had to be at least five hundred people gathered around, and he didn't need to have them call roll to know it, either.

A flash of insight filled his mind. He knew how to start.

"Hello," he said much too quietly. The chattering continued. Andrius looked down and kicked the dirt. Gathering his courage, he lifted his head again and shouted this time. "Hello!"

The crowd was startled into quiet, as was Andrius. He had no idea he had such a voice. He'd never used it before. The villagers were paying attention, patiently waiting.

Andrius's stomach was trying to tie itself in knots, but he was resisting. He cleared his throat.

"There are about five hundred of you here this afternoon," he said, doing his best to project. "No one told me that. I can just tell. I don't need you to call out your names for roll or anything. I just count you, like if we were playing Akmenys. I don't even have to come around and touch you to know."

People were listening. Andrius could not believe it. The only person who ever listened to him was Aleksandras. The momentum carried his shaking voice onward.

"And . . . and I can read! Without touching the bumps on the page, even. I don't get lost. I recognize people really easily, and . . . and I'm good at finding things. Whenever one of my age-peers loses something, they talk to me to find it. It's pretty much the only time they talk to me, actually," he added dryly.

A most curious thing happened then. The people laughed. It wasn't in a mean way, and they weren't mocking him–it was a delighted laugh. They thought he was telling a joke, and so they laughed.

Andrius stood a full inch taller. He felt strong.

"I hardly ever fall down, and I love running! Running is so great, so free. I can climb trees, and I always know what's around me, even things that don't make any noise. And I can hear the sun's song every day, and the mountains all around us, and did you know there's a night-sun? It's true. I hear it sing almost every night. It's mysterious and . . . misty and beautiful. It isn't hot like the sun; it's cold so you don't feel it. And I can hear a million other things in the sky at night. The universe is a great big band making the best songs every night and I can hear them!" He paused and lowered his voice. No one stirred or made the least sound. Andrius raised his finger to his eye. "Because I can hear out of my eyes. And I want to teach you how too."

Somewhere in the back a lone villager started clapping. Then it was like the sky had opened up with a crack of thunder. Every man, woman, and child applauded uproariously. Andrius could not believe it. He actually had to quiet them down again. They had started chanting his name. "Andrius, the Prophet's own! Andrius, the Prophet's own!"

Once they had settled down, Daumantas stood and let his voice boom forth.

"How do we learn this skill from you, Andrius?"

Andrius opened his mouth before he realized he hadn't the faintest idea. It was too late to restrain himself from speaking.

"Open your eyes!" he shouted, arms outstretched over the crowds.

Andrius gained confidence then. He had stumbled upon the answer.

"When my eyes are closed, I can't hear out of them," he said quietly. "It's no wonder, people keeping their eyes shut all the time." He had a bad habit of talking to himself.

One by one and two by two, eyes were strenuously

opened throughout the crowd. Andrius looked on in amazement. No one's eyes looked like Daniel's—or like his own. They were all hollow, like the night somehow. It was a chilling and exhilarating sight, seeing so many eyes open.

Andrius raised his arms again, grinning so big that he showed his teeth. He couldn't remember any other time like this.

"Now!" Andrius declared, searching for the words. He waved his hands as he struggled to explain, and finally he shouted, "Look at things!"

The crowd was befuddled at that. Many people scratched their heads or murmured to one another. Andrius's hands fell down to his sides and his grin evaporated.

"Psst!" Andrius heard from the front row. "Psst! Andrius!" His eyes lighted on Aleksandras, who was leaning forward, cupping his hand around his mouth. "What does 'look' mean, my boy? You're using smart words we common people might not know." He laughed.

Andrius nodded earnestly and raised his arms again.

"'Look' means pointing your face at something. I can look at the sky or look at my father or the fire or anything. Look at something and listen with your eyes!"

Understanding fell on the crowd with a collective chuckle and sigh of relief.

But nothing seemed to be happening.

Finally, the apothecary spoke up. "What should we be experiencing, exactly? I don't think I'm doing it right."

She was met with a chorus of agreement.

"Well, uh, I—" Andrius began, uncertain what to say. When he opened his eyes he could hear out of them. Why couldn't they? "Learning to listen with your eyes is a . . . process. It's going to take some time. But that was the first step and today's lesson: open your eyes and look at things."

The crowd understood now. They politely clapped, but Andrius wasn't sure what to do. He was sweating profusely and it wasn't even hot out. He felt like he needed to say something.

"I promise you," he raised his voice, and the crowd listened, "that I will find a way to make this village hear with its eyes, just like me. I promise!"

The gathered villagers erupted in thunderous applause and shouts of acclamation once again. Andrius startled himself with a chuckle, and then a full-blown laugh. Then he was smiling and looking at the sun as people came up to congratulate him and pat his back. A chorus of canes tapping the earth made steady percussion that paired with the chants of "Andrius, the Prophet's own! Andrius, the Prophet's own!"

Andrius had felt many emotions in his life: disappointment, doubt, fear, relief, despair, occasionally even happiness. But what he felt now was entirely new to him. It was triumph.

At the same time, in the back of his mind, Andrius knew that he had to figure out how to teach these people to use their eyes, to learn this new sense. It would take a lot of thought.

He wished he could talk with Daniel.

Where was Daniel, anyway? He would have to find him. He needed some help and some advice.

Someone kissed Andrius on the cheek as he was lost in thought and taking it all in. There were so many people pressed in around him that he couldn't tell who it was who had done it.

The excitement was real and palpable. People were counting on him. Andrius, the Prophet's own, was here to teach them another sense they had never known.

Andrius's heart felt near to bursting as hands continued to pat him and shouts went up declaring his location for the other well-wishers to find. His cheeks hurt from smiling so long.

The sun sang gloriously.

ANDRIUS WANTED TO GO AND DETERMINE IF HE could find anything out about Daniel's whereabouts, but he didn't have a lot of time before lessons. He figured it was bad enough being late once. He couldn't possibly risk being late a second time. There might not be a Prophet to save the next time he got in trouble.

After the excitement from his speech atop the hill earlier, Andrius quickly forgot that he was supposed to be somebody. Unconsciously he went back to staying out of the way and looking at rocks and trees and whatever creatures happened to fly by. No one noticed him on the road, which was nothing unusual, but now he was beginning to understand why. They couldn't . . . sense him, hear him, the same way that he could them.

As he passed by Fourth Brick he noticed a group of women drawing water from a well. Several of them had their eyes open. Andrius had to smile, though his glee faded when none of them acknowledged his wave. They couldn't hear from their eyes yet, but at least their eyes were open. Andrius was mostly convinced that it would come to them with time and practice. He was confident.

But somewhere else inside of him, he was afraid. Maybe he was teaching it wrong. There must be more to it.

Daniel had said there were people where he came from that could help.

"We could fix all these people if they came down from here–down the mountain to Brezno," Andrius mumbled to himself. He was curious to experience this Brezno that Daniel had spoken of. Crazy or not, he had a lot of insight. Andrius wondered if Daniel's instructions would actually lead to another village. He wanted to investigate and find out.

But following Daniel's directions meant crossing the barricade. And besides, there were no villages outside in the Regions of Death. The disease had destroyed them all.

A leaf floated across Andrius's path and he kept his eyes on it as it danced and played with the wind. A chill went up his spine and he was captivated for the moment. He stopped to follow its motion with his eyes.

Voices coming down the road brought him out of his trance. It was Milda, Berena, Ugna, Viktoras, and Tomas, all walking as a group. Their canes tapped against the road continuously.

Andrius lifted his pitcher to his lips and listened as they walked by.

"But do you really think he can hear with his eyes?" Ugna was saying. She was clearly skeptical.

"How else could he have known that the ex-Regent was going to attack the Prophet?" Tomas argued. "His ears didn't tell him, or else somebody else would have noticed too."

"Maybe he just knew," Berena offered.

"Yeah, Tomas. Maybe he just knew," Ugna agreed.

Andrius nearly spit out his water. They were talking about him. They had no idea he was around and they were *talking* about him.

Tomas couldn't keep the disdain out of his reply. Andrius had always thought he had a squeaky speaking voice. He wasn't a bad singer though.

"You're trying to tell me that an eleven-year-old knew about a plot to commit the greatest crime possible, that no one else found out, that he didn't tell anybody so he could pretend that he had magic eyes, *and* that he jumped in at the perfect moment to save the Prophet?" He shook his head. "I don't think so."

"But it wasn't the perfect moment," Ugna replied. Andrius let his pitcher hang down by his side and he tiptoed after his peers to hear the rest of their conversation. "I heard the Prophet was stabbed in his legs. Maybe he'll never walk again." She fought back tears for a moment, as did a few others. The thought of their beloved Prophet being crippled was too much. "If Andrius had this extra sense, why couldn't he stop that from happening?"

Viktoras was conspicuously absent from the debate. His head hung low and his shuffled steps seemed forced, as if living was a dreaded and grudging necessity.

Tomas threw his hands in the air.

"He's eleven!" he shouted. "Like us. Can you stop a man with a knife on the first try?"

"How did he do it at all?" Ugna wondered.

Berena sighed.

"Milda, you're his friend. What do you think?"

"Yes, he's my friend," Milda agreed casually.

Andrius jumped and actually said "What?" aloud. His hand immediately went to his mouth. Milda halted in the middle of a sentence. All of the children strained their ears.

". . . Andrius?" Tomas asked. "Is that you?"

Andrius's heart was racing. Why couldn't he ever just think

things instead of saying them? He had a terrible habit of saying things out loud.

He panicked.

"No!" he answered in the deepest, strangest voice he could manage. Then he clutched his wooden pitcher to his chest and hurried past them, careful not to spill.

"Was that him?"

"That was weird."

"Who was that?"

ANDRIUS WAS HAVING TROUBLE CONCENTRATING on his lessons. The instructor's opinion of him had changed entirely, so that at least was nice, if strange. He even recounted Andrius's heroics to the class and had them thank him for his service to the Prophet and the village. He didn't know how to take it. He wasn't used to approval.

So while the instructor lectured on the principles of communal living, Zydrunas's early philosophical works, and punching dots into writing paper, Andrius's mind was elsewhere.

An insect was clinging to a tall blade of grass. The little bug seemed to have its eyes fixated on Andrius, just like his were on the bug. He thought it was a grasshopper, but he wasn't sure. People were always so vague when he tried to ask about the different kinds of bugs.

The grasshopper, if that's what it was, blinked, and Andrius tracked the motion of its eyes.

"You can hear from your eyes too," he whispered, too soft for anyone to hear over the class's recitation of the village code for conduct and community.

Teaching this idea of hearing from the eyes was difficult. He did not even understand it himself–he could just do it. It was like trying to understand breathing. It just happened.

As Andrius sat with his hands propping up his face, a most peculiar thing happened. A second grasshopper flew past and landed on a rock, then hopped onto Andrius's knee, where he lingered.

Andrius only narrowly kept himself from loudly gasping. He looked from one grasshopper to the other; first at the one swaying in the breeze, attached to the grass, then to the one resting on his knee.

Something important was in front of him, just barely beyond his grasp. He sensed the truth more than he comprehended it, but those grasshoppers . . . they were different somehow. They weren't different in any way he knew how to describe, and yet they were not the same. They were very different.

What did it mean?

He listened intently with his eyes until the second grasshopper grew bored, or else disenchanted with the young boy who seemed so inexplicably fascinated. The other leapt into the air and flew away soon after, but they had served their purpose. In some small way, the world had shifted for Andrius. Something tremendously important was right under his nose.

He spent the rest of the day's lessons looking at the sky and thinking about what had happened.

LESSONS WERE FINALLY DISMISSED, AND ANDRIUS was almost too distracted to notice that all of the other children had stood up and started talking. They cleared out quickly like they typically did at the end of the day.

Andrius remained sitting, lost in thought until he heard Milda saying his name.

"Andrius? Andrius, where are you? Want to walk with me? Andrius?"

He shook himself back to reality and looked over to Milda. Her hair was pretty today. The sun's triumphant chorus weaved between strands of hair.

He did not know what to think of her.

As he considered whether or not to answer, he raised his wooden pitcher to his lips and took a sip. Milda must have heard the sound, because her ears perked up and she turned.

"Andrius?" she said sweetly. Her tone was light and airy. It captivated Andrius, who swallowed the rest of the water in his mouth much too quickly.

"Ahem. Yes. Hey. Hi, Milda."

She smiled. Andrius wasn't sure if she knew that he could hear it.

It was quiet as he looked on. Finally Milda crossed her arms and laughed. "Well aren't you going to take the road?"

"Oh. Yes. Thank you, yes."

He scrambled to his feet and then he bent down to retrieve his pitcher, which was the only thing that he was never separate from. He had been leaving his cane at home more and more these days. He didn't need it like everybody else.

Milda turned and began walking, tapping her cane in front of her from left to right, left to right to offset her steps. That way she wouldn't run into anything. Andrius fell into step beside her nervously. He wringed his free hand open and closed.

"Thank you for your service to the Prophet and to the village, Andrius," she said sweetly.

He felt his insides skipping. A lot of people had been greeting him that way today, but he liked hearing it from her. A troubled feeling fell over him, however, like a heavy fog.

"You know," she began, "I don't mind practicing writing, but I think it's a lot more interesting when the instructor talks about Zydrunas. Don't you?"

"Oh. Yeah. I think so too."

Milda smiled graciously and they walked on. The subject died on the table. A minute later she tried again.

"I bet if you start working on next year's offering they'll pick you to represent us for the next Day of Remembrance. Everyone would want you to win now."

Andrius was still distracted and a little morose.

"People don't like the things I make. The patterns."

"Well, maybe you just need to explain them better. Have you kept them all?"

"Yes."

"Do you have your water pitcher with you?" She laughed. "Of course you have it. You're always carrying it everywhere. Can I hold it?"

Andrius handed it to her indifferently and she stopped near Thirteenth Brick to receive it from him.

Her head was pointed slightly upward in a totally different direction from the pitcher. Andrius never would have thought this to be odd before, but now he did. She wasn't even looking at it. She couldn't.

Milda ran her fingers along the grooves carved into the wood, tracing the long, intricate borders and the accent ticks in the shape of leaves. Near the belly of the pitcher it was carved inward such that parts sticking out were like little people. Some of them were sad, others happy, others angry or bored or amused. One figure bought bread from another as someone else drove pigs down the road. It was very detailed, but though she was trying, Andrius could tell that she didn't appreciate it in the same way he did.

When she was finished rubbing her smooth, white hands across his pitcher, she nodded and handed it back to him.

"You should make something like this again if you don't want to write a poem or a song or a story or anything normal. It's kind of fun to feel the grooves in it, and it's something you can use too."

Andrius took a drink from the pitcher. He would have liked to make another, but it hurt him to even consider the possibility. He put so much of himself into the work and no one had really understood it.

"I don't know. I really do more of the patterns now. And not just for the offering, actually. I have a bunch that I've made just for fun. I could show you sometime."

"Oh, sure, Andrius." She didn't sound interested. "But how did you make the pitcher like that? You should do that again." Her cane tapped against the protruding brick on the side of the road, so she knew they were passing Eighth Brick.

"Leonas let me borrow his tools. I don't want to make one again."

Milda had opened her mouth to say something, but she let out a breath and closed it instead.

Something was still gnawing at Andrius. "Milda," he asked, "are you my friend?"

"Of course I'm your friend, Andrius. I was nice to you before people liked you, remember? I'm your only true friend, really."

Andrius dropped his eyes to the road. That was true, sort of. "But I heard you say that you weren't."

Milda laughed. Andrius liked the sound of it. He couldn't help himself. "I never said anything of the sort. Why would I say that?"

"Oh."

He remembered though. It wasn't that long ago when she had been talking to Berena and he overheard.

Nobody noticed things, so Andrius sometimes heard comments he wasn't supposed to hear. It let him know usually what people really felt. He wondered momentarily what the village would be like if everyone could hear with their eyes and notice people better. Maybe there wouldn't be so many secrets.

Maybe he had misheard her or something. He didn't have a lot of friends.

Just Milda, really.

They passed a field of cartwheel flowers on the left. It was Stephinius's second field, Andrius thought, but he wasn't sure. Everything belonged to the village anyway, especially the plant that supplied the cure to the disease.

He always liked looking at the tall, thick plants. Cartwheel flowers were almost always taller than him, and usually by quite a bit. They had large, fanned, jagged leaves that sprawled out every which way and round stalks that shot up and sprouted a wheel of hundreds of tiny flowers. He didn't often stop for them, but he always noticed as he passed.

"So," Milda began. She was trying very hard to have a conversation. "What did you think about lessons today?"

"I don't know," Andrius replied distractedly. "I wasn't paying attention."

Milda gasped and Andrius felt ice shoot through his veins. What had he just admitted to?

He took her by the shoulder.

"Milda, calm down. Please, just wait a second okay? I didn't mean– It's not that–"

She was breathing fast, nearly hyperventilating.

"I had a good reason!" Andrius insisted. He closed his eyes while Milda panicked. He was going to die before he reached twelve; he was sure of it.

The cartwheel flowers swayed in the gentle breeze, oblivious to the affairs of the people passing them by.

"You mean that you," Milda said between breaths, "weren't *listening* during lessons? That's worse than being late, Andrius!"

"Shh, listen. Just wait, okay? I can explain, I think. I can. But you can't tell anyone. Just calm down okay?" He felt her slow her breathing a bit, and some of the tension went out of her shoulders. She was still panicked, but she was trying to remain calm.

Andrius sighed. He felt sick again.

"Milda, please calm down. No one knows. It's . . . Well, it's not okay, but it's all right. I had a good reason. I promise."

Milda wiped her eyes with her sleeve and tried to regain composure. Her nose seemed funny now that she was so upset. The tip was different somehow.

"Blizzards, Andrius! Are you trying to get brought to judgment again? If you think that he's going to let you off easy because you're a kid, you're wrong."

She was sniffing between her words now and then. Andrius's heart beat faster. He thought it was adorable. He couldn't help it.

He waited for her to relax, and then, with a sigh from Milda, they continued walking. Her cane tapped regularly in front of her.

"So what is it?"

"Huh?" Andrius asked.

"This great reason you had. For," she lowered her voice, "not paying attention."

Andrius looked at her out of the corner of his eye.

"Do you really want to know?"

"Yes I want to know! Is it good? Tell me."

"I still haven't quite figured it out. That's why I had to think so much instead of listen. I heard this grasshopper in front of me—"

"An ant?" Milda interrupted.

Andrius shook his head.

"It was a grasshopper."

"How can you tell?"

"Because there was only one instead of a bunch of them, and he was bigger than an ant," he said, a little frustrated. "Anyway, there was a grasshopper and I was looking at him when another grasshopper shows up."

"Are you sure it wasn't an ant?" she interrupted, skeptical.

"I'm sure. Listen, this second grasshopper was exactly like the first one, okay? But it was different. It was different, Milda!"

He was getting excited, but his enthusiasm didn't spread to Milda, who seemed confused.

"Was he bigger than the other one?"

Andrius shook his head. "No, they were the same size."

"A different shape?"

"No, the same."

Milda thought really hard as they passed Fifth Brick. It hit her suddenly. "It was missing a leg!"

Andrius frowned. "No, nothing you would usually think of. I can't quite figure it out, but it was really different. I know it's important somehow, I just can't name it."

"Andrius, you aren't making any sense."

"I know," he admitted sadly.

She tapped him with an exaggerated swing of her cane.

"Are you sure one of them wasn't an ant?"

Andrius shook his head and took a drink of water. He didn't feel the need to answer her again.

The water felt good on his lips. It was cool and refreshing. He closed his eyes in satisfaction, but a bump in the road made him stumble.

Water fell down his shirt and splashed onto his feet, wetting the dusty road around.

He stopped in his tracks. The road was different where the water had hit.

Milda continued walking, unaware that he had stopped. She laughed.

"Did you spill, Andrius? Maybe you wouldn't be so clumsy if you used your cane like a normal person."

She smiled smugly, but Andrius didn't care. He was onto something.

He jerked his head up and began looking around. The clouds, the trees, the road, the huts . . . It suddenly started to make sense.

"I've got it!" he declared excitedly.

"What?"

Andrius jumped and let out a whoop, causing more water to splash onto the road. He looked at it change.

"I know what was different about the grasshoppers."

"Is this part of hearing with your eyes?"

"Yes, Milda, it is. I've got it."

"Well spit it out. They weren't different sizes?"

He shook his head. "I don't know if there's a word for it, but they were different . . . Snow and hail! This is hard . . ." He furrowed his brow. Gimdymo Namai began rising up before them. "Okay, you know how when you hear a song, you can sing the same word, but in a different way?"

"Like with a different note?" she offered.

Andrius snapped his fingers. "That's it! Milda, you're a genius. A different note, exactly. Just like in a song a word can have the same volume and everything but a different note. The grasshoppers had different notes, but notes that only your eyes can hear. One was like grass and the other one was like . . ." He looked around, then grabbed at his clothes. "Like my shirt! Or dirt, that would work too. They had different notes."

Milda considered this for a while. Andrius waited expectantly.

Finally she shrugged her shoulders a bit and said, "That's neat?"

THE EVENING HAD PASSED IN STUDIED SILENCE FOR Andrius. People spoke and argued about every topic of conversation at the Stone Gathering, but Andrius ignored them. He was looking at things by the fire, comparing them.

Now as he stood on top of his little hill again and the people gathered, he was lost in thought. More people had come today, but Andrius was for the moment more interested in all of the beautiful, varying notes around him that he could hear with his eyes. When he looked over the crowd at last, it filled him with delight.

They were here to hear him.

"Today," Andrius announced, "I want to explain some more about this new sense. It lets you know where things are, but your ears do that sometimes, and so do your hands, your nose, and maybe even your tongue. It lets you know how big something is, or you can tell what it feels like without touching it, which is good when things are far away or really hot. But still, you can know that with your hands, I guess.

"Today I want to tell you about something your eyes can sense that no other part of you can: notes!"

The crowd remained silent, and Andrius's stomach tightened at the lack of response. He remembered, however, that they were here to hear what he had to say. They would listen.

"No, wait," he said, raising his hands. "It's not like the kind of notes you hear with your ears; it's something completely different. There just isn't a word for it, so I call them notes."

"Do you hear them when the sun is singing?" someone shouted from the crowd.

Andrius nodded. "Yes. There are such amazing notes when the sun sings! A leaf can be like grass or like dirt. A chicken's feathers are like the clouds. A rock can be like the sand or like the mountains or like the fog."

The people seemed to be following, and Andrius was pleased. He continued in the same vein until their time was up. He ended with an urging for the people to open their eyes and look at things.

This was met with great applause.

His satisfaction was dampened, however, when he overheard several groups of people leaving the session saying things like, "A chicken's feathers are like a cloud because they are too soft," "What's a cloud again?" and "A leaf can feel fibrous like grass or crunchy like dirt." "Notes are like textures."

He tried to correct one such group, but he was out of time and needed to get to lessons. They left very confused as to why he was upset.

At lessons, Andrius didn't pay attention again. He was thinking.

THE WALK HOME WAS ODD. BERENA AND A FEW OF the other children all asked Andrius if he wanted to walk with them. No none had ever asked him that. It had been strange enough when Milda asked, but now there were others.

What's more, his classmates complimented him when he spoke—which he did not do often—and patted his back. Tomas had linked arms with Andrius on the way back from lessons and declared the two of them to be good friends. Tomas had always dismissed Andrius in kind of an arrogant way, but now he said they were friends. He couldn't tell him no.

Several others from his age group asked to be friends with Andrius also. He said yes to them all. What else was he supposed to do? Was he even allowed a choice once the question was asked? He didn't really have any friends, except maybe Milda lately. It was complicated, and he was new at this whole friendship thing.

His walks to and from lessons were usually peaceful, if a bit lonely. Today it was a cacophony. So many boys and girls talking at once—at him, at each other. Andrius's head was on a swivel trying to keep up with it all.

Needless to say it was a bit overwhelming, and by the time the others had reached their homes and Andrius approached Twenty-fifth Stone he felt relieved. Though, in truth, he had enjoyed the attention.

On the other hand it made him uncomfortable.

He hadn't decided how he felt just yet.

Caught up in thoughts, Andrius followed the fraying rope from the main road to his house. It had been a long day. He undid the latch and gently pushed the door inward.

"Well look who decided to show up."

Daiva sat on her stool, fat and disgruntled as ever. She was in a bad mood from the looks of it.

Aleksandras stood at the counter with an apron on, putting the finishing touches on dinner. He had roasted a couple of chickens outside. One entire chicken would be for Daiva, of course, in addition to sides.

Andrius glanced about the room. The sun was still singing softly.

"Why are you upset, Daiva? I'm not late."

She snorted. "Oh, and you make the rules around here, don't you?" She shifted her huge girth, and for a minute Andrius was worried that she would get up and beat him.

"No, Daiva. It's just that–"

"It's just that what?"

"Dear," Aleksandras interceded.

"Shut up!" she screeched. She rose from her seat and lumbered in Andrius's direction. "The Prophet's own," she said in a high, nasal voice. "The Prophet's own, the Prophet's own." She spit. "Well even Prophets have a chamber pot. That's the Prophet's own too."

Andrius reached across the room and set his water pitcher against the far wall of the hut. If he was going to get beaten, he didn't want that to get damaged at least. He couldn't help trembling as he waited for the worst of it.

"It seems to me," Daiva shouted, groping about with her rough, meaty hands until she gripped the boy by the shirt, "that you think you're too big for your pants now."

Andrius looked down at his pants. They were loose. He had been losing weight from skipped meals.

She shook him by the shirt, and Andrius felt a heaviness come over him. It was happening again. He didn't want this anymore. He still had bruises from the last time, and he was very afraid.

"Dear, I think that Andrius is a–"

"Shut up!" she screamed, louder this time. Her face shriveled up in a rotten grimace as she tightened her hold on her stepson. "You sack of manure. You trip into someone who happens to be committing a crime, and I bet you think you're some kind of hero now." She rattled him. "Don't you?"

"No..." Andrius tried to protest. His lip quivered uncontrollably and he felt tears on the way.

"You accidentally do one thing right for once in your life," she yelled, "and now you've got this big head. Look at you, you teach classes. Look at you, you have another sense." She slapped him across his face, hard. The sting spread from where she hit him to the rest of Andrius's face.

Aleksandras wasn't preparing dinner anymore.

"Daiva."

"You're worthless. Worthless! I wish you would have died that day in the cold. I swear I do. When you were little–"

Aleksandras laid a hand on his wife's shoulder. "Daiva, is this really necessary?"

She didn't waste any time swinging at Aleksandras with her free hand. It was a wild punch, but it connected with his nose, and Andrius heard the crack. The old man staggered backward, hitting the counter and holding his face in his hands. Blood was seeping through the gaps in his fingers within moments.

Daiva did not calm down. She hit Andrius again.

"When you were little I thought about killing you while Aleksandras was out with his cows. I thought I should just lay on you and crush you, or smother your little lungs, or poke your eyes out."

She hit him again, in the stomach this time. Andrius mumbled.

"What?" she cried. She slapped him across his face. "Speak up, boy!"

Though tears, Andrius said, "I only wanted to eat some dinner."

Daiva laughed–an evil, menacing fit of cruelty.

"Oh are you hungry now? You don't like that I keep meals from you?" She slapped him again, over and over. "Well you'll be starving by the time I'm done with you! And you'll have had the beating of your life too."

She stumbled against Andrius, crushing him into the wall and forcing all of his breath out.

"Daiva . . ." Aleksandras pleaded in a breathy, congested tone.

Her fingers closed around Aleksandras's harvest shears. Why they were inside the hut, Andrius didn't know, but her groping fingers knew what they touched upon.

A smile of grim satisfaction crossed her lips, and Daiva raised the blade above her head.

Andrius was blubbering now. He was going to die. He pled for his life in a series of squeals. "Please don't kill me. Please don't kill me."

A rush of wind gave them pause, as did the creaking of the wooden door to outside.

Daiva growled.

"You think you can get away, Andrius? Are you so foolish? Did you open this door?"

"No," another voice said. "I did."

Everyone stopped. Andrius's eyes were blurred shut. His father's feet slipped where he leaned against the counter and he nearly fell.

The voice sounded familiar.

"Who are you?" Daiva barked, surly once again. "Don't you know it's rude to barge into a person's home?"

"Homes belong to the village," the voice said, "and should not be treated as personal property. To answer your question, my name is Petras, and my wife's is Simona."

The harvest shears clattered to the floor. Daiva's face registered shock as she let go of Andrius and backed away.

"And furthermore," Petras declared, "the visitation of a Regent is to be considered an honor."

IT WAS THE MOST AWKWARD DINNER OF ANDRIUS'S life. Daiva tried to overcompensate by being extremely attentive to the needs of their guests, but it didn't help. Every once in a while she would begin a sentence with the intention of praising Andrius, but it would always die on her lips halfway, as if she lacked the capacity to go through with it.

Aleksandras was proud of his son, of course, and he spoke many times in his favor, telling Petras and Simona how honored he was to be the boy's father.

Unfortunately, in addition to pride he also had a broken nose, and his voice was consequently very nasal. He had to excuse himself several times before finally heading out to find the healer of Stone.

At least there was plenty of food.

Petras spoke little, asking questions here and there but mostly preserving his reticence. His wife Simona did not speak at all.

When it came time to leave, Daiva fawned over them as Andrius instinctively went over to begin cleaning the dinner things. It would be harder this evening, since Aleksandras wasn't there to help him. The Regent of Stone spoke up, however, and altered him from his intended course.

"Andrius," the large man said, interrupting Daiva's meaningless blathering. "Walk me outside."

The door creaked open and the hut was filled with a rush of cold air. Andrius stood frozen for a moment, then hurried out after the honorable couple. He just narrowly avoided running into Daiva as she collapsed onto one of the wooden stools. It cracked audibly, followed by Daiva's expressive swearing. Andrius let the door swing shut behind him, relieved to feel the evening mist on his face.

"Walk us to the road, Andrius," the Regent said as he led the way. He held onto the rope and his wife held onto his shoulder. There was silence for a while, then the questions came. Very calmly he asked Andrius about his home and his daily life–where he slept, if he was ever hungry or needed things that were not given to him. The only time he seemed to get upset was when Andrius replied to him that he didn't use a cane. He quickly explained to the Regent that with his other sense he didn't need one.

As if on cue, Andrius tripped over a loose rock in the pathway to the road. Petras frowned but said no more of it.

When they reached Stone Road, Simona gave Andrius a hug and the Regent clapped him on the shoulder, thanking him for dinner.

Andrius looked at them walking away, fidgeting where he stood. He wanted to ask a question, but he was nervous. After all, the second most important person in the village had seen his family at its worst. It was shameful.

"Regent!" he blurted out before they went too far. They stopped to listen.

Andrius felt sick, but he had to know.

"Regent," he said softer. "Did you . . . Why did you come to our hut tonight?"

The barrel-chested man nodded once and tapped the end of his cane against the ground.

"The Prophet is fond of you, Andrius. So am I."

The Regent and his wife did not stay to chat. Arm in arm they quietly set out into the night, waving their canes in front of them as they went.

Andrius stood there a long time, ostensibly thinking, but it seemed as if he couldn't think of anything at all.

DAIVA WAS PARTICULARLY BITTER IN THE MORNING but wary also. Andrius was able to avoid her for the most part, tiptoeing around and pretending not to hear her threats and insults.

Sometimes Andrius wondered if he ought to just lie down and never get up, but that would be too much like Daiva, and Daiva wasn't even his mother. Besides, he had his class to teach.

He wouldn't have thought it possible, but there were even more people in attendance this time. He tried to describe how to hear movement with the eyes, and the crowd seemed to follow him fairly well. He finished his lecture with an encouragement to open their eyes and look at things. This was met with great enthusiasm and support. The heaps of praise that the villagers laid on him made him feel better. He was trying not to think about the previous night.

More and more people seemed to be traveling about with their eyes open. A few would open then close them alternatingly, others seemed to try and keep them open at all times.

"I'll have to tell them to close their eyes sometimes," Andrius said to himself as he walked down Brick Road, thinking about his students.

It was encouraging to have such a large group coming to meet with him again and again, but Andrius wondered how much progress they were making.

When the villagers opened their eyes it looked hollow, like they were dead.

It was not like his eyes or Daniel's eyes. For the hundredth time, Andrius wondered where Daniel had gone. He had so many things he wanted to ask him.

Andrius thoughtfully lifted his wooden pitcher to his lips and took a drink. The water sloshed noisily.

"Andrius?"

Andrius turned his head and there was Tomas, grinning big.

"Andrius, is that you?"

He choked on his water trying to answer too quickly. He spit it out as he coughed, but he managed a weak "yes."

"Great job on the hill today! You're the Prophet's own, Andrius." He excitedly raised his hands as Andrius wiped the water from his own chin. "I could tell where you were because of the water's movement. It's like I can hear with my eyes already. You're the best, Andrius–the Prophet's own!"

Andrius thanked him and listened as Tomas went on about how he thought that maybe, just maybe he was starting to softly hear things with his eyes.

Of course, as he went about trying to prove this, he neglected to open his eyes.

Andrius wasn't sure if what he was hearing was flattery or wishful thinking, but still, it lifted his spirits a bit. He kept sinking down into sadness whenever his mind wandered.

Tomas chattered all the way to Eighteenth Brick, and Andrius let him. He was happy to have a companion during his walk, and besides, he did not know what to say.

The tall, strong oak tree that he and his age-peers sat beneath rocked gently in the wind. Andrius stopped in his tracks and listened. He even closed his eyes so as to better hear the melodic rattling of the leaves high above.

That was music to him.

"Ow!"

Andrius was jostled forward as someone crashed into his back. He only narrowly avoided an actual fall by putting his hands on the ground. He was pulled from his reflective moment, but at least he had not fallen on his face.

Viktoras, who had run into him, had not been so lucky. He wore a muddy scowl as he rose, cursing under his breath. He irritably wiped himself off.

"Who is the idiot who didn't hear me coming and move?"

Andrius swallowed hard, expecting the worst.

"I'm really sorry, Viktoras. It was me."

Viktoras's countenance changed, like he was placing the voice. Then, his demeanor was completely different. "Andrius? Is that you?"

"Yes," he croaked.

To Andrius's surprise, the other boy didn't get angry. He didn't seem happy exactly, but he wasn't angry anymore. It was like he deflated.

"Don't worry about it. I didn't know it was you."

Andrius raised an eyebrow.

"Sorry," Viktoras continued as he took his seat.

Andrius stood still as his age-peers gathered and sat nearby. The instructor was starting roll, but Andrius could hardly hear him.

No one had ever apologized to him before.

"Andrius. Andrius?"

"What's that?"

His classmates giggled.

"Well," the instructor chuckled. "I suppose the question is answered now, but are you here? We're calling names."

"Oh, yes. I'm here."

He quickly sat down on the grass, setting his pitcher beside him.

The children still giggled softly, but there was something different about the sound. It was more like delight than mockery.

"You're so silly, Andrius," Ugna whispered playfully.

Andrius wasn't sure how to handle that, so he let a stupid grin on his face and waited for the instructor to move on, but he didn't.

"Did you sleep well last night, Andrius?" the instructor inquired, genuine concern apparent in his voice. "No, probably you were just being funny. Never mind."

The kids laughed again.

A strange feeling welled up inside of Andrius. He wasn't sure what it was, but he liked it.

"All right, children, today we will be talking about– No, wait a moment." The instructor folded his hands. "Children, I just want to reiterate what a debt of gratitude we all owe to Andrius. He saved our Prophet, he is expanding the limits of human knowledge with his lessons, and this new sense of his . . . Let's applaud for him, children. Clap your hands for Andrius, the Prophet's own!"

The children broke into uproarious applause, and Andrius felt a wave of that feeling come over him again. He wasn't positive, but he suspected that it was acceptance.

Someone patted him enthusiastically as the cheers wound down. The instructor seemed very moved, but he pressed on.

"Thank you, children. All right, yes. Thank you. And thank you, Andrius. Truly."

The instructor stood and then nearly fell, being on uneven ground, but between his cane and a hand on the oak's trunk he was able to catch himself. He took a deep breath as the children settled down.

"All right. Today we will be primarily discussing mathematics and memorization. You can't have the first without the second, after all. Mathematics–which was invented by Zydrunas, of course–helps us to solve problems in our daily work for the village. It also trains us to hold complex thoughts and patterns together in our minds. Now, before we get into anything else we will be discussing measurements. I took the pains of measuring Brick Road this morning before lessons. Does anyone have a guess as to how long it may be?"

"3,422 paces."

"Not in paces, Tomas. Everyone should know it in their own stride. We are speaking of standard measurements for more accuracy."

Andrius happened to turn around as the instructor continued speaking and he noticed a young woman coming down the road. She wasn't young enough to be in his age group, but she didn't seem to be much older than he was.

She was still too far away to hear–with ears, that is.

"No, no. First we want answers in the standard foot, and then we can estimate particular measurements."

The class went on guessing, and the instructor made them give justification for their answers, which were invariably incorrect.

Andrius, as per usual of late, was not paying attention. He was looking at the girl.

He recognized her.

"We have the pirstas, the span, and the foot. Larger estimations of distance have existed far away in the past, as you may or may not be aware, but after the disease wiped out the rest of the world and reduced man's population and living space to this village, those larger units became obsolete. They are archaic now. Does that answer your question?"

She was thirteen years old, and her hair was like the hay as it swayed in the fields. He knew her from the Day of Remembrance, when her father tried to kill Valdas.

It was Jehena, the Prophet's newest wife.

"Well, Milda, it's nice that someone is finally asking the right questions. First, I took–"

"Excuse me."

The young woman interrupted the instructor. She seemed poised and yet so frail. Andrius wondered what it must be like to be so close to the Prophet all of the time. It couldn't help but rub off on you.

"I'm sorry," the instructor responded, irritated. "Who was that? Berena, was that you?"

"No, Teacher."

"It was me, Instructor. Jehena."

"Well this is quite irregular, Jehena. Aren't you aware that we are having lessons here? This is quite irregular."

She dipped her head.

"I know that, sir, but it is the Prophet's will."

The instructor huffed for a moment, still incensed at being interrupted.

"What is?" he inquired at length.

Jehena looked off with her eyes closed, not even in the same direction as the man she spoke with. This struck Andrius as odd, suddenly.

"I have been sent to retrieve the boy called Andrius and bring him to Gimdymo Namai."

The wind replied with a light breeze, but everyone present was silent.

"But," the instructor protested, "he's in lessons."

"He knows that, Instructor."

"Are you– Did he–" He scratched his head. "Are you sure you heard him correctly?"

"Yes, Instructor. I was sent to bring him to Gimdymo Namai."

Andrius's heart dropped into his stomach. He was under the impression that the Prophet liked him, but why would he pull him away from a lesson? He didn't know if that had ever happened before.

It couldn't be good.

"All right," the instructor said slowly, hesitantly. "If this message was brought in error I am not to be held responsible. A child needs his education."

"It is not in error, sir. The Prophet sent me to do his will only just now. You do his will by releasing the boy to me."

"Very well. Andrius, get your things and go with this woman. Perhaps tomorrow you can stay after class to hear the material you will miss."

Andrius stood up quickly, then stooped to pick up his pitcher of water. His fingers dipped into the intricate grooves on the sides.

"Yes, Teacher."

"Very well then. We will continue straight off, class, and no gossiping. Standard units."

Andrius weaved through the scattering of his age-peers to where Jehena patiently waited. He stole a look at Milda, but she did not seem concerned. She was happily listening to the instructor's lecture on mathematics.

"Are you here yet?" Jehena inquired kindly.

"Yes."

"Good."

The young girl turned around then, and using her cane to guide her, she began walking, tapping roadstones as she went. Andrius fell in beside her.

Already the instructor's didactics were fading into the background of a place far away and forgotten.

A butterfly the same note as Jehena's hair floated by. Andrius tracked with it distractedly.

"I don't believe we've met officially," she said cheerily.

"No, I don't think so," Andrius replied, coughing halfway through the sentence. He lifted his pitcher to his parched lips and took a drink of water.

She smiled in response, a secret smile.

He was expecting her to say something more, but nothing was forthcoming, which was fine. He was accustomed to keeping company with his own thoughts.

They passed the field of cartwheel flowers. Stephinius had several men helping him chop down the giant stalks and load them onto a mule. It was harvesting time for the cure. Andrius's instructor often said that it was a miracle how fast the plant grew, which allowed for continual reaping until the winter.

Apparently in the time before the Hausen War, cartwheel flower was regarded as a weed. Now, thanks to Zydrunas's research, it had saved every one of them.

Andrius thought that the disparity was significant somehow.

The men in the roadside field cheered loudly as another great stalk snapped and fell to the ground. They were a good distance into the labyrinthine crop.

"We're passing the cartwheel flower, aren't we?" Jehena asked with a hint of delight.

"Yes," Andrius replied. His thoughts returned to the fact that he had been pulled from class to go to Gimdymo Namai. It couldn't be anything good. Things had been going too well recently. There had to be a storm on the horizon.

"It is a joyous occasion," she said. The men began to sing as they worked. They were excellent singers, mostly basses and baritones.

Andrius did not respond to her as painful realization washed over him. Probably he was being called because the Regent of Stone had reported to the Prophet how unruly and undignified his home was.

The Prophet would strip him of his class teaching eye-hearing and maybe something worse, even. His footsteps felt heavy beneath him.

"They say," Jehena continued sweetly, "that it's good luck to rub a freshly cut bunch of cartwheel across your eyes, in remembrance of the cure and your birth. It honors Zydrunas."

Andrius grunted, only half listening.

"Want to?"

Jehena smiled widely. Her cane tapped against a roadstone—Sixteenth Brick. She stopped, waiting expectantly.

"No," Andrius replied, but he noticed Jehena looking sad, so he qualified his refusal. "I mean, because it would slow us down. We should hurry to do the Prophet's will."

Really it was just because he was sad that he said no. He hadn't ever done it before. The others sometimes went in groups.

"I suppose that makes sense. Thank you for thinking of the Prophet, Andrius."

He grunted in assent, still thinking about his coming punishment and what they might do to Aleksandras. If only he had more time, he was sure he could show people how to use this other sense. He needed to research the problem, but who could he ask? Where was Daniel?

"Andrius, I haven't gotten the chance to thank you for what you did on the Day of Remembrance. I owe everything to you. We all do. Without the Prophet, what do we have?"

Andrius wiped his face, then looked at the encircling mountains. People sure talked to him a lot lately. It was nice but also difficult and tiring. He never knew what he was supposed to say.

The sun sang down on them in glorious lines.

"You're welcome," he said cautiously.

"I know what you're thinking, though it's a scandal to have such thoughts. You're wondering if I actually resent you because of what happened to my father."

"Yes," Andrius agreed, then he kicked himself. He hadn't meant to say that out loud.

"I loved my father, but he just didn't understand. For all of his wisdom and years of serving the Prophet–I know he won't be remembered this way now, but he served him faithfully for his whole life until the end. He started to change when Valdas–the Prophet, I mean–decided to claim me. My father said that I was too young, but he didn't understand the magic that's between us. He said I was being manipulated. Ha!" She tapped her cane extra hard against the Brick Road. "Can you imagine? The Prophet manipulating someone? Then he started questioning things, things you shouldn't question. Why does the Prophet keep more than one wife if it's a great evil for the rest of us? How does he possess the wisdom of Zydrunas if he never met him–nonsense like that. I overheard him talking to my mother about it once. It wasn't something he'd say openly. He became really possessive, and when the day came—"

She cut herself off suddenly. Andrius heard her sniffle. A trickle of tears began to slide down her face.

"He snapped. I love my father, Andrius, but no one can defend what he tried to do. What he did. I wish it wasn't true, but he got what his actions deserved, if not better. I know my place, though. What is the family without our Prophet, without our village? I love the village first, and so I will always thank you, Andrius, and I'll never be cross."

She cried for a while as they walked, but Andrius did not say anything. He almost piped up a few times, but he decided it would probably do more harm than good.

It wasn't until Third Brick that she was composed again, but they did not speak until First Brick when her cane missed a branch that had fallen in the road, and Andrius had to catch her and lead her over it, for which she was very grateful.

Then, they were at Gimdymo Namai.

The round building's double doors were imposing, shut today as were the shutters. It seemed to Andrius almost like a creature of malintent, shut up against him and his interests, yet beckoning at the same time.

Most boys only entered Gimdymo Namai once—in their mother's womb on the day of their birth. Coming here was a weird feeling.

Jehena knocked and announced herself, and the large doors swung inward. Andrius lost his foreboding as wonder overtook him that he was for the second time walking into Gimdymo Namai.

They plodded on top of slick stone that was the note of

night, past the birthing room and several rooms Andrius had no previous knowledge of before they reached the beginning of the stairs.

Andrius grabbed his escort's arm as she went to take the first step. His eyes couldn't hear well in the stairway.

"Jehena," he whispered, "why did the Prophet want me to come here? Am I in trouble?"

She shrugged, not bothering to turn her head. "I don't think so. He wants to talk with you. He's right at the top of these stairs in his sitting room with Petras, the Regent of Stone."

Andrius's stomach sank. It was trouble. It was exactly as he feared.

The stairs felt like a death march, and the stillness of the cool hallway was eerie. Every footstep echoed. He couldn't hear with his eyes. The sounds of strange, muffled speech tumbled down the steps.

The Prophet and the Regent were having a conference with each other; probably talking about him.

That was a strange thought. They were talking about him.

As they reached the top of the stairs, Andrius began to faintly hear the sun singing once again, and when Jehena opened the door he was bathed in its melody.

"I've returned," Jehena declared.

"Jehena, my wife, my love, is that you?" the Prophet asked. He was as regal as always, dressed in a flowing robe and reclining in his leather chair. The Regent of Stone stood at the far end of the sitting room, and the Regent of Brick sat on the sofa.

She giggled girlishly, betraying her thirteen years, and the notes of her face changed from like snow to like cherries.

"Yes, my love."

The Prophet chuckled as his very young new wife tapped her way to him and fell into his arms. He kissed her.

"Have you brought him?" he asked. "Andrius?" he said, raising his head. "Are you there?"

"I'm here," Andrius replied. He realized that his foot was shaking. He stopped the motion right away.

With a gentle pat the Prophet urged Jehena away. There was business to attend to.

"Good! Good, Andrius, my most faithful servant, you're here. I've been hearing wonderful things about your lessons on this sense that you have."

The Prophet's voice was like warm butter spread on freshly baked bread. Andrius's lips curled into a weak smile at the compliment.

"Thank you, Your Excellence."

"Andrius, please, address me as a friend. Do you know Tadas, the Regent of Brick? And you've met Petras of course."

"Hello, Andrius."

"Andrius."

"Hello," Andrius replied.

This didn't feel like he was in trouble. The men seemed to be in too good of a mood. He remembered that the Regent of Stone had spoken kindly to him on their last meeting, even if he had spoken sternly as well.

"I trust your age-group lessons are going well?" the Prophet inquired. "Adomas is a good man and a capable instructor."

"Oh yes, Your Excellence– Sir. I mean . . ." Andrius was stumped. "What should I call you?"

The Prophet waved dismissively.

"Oh, whatever you like. Something more familiar than 'Your Excellence.' I think we're closer than that."

"Valdas?" Andrius asked tentatively.

The Prophet's voice dropped slightly. "I don't think we're that close."

Andrius felt a wave of panic, but the Prophet broke into a booming, infectious laugh, and the Regents laughed with him. It took Andrius a moment, but soon his nerves were gone and he was able to join the levity.

"You are a clever one, Andrius," the Prophet said. "Very clever. Let me give you a more helpful response. Perhaps . . . perhaps call me Father. After all, I am the father of the village, Zydrunas's heir in influence and responsibility. It is at one time respectful and intimate. What do you think?"

Andrius thought briefly of Aleksandras. The thought of calling someone else "Father" seemed repellent, but then he remembered who he was speaking to.

"I like it, Your–Father."

The Prophet clapped his hands. "Good! Now then, Andrius, you are probably wondering why I've brought you here."

"Out of lessons," Andrius added. The Regent of Brick chuckled at the comment. The Prophet smiled.

"Yes, out of lessons. I did not want to delay until this evening. You will be living here from now on. Petras has arranged for a mule and he will help you personally with whatever belongings you need to bring with you."

Andrius looked around the room, unsure if he had heard correctly.

"I'm sorry," he caught himself just as he was about to say "Your Excellence." "Did you . . . I mean, Father, did you just say–"

"That you will live here, yes. We discussed several options, but this really is the only possibility. The second floor here where I reside is large, and I am the only inhabitant, other than whichever of my wives happens to be with me on a given day. Solveiga has a room downstairs, and I have another servant who never leaves as well, but I wouldn't mind having a boy around. You'll give this place energy." He laughed, and Andrius's heart slammed against his chest.

The thought of living somewhere, anywhere, without Daiva was indescribably exciting, but in the Prophet's own house?

"Wow," Andrius whispered.

"You heard him!" the Prophet declared, his hands raised. "We have a room all set up for you, Andrius. Petras will ensure that everything is taken care of."

"I'm going to live here?"

"Sharp as a shear, isn't he?" the Prophet chuckled. "Yes, Andrius. You will live here with me. We ought to invest in the future, don't you think?"

It was all that Andrius could do to keep from gasping as he looked around the room with new eyes–and this was just the sitting room! He was surrounded by luxuries he had never dreamt of: comfort, prestige, and security. There were padded chairs, shelves of books, probably even a real bed.

A wide grin spread across the boy's face, and then he snorted, trying unsuccessfully to suppress his mirth.

"What is it, Andrius?" the Regent of Stone asked kindly.

Andrius continued to chuckle, and then he took several deep breaths, leaning over his knees.

"I thought . . . I thought that when I was called here I was in trouble or something really bad."

The Prophet and Tadas smiled, but anguish claimed Petras's features. Andrius did not know why, but it was as if the man's heart had broken.

"You always think you are in trouble, Andrius," the Prophet declared cheerfully. He leaned forward. "Is there something I should know about?"

Andrius's blood froze.

"No, sir."

"Father."

"No, sir, Father."

The Prophet, Andrius quickly realized, was joking. He was so full of life and kindness.

"Good, then it's settled. Andrius, go with Petras and collect whatever you wish to bring, if you have any such articles. You will be given new clothes, naturally, so don't bother about those. Whatever you need will be provided."

Andrius felt weak in the knees. It was all too good to be true.

"Thank you," he stammered.

"You're welcome," the Prophet returned magnanimously. "Now go along. The Regent of Brick and I must return to discussing who ought to succeed Aras as the Regent of Wood. Petras, I am already aware of your opinion."

"Yes, Prophet."

"Good. Goodbye, Andrius. We shall meet soon."

The Regent of Stone had already crossed the room and was beginning down the stairs.

"Oh! Oh, okay. Thank you, Father. Thank you very much."

Andrius wore a grin a mile wide as he walked down the marble steps. He was going to live in the Prophet's house, in Gimdymo Namai.

Tears came to his eyes. He wiped them away and tried to keep up his smile. Petras was waiting for him at the base of the stairs, and there was a dull, echoing thud as the heavy door at the top of the staircase shut. Andrius felt tears coming again, and this time he broke down. He couldn't help it.

"Andrius?" The Regent of Stone turned around, panicked.

Andrius's chest heaved. "Andrius, did you fall?" Petras urgently followed the sound of the boy's tears.

The big man sat down next to him. Andrius was breathing hard, trying to calm himself. He could tell that Petras wasn't sure what to do. He almost put his arm around Andrius, then decided against it and folded his hands.

"Why are you crying?" he asked.

Andrius's laughter mixed with tears. He was bewildered.

"I don't know."

Then the laughter left him and only sobbing remained. Petras reached his arm around the boy's shoulders and pulled him in. He didn't say a word; he just let Andrius cry.

Finally he wiped his eyes and smiled at the Regent.

"I'm going to live here. Why am I crying?"

"You've been holding this in a while, I think."

Andrius nodded. Petras opened his mouth to speak, then stopped, letting silence reign for several moments.

"Is it because you won't get hit anymore?"

Andrius wiped his nose with his arm. He nodded again.

"Yes." He sniffed a few times. "I feel relieved, and I feel guilty for feeling relieved. I have to leave, but how can I leave my father alone with her? She's so awful. I'm excited, but I'm so scared I'll . . . mess up. It's–"

"Overwhelming," Petras offered. Andrius nodded.

His eyes had mostly dried. He took a deep breath, speaking but refusing to look at the Regent, just like Jehena had done with his instructor.

"She isn't my real mother. A woman who died is. Her name was Janina."

"I know."

Andrius lifted his head. "You do?"

Petras nodded. "The Prophet told me."

"He knows?"

A wry smile crept across the stern Regent's lips. "The Prophet knows everything."

Petras removed his hand from Andrius's back and folded his hands again. The silence was comforting to Andrius. He was used to it.

After a respectful interim, the Regent of Stone inquired, "Are you all right now?"

Andrius sniffed, and then he sighed. "Yes."

"Are you ready to go?"

"Yes."

The Regent stood, but Andrius remained sitting.

"My father Aleksandras can't come, can he?"

"No, Andrius. I'm afraid not."

Andrius took a deep breath and stood. "Okay. I'm ready to go."

"The mule and the man helping us are right outside."

They began walking down the round hallway toward the entrance.

"We won't need him," Andrius said.

"You don't have many things you will be bringing?"

Andrius wiped the blurriness from his eyes and wiped his fingertips on his pants. "No. Just my patterns."

The late sun sang a dirge as it lowered behind the mountains. Walking through the heavy double doors and out into the breezy air, Andrius felt a memory of peace. He stopped suddenly, overcome by the feeling that everything was going to be alright.

"What sort of patterns?" the Regent asked as he broke the threshold after him, emerging into the village.

"I'll show you," Andrius returned softly. He looked at the growing night upon the face of the mountains and felt strength in his chest, as if a weight had been lifted off of him.

His skin tingled with the sensation. It was a day of firsts.

"I shall look forward to experiencing them," the Regent politely replied.

There was a rush of sudden activity coming from Wood Road. Andrius furrowed his brow and looked back to the Regent. He did not seem concerned.

The sounds grew louder, and Andrius perceived a group of people urgently passing First Wood. Without thinking, he ran to the boulder by the side of Gimdymo Namai and climbed on top to get a better look.

Five men were carrying someone, and a group of women followed nervously behind. Everyone was speaking at the same time.

There was a scream amidst the men, and Andrius noticed a pregnant woman. Suddenly he understood.

"She's in labor," he said aloud.

Petras turned his head, surprised at the direction of Andrius's voice.

Andrius looked back to the group as it rushed ever nearer to Gimdymo Namai.

"She's in labor!" Andrius exclaimed.

When the flurry of activity was almost upon them, Andrius shouted over the noise to Petras. "What should we do?"

He seemed somewhat amused by Andrius's enthusiasm but otherwise uninterested. "Nothing."

"Nothing?"

Petras shrugged.

"There will be plenty more."

The small crowed buffaloed past and Andrius grinned broadly.

The Regent was right, of course. He lived in Gimdymo Namai now, and the Prophet himself was his benefactor. There would be plenty more births to witness.

How incredible to be so familiar with miracles as to be uninterested in them, Andrius thought. He got a better look at the soon-to-be mother being carried along as she screamed again. Andrius laughed aloud as they burst into Gimdymo Namai.

It was his instructor's wife, Audra.

"Now they'll have to pull him out of lessons," he giggled.

APPROACHING THE FAMILIAR HOUSE AT TWENTY-FIVE stone was a confusing experience. Part of Andrius was elated, but the smallest seed of guilt had now sprouted and grown to such a size as to demand attention. He would not miss Daiva, but he was abandoning his father.

"Get your things," the Regent of Stone said softly. His cane had just clacked against the roadstone and they made their way toward the only home Andrius had ever known. The night was suddenly colder.

"Can I say goodbye first?"

Petras acquired a hard look, as if the heat of anger suddenly steamed off of him, but then he softened and seemed sad.

"You'll miss Aleksandras."

Andrius nodded, wiping his hand across his face.

"Very well," the Regent relented.

The door creaked open and Andrius could not hear with his eyes, though his ears told him that the room was occupied. Aleksandras was sitting in a chair facing the wall.

"Andrius?"

"It's me, Papa."

"And I am here as well," Petras added. Andrius's eyes began adjusting to the room, and he could now faintly hear with them. His father had grown animated at first, then forlorn, hearing the Regent's voice.

"They've decided to take you away from me, haven't they?"

Andrius's stomach tied in the worst of knots. He took a lunging step forward.

"No, Papa! It's–"

"Yes."

Andrius stopped dead in his tracks. The Regent of Stone shifted his weight, then broke the silence again. "Yes, Aleksandras. We are taking him away from you."

Andrius frowned at the Regent, and then he remembered bitterly that the man did not perceive his look. Andrius took his father by the hand, who shook his head as he spoke.

"I can't say I'm surprised–or that I blame you." He chuckled bittersweetly and ran his hand over Andrius's hair. "You always were a special boy. Destined for great things."

"Papa . . ."

"You belong to the village, Andrius, though I liked to think you belonged to me. We have to obey the Prophet and his Regents, don't we?"

Andrius sank to his knees, still clutching his father's hand. The night-sun's song had followed them in, and Andrius noticed how large and swollen Aleksandras's face was. Dried blood missed during washing dotted his face here and there.

"Papa," he whispered, heartbroken. He reached out to lightly touch the affected area.

"Ah! Ah! Andrius, please. It's sensitive still. The healer tells me it's broken." He inhaled hard and long, making a strange sound through his congested and swollen nostrils.

"Andrius . . ." the Regent gently urged him. They could not delay forever.

"Go, Andrius," his father said with a tremor in his voice. He was crying and trying to hide it. "Daiva is asleep. Now is a good time. I'll miss you for my sake, but it is better for you to be away from here. I should have protected you better."

Andrius looked down. "You saved my life."

Aleksandras warmed to a tired smile.

"Yes, I did. And now the village recognizes how special you are." The old man stood up and pulled Andrius into a tight hug. "I know you'll do great things. I believe in your new sense, and I believe in you."

Andrius felt the old man's tender arms release him then.

He sighed, trying not to cry again. "It seems like everyone does, these days."

Aleksandras smiled frailly and hoarsely whispered, "I believed in you first." He took the boy's head in his hands and kissed it. "Go. Daiva is asleep and won't bother you anymore. I'll be all right."

"But Papa . . ."

"It is time to go, Andrius," the Regent of Stone interjected. "Let us collect your things."

Andrius looked sadly at his old father who trembled as he groped back toward his chair and sat down. He was crushed.

A large, gentle hand came down on his back.

"Come on. It's for the best," Petras said, leading him out. The door squeaked as they pushed it closed behind them, but still Andrius looked back, imagining his father when he could no longer hear him with his eyes. "Where are your belongings?"

"In the barn," Andrius replied lifelessly.

"And you say we won't need the pack mule? Do you have clothes, toys, blankets to bring?"

"Only my patterns."

"Patterns?"

Andrius nodded.

"A stack of patterns. I make them."

Petras said something else then, but Andrius did not hear him. For all of his elation at being invited to live in the Prophet's house, to get away from the abusive woman who had tormented him for so long, all he could think about was Aleksandras–old, alone, and trembling from sorrow.

WIND TUSSLED ANDRIUS'S THICKENING HAIR AS HE stood upon the grassy knoll where he taught his lessons. It had been growing out lately, a fact which would have bothered him in the past, but since he had traded a rotting pile of straw for a real bed and a pillow, he didn't mind the extra inch of hair. Nothing got stuck in it.

The gathered crowd was rapt in attentive silence, waiting expectantly for Andrius to begin the day's teaching so that they too might one day hear with their eyes. Some days Andrius's lessons made more sense than others, but enthusiasm was at an all-time high. There were groups that met at Stone and Wood and Brick Gatherings to discuss Andrius's methods each night and compare progress. Many of the villagers now tried to keep their eyes open for at least part of the day.

Andrius's prestige had risen with his move into the sacred Gimdymo Namai. He didn't feel much different, but he had grown to like the attention–even if he still thought it was a little weird.

"I wish the enlightenment of Zydrunas on you all," Andrius greeted them.

"And on you as well, with all his wisdom," the crowd responded.

"I've decided that we need to talk about things differently." Andrius scanned the crowd. There were around six hundred fifty people present, sitting on the grass. Maybe six sixty. "When I'm describing notes to somebody it takes a long time to say. 'Its note is like the way the sky sings in the evening' is too much for normal talking. I've thought a lot about a better way to describe things. Their notes, I mean.

"We'll have names. I've counted, and there's really only about eight different notes that things can be."

Andrius fidgeted where he stood. It was one of his crazier ideas, and he was nervous about presenting it.

"Anything that's the note of grass, for example, we'll call 'grass,' as long as it's close. Anything where the note is like dirt we'll call 'dirt.'"

Andrius felt a swell of hopefulness, but it ebbed as he noticed the looks of bewilderment in the crowd.

"I . . . I have other names too. For the other notes. It will make it easier for us. At least, I think it will."

Elze the apothecary stood up. "Permission to ask a question, Andrius?"

Andrius hated when people asked him that. It made him squirm. They shouldn't be asking him for permission. He was just a kid, and an abnormal one at that.

Still, it gave him a boost of confidence that people thought of him as the expert. "Of course you can."

Six hundred fifty pairs of ears tilted up toward the speaker, awaiting the question.

"So what am I to say when describing grass or dirt? Dirt is dirt? And I thought trees had the same note as grass, so a tree is grass, and grass is grass?"

"It's baffling," someone else said. A chorus of agreement joined them.

This was not going how Andrius had hoped, but he was not very surprised.

"It was a stupid idea," he said aloud, intending to think it instead.

To his horror, several women nearby agreed.

"The leaf is grass? It's too confusing. A person would sound crazy all of the time."

"Just forget it," Andrius said, wiping his face with his hands. "Maybe I can think of a better system. It was a bad idea."

The murmurs grew until one voice broke through the noise. "It's a brilliant idea."

Andrius looked up sharply. He knew that old voice.

There, not fifteen yards away, sat Aleksandras, who came faithfully to every lesson, listening intently. Andrius had looked for him earlier but did not find him, and now here he was.

"It's a brilliant idea," Aleksandras said again as the people quieted down to hear him. "It is an easy thing to come up with a different name, or a made-up name so it isn't so puzzling. Let the boy explain. We should trust him, don't you think?"

The apothecary considered this, then she sat down. The crowd was thinking too.

Andrius smiled weakly. He was grateful, though it was odd to be near Aleksandras these days. He couldn't put his finger on why.

"Well," Andrius began, "it's true that calling something like a tree 'grass' would be sort of confusing, so we'll add to it." He tilted his head, musing. He was speaking mostly to himself now, forgetting the people, but they were listening. "It can't just be totally random because it would be hard to remember, but it can't quite be a real word either . . . What if we called the note of grass and trees 'grassentree'?"

"Grassentree?" Milda wondered aloud. She had been sitting up front with Berena lately.

Andrius was engrossed in his thoughts now, excitedly sharing them as they came.

"Yes! That's better. And the note of dirt we'll call 'dirtyshoe,' because it's the note of dirt and shoes, and no one will get that mixed up. That's much better!" The boy looked up with wide eyes at the crowd listening. "I'm going to go and come up with new names for the other six notes. Until then–" The people joined in to recite his closing line, now well-known to them all. "Open your eyes and look at things!"

Andrius couldn't help but smile. Before the crowd could come up to him, however, he was off running so he could think in peace–and out loud.

"Daisy sun. Sundaisy. Sudaisy! Cloud and chicken . . . milk . . . Milkcloud. Milkoud. That would be good."

He darted across the meadow, thankful that his eyes allowed him the freedom to run with hardly any fear of falling down. All the while he played around with the different words he could combine to name the notes, changing his mind several times. He stopped to pick a dandelion and blow its seeds into the wind, then he was off again.

He circled back to the village, skirting around some of the huts in Wood.

The sun's song was marvelous today, and every part of nature accompanied it beautifully. The fields of cartwheel flower stood tall and healthy, swaying in the breeze, and birds swooped down from the trees to snatch at the little insects that buzzed about.

Andrius stopped jogging and slumped against the side of a house, sweat on his shirt and a smile on his face.

He was happy. Happiness was a rare sensation for him, but he felt it now.

A group of his age-peers, Tomas and Ugna among them, passed

by on the road and Andrius knew that if he left his resting spot to approach them, they would welcome his company. They would talk with him and ask his opinion and thank him for walking with them. It sounded ridiculous, but it was true–it had happened several times.

Andrius sat on the ground and closed his eyes, breathing in the pure air and enjoying the cool of the shade. He had some time before he needed to leave for lessons, and he was going to cherish it.

Approaching footsteps and muffled voices came to his resting ears, drawing him from his thoughts.

"I can think of no reason why."

"Oh come off it, Petras. You know exactly why."

"You are going to say 'leadership,' as if that is a virtue in itself. We need wise leadership for the people of Wood, not just a man to fill the void."

Andrius opened his eyes and peeked around the side of the building. A large, barrel-chested man conversed with a wiry one as they slid their canes back and forth in front of them. It was the Regents of Stone and Brick.

His chest tightened. He probably was not supposed to be listening, but he had no desire to alert them of his presence. He'd stay put until they passed.

But then Tadas, the Regent of Brick, halted Petras, clapping him on the shoulder.

"Dovydas is a good man."

"I don't doubt it, but he isn't the right man. A Regent must be unwavering in his decisions, particularly in a section like Wood."

"You doubt his decisiveness?"

"Yes."

"He is resolute!"

"No he isn't."

Tadas thought for a moment, then let his hand slide off of his companion's shoulder.

"No, he isn't," he agreed, "but he's a good man."

"It isn't enough. Do you think he would have had the will to deal with that stranger Daniel?"

Andrius perked up at this, almost falling over.

Petras sniffed the air and rubbed his fingers together. "Winter is coming. It will be here early this year."

"You always talk of winter."

"And I thus I am alive to do so. Soon the snow will come and cover the paths, cover the crops, cover the roadstones, and make us deaf. If the people of Wood are not adequately prepared, there will be too much death."

"They have endured many winters before, and we had a good season of births. Our numbers will grow this year, not diminish."

"Let us hope."

It was quiet then, and Andrius was suddenly aware of how dry his mouth was. It was sticky and hot from all the running he had done, and his carved wooden pitcher tempted him. Yet taking a drink would make a sound, and so he waited.

Petras spoke again.

"That we must find a new Regent of Wood quickly, I agree, but it has to be the right man. The people will be shut in their homes from snowfall to springmelt. Someone competent is needed."

Tadas sighed, and then he started walking again. "So not Dovydas?"

"No," Petras agreed in his steady, deep voice. "We seek another."

They were quiet then as they walked along until they had passed out of earshot.

Andrius pensively lifted his pitcher to his lips and drank a full third of his water. He got up and walked to his class, feeling waterlogged and thinking of all he had heard.

Notes still sang in the back of his mind. And why were the Regents talking about Daniel?

ANDRIUS RAPPED ON THE DOOR OF GIMDYMO Namai, tired from lessons and from thinking. It had been an eventful and confusing day. The doorman answered him.

"Who wishes to gain entrance to this sacred space?"

"It's Andrius," he said, perking up for a moment. The novelty of being allowed into Gimdymo Namai had not faded.

The locks turned, the door opened, and Andrius was inside. He noticed, to his delight, that the doorman had his eyes open–though they seemed hollow and empty. Andrius nodded at him. He did not nod back.

"Is the Prophet here?"

"He is."

The doorman continued standing erect, looking nowhere in particular. He was a stiff man. Andrius was used to people not wanting to engage with him, however.

Footsteps reverberated through the strong stone structure as Andrius climbed the marble staircase to the second level. It was quiet today, as it often was. The sun's singing, too, was now only very faint.

A murmur of voices grew louder as he approached the heavy door at the top of the stairs and eased it open. Valdas the Prophet was inside, speaking with Petras and Tadas, Regents of Stone and Brick.

"He's an eleven-year-old boy," Tadas was saying. "We can't possibly allow him to—"

"Who's there?" Petras interrupted, the three men stopping upon hearing the door. Petras stood, facing the side wall. Tadas reclined upon the padded couch, and Valdas sat majestically on his favorite dais.

"It's Andrius," the Prophet replied with quiet assurance. "Isn't it?" He laughed congenially, taking some of the knot out of Andrius's stomach, but the two Regents seemed very uncomfortable. "Andrius," the Prophet implored in his honey-rich voice, "say something or we'll all think we've gone mad. How were your lessons today?"

Andrius sighed, loosening his grip on the wooden pitcher that might as well have been glued to his left hand.

"It was good. Our instructor spoke to us for a long time about the fires of purification, when our village was founded and its members burned all traces of their former lives."

Tadas coughed. The Prophet smiled.

"A wonderful topic. What dedication and wisdom those men possessed! But Andrius, I was asking about your lessons."

"Oh! I thought you meant the normal lessons, for my age-peers. I'm so sorry, Pro— I mean, Father." Andrius laughed nervously, but the Prophet's gracious smile set him at ease. "My lessons went pretty well, but they started off weird. I thought I had a good system for naming notes, but then the people didn't like it, so I had to change it. I think it's good now."

The Prophet nodded wisely and opened his arms.

"Good, Andrius. But remember, don't put too much weight on what people think. You have a gift and a tremendous mind. Teach what is best, what would make Zydrunas and I, his successor, proud."

"Thank you, Father. I will."

There was a lull in the conversation, and Andrius wasn't sure what to do until Tadas cleared his throat.

"Would you mind leaving the room for just a while longer, Andrius? You entered as we were discussing important matters for the village."

"Oh." Andrius kicked himself. Of course he should have left. "Okay. I'm sorry."

"Don't be sorry," the Prophet chided. "Your presence lifts my spirit. We will no doubt converse all about your lessons soon."

"I'd like that," Andrius began, making his way to the door that led to his quarters. He stopped just as he reached for the handle, and he turned around. "Father?"

"Yes, my son?"

Andrius debated within himself, but suddenly the words came gushing out. "What happened to Daniel?"

Tadas looked away. Petras folded his arms. The Prophet, for his part, was unfazed.

"Who?"

"Well . . . Daniel. The man I saved. The one we found on the other side of the barricade protecting us from the Regions of Death. What happened to him?"

"His name wasn't Daniel," Petras interjected. "It was Drunas, and he was not well."

"Ah, yes. You speak of Drunas, brought here some time ago? You really are perceptive, having found him out there. But Andrius, I have to tell you . . . Petras is right. He wasn't well in the mind."

"Oh, I didn't . . . I mean, he didn't seem crazy."

Tadas sat up suddenly. He was a lot jumpier than the others.

"You spoke with him?"

"You spoke with him?" Petras echoed.

The Prophet raised a hand.

"Gentlemen, please. Andrius, they didn't realize you had spoken with him. It was thought that he was unconscious when you found him."

Andrius fidgeted. The way the Regents were acting was so strange.

"Well, he was, but the next day on my way to lessons he was sitting outside of Gimdymo Namai and he called me over."

The Prophet seemed sympathetic and a little sad. "I understand. He didn't make much sense, did he?"

Andrius looked down. "No. He used a bunch of words Milda and I had never heard before."

"Milda was there? From your age group?"

Andrius nodded.

"Berena too. Well, Berena wasn't there with us, but she talked with him too."

The Regent of Stone took a seat on the luxurious couch, clearly in thought. The Prophet stroked his beard.

"I didn't know that. Thank you for telling me, Andrius. You are a loyal servant of me and my village."

"You're welcome," he said quietly.

The Prophet sighed. "Andrius, I wish we knew what became

of Drunas, or 'Daniel,' as you call him. We tried to help him, reintroduce him to his parents. He was a runaway from the village, you know. Living in the meadow, eating off the land like an animal . . . I had such compassion for him, but he ran away from us and we couldn't find him again. I'm so sorry."

"He ran away?"

"Took his things and left," the Regent of Brick interjected. The Prophet looked momentarily displeased, then reassumed his typical, comforting air.

"It is a tragedy, but he wouldn't let us help him. Perhaps we will find him again someday, but winter will be here soon, so for your sake I don't want you getting your hopes up. We just don't know."

Andrius nodded. "Okay."

"All right," the Prophet concluded warmly. "Now if you'll excuse us for a short time, Andrius. We're finishing up a discussion. I have a decision to make, and as you know, these men advise me."

"Yes, Father."

"Thank you, Andrius."

The Regents added their goodbyes, and Andrius opened the door and stepped through it. As it closed, he heard the Prophet's voice distinctly say: "Touch four walls and begin."

GRASSENTREE, SUDAISY, DIRTYSHOE, MILKOUD, highsky, bloodnote, fuzzymum, and nightish. These were the words that Andrius had chosen to describe the different notes he was hearing with his eyes. He decided that he couldn't keep calling it "hearing," but since he didn't have a better term for his extra sense, he did not immediately press the issue.

Most of the village liked the new names. They were delighted to hear Andrius excitedly describe that flowers come in basically every kind of note except nightish. Some raised objections to this, but Andrius's father spoke up in his defense again, saying, "If different sorts of flowers have different smells, it would make sense for them to have different eye notes too," and, "My boy's a poet!" The others accepted this explanation.

He had begun sheepishly, describing that clouds, milk, and most people's eyes were milkoud. The sun was sudaisy. Weeds were grassentree, the wildflowers that sprang up after a rain were fuzzymum, and so was fire. He grew in confidence as the crowd soaked up this new revelation. It was like a breakthrough into a whole new subject of learning.

Not many things were bloodnote, except for blood, obviously, some types of bugs, and people's lips, sort of. The people were amazed when he told them that when the sun stopped singing in the evenings, everything lost its note or became nightish.

It had been his most spectacular success since his now-famous "open your eyes and look at things" speech. He was not as dismayed by the confused comments floating around as he typically was. People were trying to determine how to make notes change, which didn't make any sense to Andrius, and he heard comments like, "I'm highsky. What note are you?" and, "Anything tall is highsky. Anything low is dirtyshoe."

There was still much work to be done, but the response had been wonderful, and even now as Andrius walked down Brick Road, he replayed moments of it in his mind.

He wasn't paying much attention in his age-group lessons these days. Either he was looking at Milda or he was thinking of new ways to describe his extra sense and how to teach it. It happily consumed him.

It was cold in the air, and Andrius shivered a bit, but he didn't mind. He was used to the cold, and it would be at least a month until the snows came, so he didn't have to fear being caught outside during a storm.

The sun was singing, but its song was dulled by the thick cover of clouds, which weren't milkoud like usual, but sort of a mixture of milkoud and nightish.

"Can notes mix with each other?" Andrius wondered aloud. It was an intriguing thought. He had never considered it before.

"Andrius?"

He turned around. Milda was heading in the same direction as he, bundled in warm clothes and bouncing her cane back and forth like she always did. He had been one of the last students to leave lessons, but he had been so wrapped up in his thoughts he didn't notice who else was still around.

"Andrius, is that you?"

"Hi, Milda."

He couldn't help a slight grin. He liked Milda.

People passed by on all sides as he waited for her to catch up. It was a showcase day, where all of the villagers set up their wares that they had produced that others might need, so it was busier on the roads than usual–particularly near Gimdymo Namai.

"I didn't know you were still around," Milda said as she reached Andrius. "What were you doing?"

He shrugged. "Thinking."

"Can I have some of your water? Do you have your pitcher with you?"

Andrius placed it in her outstretched hands and shivered as she took a drink. It really was cold today.

"Thanks," she said, holding out the pitcher to be taken again.

"You're welcome."

They resumed walking then, occasionally dodging passersby carrying bundles of walking canes, firewood, or extra food.

"So did you hear me?"

"Hm?" Andrius had been thinking again, and the noise caught him off-guard.

"Did you hear what I said to our teacher? Since you were staying behind too."

"What? Oh, no. No, I was just . . . I didn't notice."

"You didn't notice?"

"No."

"But you must've been right there."

"I was thinking."

"Thinking?"

Andrius didn't know what to say. She kept repeating him.

"What were you thinking about?"

"A lot of things. I heard the Regent of Stone and Brick talking the other day. I'm trying to make sense of what they said."

"*The* Regent? Our Regent?"

"Petras III, yes."

He stopped to think for a moment.

"Talk, Andrius, please! It's like you're not even there sometimes."

"Sorry," he said, beginning to walk again. "I was just remembering. They talked about finding a new Regent of Wood. The Regent of Brick wanted Dovydas, but Petras said no."

"Good. He'd be terrible. What else?"

"You know Dovydas?"

"I don't know him personally, but I know someone else should be Regent. Though the Prophet and his Regents know best, of course. Zydrunas has my allegiance."

"Zydrunas has my allegiance," Andrius repeated from rote. "But how do you know about him? He's in a totally different section of the world."

Milda smirked. "Well, some people are just better informed than others, Andrius. Pranciskus on the other hand . . . He's in Wood too, and I think he'd make an excellent Regent. Or Marijus, he'd be good too. He's the other blacksmith, not Dominykas."

Milda kept talking, but Andrius stopped dead in his tracks. His eyes went wide. Something floated lazily to the ground in front of them, but Milda didn't notice.

"I know people in Brick too," she continued. "Almost all of them, probably. Well, there's too many, but I know a lot of them, anyway. Zydra and Stephinius raise the cartwheel flower. Ganytojas raises sheep."

"Milda . . ." Andrius interrupted.

"I'm not done yet. Rasa makes clothes for Brick. This jacket is from her, actually. My mother and her were age-peers when—"

"Milda."

"When they were children. Same lessons and everything, their whole life. It makes you wonder if we'll be friends when we're old. The people in our class, I mean. Some people, like Berena, I have no doubt, but—"

"Milda."

There was a gravity to Andrius's voice that finally got her to stop walking and turn around. She put her hands on her hips.

"Andrius, are you all the way back there? It is like you're not even there during conversations—sometimes you aren't. At least have the decency to say something first."

Andrius's eyes were fixed on the sky, filled with a nightish and milkoud layer that separated them from the sun.

"Hold your hands out," he said.

"What, is this another one of your eye things? I have to be honest, Andrius; nothing has really worked for me so far. And if it did, I wouldn't even know what was—"

She stopped. Something cold and wet fell on her hand and dissolved. Then another, and another. They were increasing in frequency moment by moment.

Her face disfigured into a look of horror, and Andrius's grave assertion confirmed her greatest fears.

"It's snowing."

The whole village stopped at these two words. All of the bustle along the roads jolted to a halt, all of the noise suddenly ceased. The whispering, taunting wind snaked among them as a hundred and fifty pairs of hands let go of what they were doing and reached out into the air.

The snow continued to fall.

"It is!" a terrified man shouted. "It is snowing!" A woman shrieked. A child began wailing.

"That's impossible!" a man carrying a bundle of horse feed shouted back, sounding unconvinced of his own objection. "It's a month too early, at least."

"Then what is this falling from the sky, Matas?" came the bitter reply.

"It's snow."

"No . . . no, not now."

"It's snowing!"

In an instant, the momentary stillness was gone, and there was panic. Bundles were dropped, animals carelessly let loose, and everywhere villagers shouted. Some shouted for companions, others in hopes of receiving instructions, and others simply shouted because terror had fallen upon them. Andrius saw a man running toward his cart take a misstep and fall on his face. Several others had the misfortune of being in his path, and they fell also.

The temperature continued to drop, and a thin layer of snow and ice now appeared dusted over the ground.

"I have to get home," Milda declared. Andrius wanted to shout after her, to ask her if she would be all right, but the words did not come. She was right, after all. She had to get out of the storm before the road was covered. Speed was of the essence.

"We'll freeze to death!" a boy shouted, turning Andrius's attention back to the town center. A murmur of agreement went up from the others nearby. A hulking villager in a woolen cap lumbered by, crashing into Andrius's shoulder, nearly bowling him over. He didn't apologize. He simply continued brazenly groping ahead. As it was, Andrius found himself having to evade streams of villagers travelling in all directions. It was madness.

Another scream caught Andrius's attention, but this one stood out from the din.

"No! That's mine! I'm only eleven–give that back!"

A short distance down Stone Road, a middle-aged woman accosted Milda. She had one hand on Milda's cane–apparently she had lost hers–and with the other hand she tried to swat the young girl away. Milda held on with both hands, screaming and crying, fully knowing that having her cane could mean the difference between life and death.

Andrius didn't waste his breath on a word. He took after her immediately, sprinting against the confused tide of panicked villagers, clutching his pitcher to his chest. He narrowly avoided collision when a big man shoved Elze the apothecary out of his way and she fell. A moment later the big man slipped on a patch of snow, and he fell also. The snow was falling faster, and the wind whistled tauntingly among them.

"I'm coming, Milda," Andrius said under his breath.

Milda's assailant succeeded in pulling away with her cane, leaving Milda weeping and lying on the thin layer of snow, prostrate and hopeless. The shrewish woman stole away immediately, deaf to her cries.

Andrius slid to a stop, coming to his knees beside Milda. He put a hand on her shoulder as she wept.

"Milda. Milda, it's all right, I'm here!"

Andrius shook her to try and get her up, but she wasn't moving.

"It's dangerous to be in the road," he said, more to himself than to her. "Milda, get up. I'll help you. Come on!"

Her crying only turned to wailing, the weeping of despair.

"She stole it!" was all Milda could manage, the words muffled by the ground that muzzled her.

Andrius looked up. Most of the crowd tried to stick to the sides of the road, but there, down the path was a horse-driven cart, and it was out of control. It was coming straight for them.

"Milda, we have to move!"

"She stole my cane!" Milda repeated, unyielding.

Andrius looked up again. Even other villagers were diving out of the way of the wild cart that trampled everything in its path. The sound it made as it approached was like thunder.

"Milda!" Andrius shouted. "Don't you hear that? We'll be killed!"

He tried to pick her up, but she was like a rag doll, and Andrius wasn't strong. He tried to push her, but she wouldn't budge.

"Milda!"

The horse was only a stone's throw away and coming right for them. Andrius's heart was pounding as he stood up and grabbed Milda's mittened hands. They slipped away from him as he tugged. He grabbed them again, and again he lost his grip.

The cart's approach was the sound of the earth coming to an end. He took Milda's hands one last time, squeezing as hard as he could. "Milda! Hold onto my hands!"

Just before the crazed horse reached them, Milda's

hands tightened around Andrius's, and he pulled with all his might. The horse's iron hooves were bearing down upon her, but just as their paths intersected, the wild horse took a staggering leap, and Andrius's pull yanked her away a mere instant before the cart's great wheels could crush her.

She screamed and Andrius fell on his back, watching helplessly as another villager was knocked to the ground by the runaway animal wreaking havoc.

Milda was shaking. "Thank you," she said.

"Let's get you home."

Andrius gently helped Milda to her feet, and she began crying bitterly once more.

"Are you upset about the cane? We don't need a cane."

"Are you crazy?" she shouted, swatting his hand away.

He felt a wave of revulsion at having to assert himself, but there was no other way. Andrius took a deep breath and her hand, stopping only to retrieve his fallen pitcher.

"Most people seem to think so," he muttered in reply.

They trudged in silence then. Wet flecks of speeding ice pelted them the whole way.

BY THE TIME HE WAS AT GIMDYMO NAMAI'S doorstep, Andrius was chilled to the bone. His numbed fingers sent sharp pangs through his hand as he knocked on the great doors.

No reply.

Then, as he raised his hand and knocked again, he heard muffled voices inside.

"Don't open that door! There's enough of us as it is."

"Poor soul must be freezing."

"There is only so much food stored here . . ."

"Keep it shut!"

"Back!" a familiar voice shouted. "I keep the doors, not you. Had your ideas been in my head before you arrived at this sacred door, you would now be languishing in the snow to die beside this man."

The door opened.

Andrius looked at the doorman and a small crowd of villagers huddled together for warmth.

"He's probably half-dead by now anyway," one of the rabble called, unaware that Andrius now stood directly before him. "It started snowing an hour ago."

"Who are you?" the doorman inquired.

"Andrius," he replied. He couldn't resist adding, "The Prophet's own."

The people began murmuring in shock and chiding those who had been most vocal about keeping suppliants out. The doorman snapped his fingers.

"Servants! Andrius is here. The Prophet will need to be told."

"Is it true that you have a fifth sense?" a young woman leaned forward, whispering.

"Didn't the blizzard scare you, boy?" Daumantas, the cane-maker, asked.

"Not really," Andrius admitted. "My friend lost her cane—"

The people gasped.

"And so I led her home before coming here."

"Amazing," the cane-maker said.

Footsteps stole Andrius's attention before he could be taken in by the fresh round of questioning all around him. The Prophet himself was descending the marble stairs, aided by his exquisite cane made of metal.

"Andrius!" He chuckled. "Forgive my nervous laughter. You continue to impress–and relieve–us."

He patted a few shoulders before arriving at Andrius. "Is that you?" he asked.

"Yes, Father."

"Andrius!" He gripped Andrius's shoulders firmly. "I am delighted to hear you safe." He took one hand off the boy and gestured around. "I'm told that we've drawn a little crowd."

The people chuckled.

"Hope fervently for the end of this storm and a warm aftermath," the Prophet instructed them, growing serious. "If this persists, we may not have enough provisions for all of you."

"We were just at the showcase," the young woman lamented, "and it is so early for this season. I fear my presence here might harm the great Prophet."

"No food or drink shall touch my lips," Daumantas declared. Others chimed in but immediately grew quiet when the Prophet spoke.

"You needed some shelter from the sudden snow; I do not grudge you that. Let us be careful not to leap ahead of ourselves. For the moment, you are welcome in this sacred place."

"But you said there aren't enough provisions," the young woman persisted. "Our presence here endangers us all!"

Panicked murmuring rose up again, coupled with

declarations of loyalty and offers to slay themselves so they would have no need of food.

The Prophet's words brought stillness again. "What do you think, Andrius?"

Andrius had been halfway into a drink of water from his pitcher when the Prophet addressed him. "What? I mean–" He coughed. "Excuse me, sir, but I don't understand the question."

"What should be done for these people?"

Andrius lowered the frigid water from his lips and looked at all the faces listening expectantly, cut off from their families, terrified of the storm. He thought of the coldness on his own skin, but that was not as important.

"I'll take them," he said weakly.

"What do you mean?"

Andrius took another drink for courage, then regretted it, feeling once again how cold the water was. "I'll guide them back to their homes."

"That's madness!"

"Really?"

"Andrius, the Prophet's own!"

"Peace," the Prophet said, and it was quiet. "You are certain that you can do this?"

Andrius nodded. "Yes."

"People die from getting caught in the snow, Andrius. Every year. They get lost, unable to hear or feel anything, and tragically they die of cold. Snow is a pernicious blanket of death, robbing us of every sensation."

"But I can use my eyes," Andrius replied. "It isn't that scary for me." He shivered. "Just cold."

The Prophet clapped twice.

"Solveiga, bring furs to Andrius. We will send the villagers out by section so that no one has to remain exposed for too long. Everyone living in Wood, stand by the door. Andrius will take them to their homes, return, warm himself, and then he will take Brick, and then Stone." He leaned down and whispered into Andrius's ear. "How will they follow you? By your voice?"

"We can just hold hands," Andrius whispered back.

"Form a human chain, my children." The Prophet smiled, and the villagers, though uneasy, responded well to his confidence.

As the people sorted themselves out by section, Andrius felt a warm, heavy coat drape over his shoulders.

The Prophet bent down and placed a hand on Andrius's back.

"It's not too late to back out, Andrius. It is dangerous–they would understand."

"No, I'm okay. I'll do it."

The Prophet nodded solemnly. "Do what you were made to. Ramunas!"

Upon hearing his name, the doorman leapt to his task and heaved the wide doors open. Swirls of frigid, icy wind swept inside.

Andrius, who had before felt no particular fear of the storm, now began thinking of how long he would need to be out in order to get all of these people home.

A groping hand batted against his fingers, then clasped over them. Andrius looked out into the howling milkoud swarm.

"Let's go."

14

IT WAS COLD, WET, AND MISERABLE, AND THE LENGTH of each trip was compounded not only by the fearful hesitation of each villager's cautious steps but also by the necessity of having to wait each time someone slipped and fell. There was a lot of falling and more than a little bit of weeping, but Andrius got everyone in the group home safe. Each time he returned to Gimdymo Namai his eyes were watering, his nose ran, and his cheeks burned, but at least Solveiga was ready with hot tea.

First Wood, then Brick, and finally Stone, where one of the villagers lived all the way out at Sixty-first Stone—the most remote address in the whole world.

When Andrius finally returned to Gimdymo Namai he was dizzy, unable to feel his hands or feet, and he was coughing.

The next several events passed as a blur in Andrius's mind: Solveiga stripping him of his wet clothes, feeling hot water rush over his skin, the soft towels rubbing feeling back into his limbs. He was suddenly in his bed with extra furs and blankets covering him, with no memory of how he had gotten there. A fit of harsh coughing shook his small frame, and the last thing he remembered was a strong and gentle hand on his shoulder.

"Did you get them home, Andrius? Are they safe?"

"They're safe," he wheezed, and then all he knew was night.

TORTURED SCREAMING FILLED ANDRIUS'S EARS. First the desperate pleas of a mother, then the howling screams of children. Notes shattered and swirled together like spokes of a spinning cartwheel, sudaisy, bloodnote, fuzzymum, milkoud, highsky, grassentree, dirtyshoe, and notes that he didn't recognize all coalesced, then shot off as dots in all directions, destroying whatever lay in their path.

Then, all of it faded to silence and nightish.

A thumping began and grew louder and louder until it was deafening. Boots striking the ground. Boots attached to feet, attached to soldiers, attached to guns.

They were there, suddenly marching past Andrius in never-ending columns.

Fire and smoke and the shouting of men and women arguing, grasping, clutching, clawing.

A freckled youth ran before Andrius, holding his ears, shutting his eyes, and singing nonsense words.

Breath failed him. The panic and pain of suffocation spread through his whole body, turning him highsky as he looked at the soldiers turning to find that a gigantic bucket, as large as a mountain, slowly tipped and began spilling its nightish, viscous liquid like a tidal wave over the land.

They tried to run, but they were overtaken, cannons and guns firing into the advancing mass, but it was unhindered as it swallowed them all.

A gasp of air filled Andrius's lungs and the stink of the unholy tar sickened him. His legs were rooted to the earth.

He watched it advance. The end was coming.

"Planned!" he heard a strained, maniacal voice shout. "Everything! Unwanted, discarded, forsaken, forgotten," and then the disembodied voice laughed high and screeching as the nightish tar advanced to Andrius's place, and the laughter turned slow, deep, and wicked.

The rushing tar split, running around Andrius in circles, then continuing on its way, destroying everything. The ground beneath him shook, then grew into a tower, a mountain, stretching the sky as the wind stretched Andrius's face.

And then the mountain was gone, and he fell—falling and falling until he was in a room. It was sealed off from the world, a circle of men, a counsel of bedraggled, grizzled men. Shadows of shadows of men.

The maniacal voice spoke. It belonged to the central man, tall and dark-haired, and winsome.

"Touch four walls and begin."

Suddenly Andrius was on the table, surrounded. All eyes of all notes, grassentree, sudaisy, singing into the emptiness from their unnatural sockets, pouring down on Andrius as he tried to scream, but no sound would escape his lips.

He tried again, but he was silent still. Terror overtook him as he drew in one more breath to try one more time.

ANDRIUS OPENED HIS EYES. THERE WAS SOMETHING over them. He couldn't hear with his eyes.

A hand pulled away from his forehead, and he heard the

sun's cheerful song, as well as Jehena's smiling face, pointed the wrong direction.

"Andrius," she began timidly. "Andrius, are you awake?"

"Yes."

A small squeal of joy escaped from her lips and she hurried from the room.

"Andrius is awake!"

Sitting up in his bed, Andrius was suddenly keenly aware of the cottony desert that was his throat. He rubbed his chest absentmindedly, and then people began to enter his room. First came Solveiga, second, Jehena, and finally Petras, Regent of Stone.

It seemed odd that there should be a welcoming party waiting for him to wake, but he said nothing.

Solveiga came first to his side. She felt his forehead, then his wrist to count heartbeats. He watched her curiously.

"What is she doing?" Andrius said aloud. He had meant to think it.

Petras cleared his throat. "She is checking your condition, Andrius. You had us worried."

"Why? Is it late? Was there something I was supposed to do?" he added quietly.

Solveiga breathed a sigh of relief, then dipped a rag in water, wrung it out, and placed it on the boy's forehead.

Andrius looked around, not understanding the strange expressions on everyone's faces.

"Do you remember those people, Andrius? The ones who got caught in the storm and had to hide in here?"

"Sure. I mean, it just happened."

Petras shook his head. "The snowstorm lasted for a week. Those people would have died had you not done what you did."

Andrius peeled the damp rag off of himself and sat up. Blood rushed to his head.

"A week? But that's–"

"You were sick," Solveiga declared. "We thought you might die."

A nasty coughing fit wracked Andrius just then, seeming to confirm her outlandish statement.

Before Andrius could protest, Solveiga's ear was pressed against his chest. "Cough again."

She didn't need have to ask. A thick wad of mucus came up through his throat and lodged in his mouth. He wasn't sure what to do with it.

"Does your chest have pain?"

"Mm-hm."

His eyes darted around the room, searching for a place to spit. There was a cup next to his bed that would do.

"Does your head hurt?"

He spit into the cup, then marveled at the strange substance that had come out. It was phlegm, but it had an odd note: grassentree mixed with sudaisy.

"A little." Pain knocked against his skull. "A lot."

Solveiga nodded, then grabbed the cup Andrius had just spit into.

"Here. Drink this."

His eyes grew wide and he could not form the words to protest. A voice saved him.

"He is awake! I've smiled on you, Andrius." The flawless beard surrounded the Prophet's smile. "Welcome back to the land of the living."

"Drink this," Solveiga insisted, pushing the cup toward Andrius's lips.

"Later," the Prophet answered for him. "Andrius, if you are feeling up to it, I have something to show you."

A change came over Petras. "But, Valdas–"

"I've made up my mind, Petras, thank you. What do you say, Andrius? Do you feel well enough for a little walk?"

Even if he hadn't been eager for the Prophet's surprise, it was better than drinking from that cup. He tried to move his legs out of bed quickly, but they felt like rubber.

"I'm up for it." He tried to stand and faltered, thankfully falling on the bed and not on the floor.

"He needs rest, Prophet."

"Nonsense. I just want to show him. It won't take long. Petras, help him."

The Regent's strong arms moved under Andrius's weak ones, helping him stand. Jehena came over to assist.

"I can help too, Prophet."

"No," Valdas said, already walking out the door. "You cannot go where we are going."

Andrius was surprised by his own weakness as he was led down the smooth, marble staircase, through the halls, leaning on Petras. The quiet tapping of canes on stone was the only sound aside from the Prophet's voice.

"Andrius, you are a special boy. You continue to prove your worth to my village."

He stopped in front of a metal door. Andrius had never seen it open.

Valdas removed a key from his sleeve and felt around for the lock.

"It has been the subject of much discussion if this was the right course of action." The key found the lock and turned with a satisfying click. The Prophet smiled. "And now more than ever I'm sure that it is. What I am about to show you only the Prophets have ever been shown, and only a few of the Regents, but now I show it to you."

He pushed the door open and spoke in a low voice. "I'm beginning to suspect you are the one, and it is time we found out."

Andrius found himself fading in and out of awareness. He realized that perhaps he was not up to a short walk after all, but the empty nightishness awaited them beyond the doorway, and led by Petras they descended a hidden stairway in silence.

"Here we are," the Prophet declared, and the ground flattened out.

"The sun doesn't sing here," Andrius said, looking around. His eyes were useless in this secret floor.

"Doesn't it? I would think of all places it would sing here," the Prophet remarked. "Perhaps you just can't hear it yet."

Andrius strained his eyes, but he could discern nothing with them. The only sound was Petras drawing in breath and the Prophet shuffling away into the uncharted reaches of the secret room, sliding his ornate cane back and forth for guidance.

"Isn't it curious?" the Prophet's distant voice called out. "Marvelous?"

Andrius blinked.

"Maybe I'm just out of it," he mumbled. He had a bad habit of talking to himself.

"Prophet," Petras called out. "May I show him the noisemaker?"

"If you wish."

The Prophet could be heard rustling through something.

Petras leaned into Andrius's ear, speaking as he grabbed his hand and guided it along the smooth wall until they came to a sudden protrusion.

"This is my favorite part," Petras whispered. "They're all over Gimdymo Namai if you search for them, but this one is the noisiest."

He pressed Andrius's hand upward and the protrusion flipped up with them. Everything changed. The room was suddenly alive, and Andrius did not know where to look first. The sun sang brilliantly into the cavernous space, revealing stacks and stacks of bizarre, unrecognizable objects. There were books too, a whole shelf of them, and one in particular set prominently upon its own stand in the center of the circular room. Everything had its note–grassentree, fuzzymum, skyhigh–moving the stick on the wall had driven away the nightishness entirely.

"Isn't that strange?" Petras asked, smiling.

"It is the most magnificent thing I've ever experienced," Andrius gasped.

"Is the sun singing now, Andrius?" The Prophet felt his way toward the books from several yards away.

"Yes," Andrius replied, breathlessly looking up to the ceiling. "It's singing from holes in the roof–round orbs of sun."

Petras laughed. "There are no holes in the ceiling here. What of the noise? Is it not strange?"

Andrius noticed then a high-pitched whine in the air, accompanied by a steady hum. It seemed to be coming from a metal monstrosity in the corner.

He couldn't stop looking around. He had no words. He was in a room of mysteries.

And then it was gone again, blinked into nightishness.

"Why did you do that?"

"Hm?"

Distressed, Andrius grabbed his hair and began searching the wall for the magical protrusion. Finding it, he placed both palms beneath it and pushed upward.

Nightishness was driven away once more. His eyes were overwhelmed.

"Oh, that?" Keep it on if you like, I suppose. It's a little annoying after a while."

Andrius couldn't believe that Petras didn't appreciate the difference. He marveled as Valdas lifted the prominently placed tome and reverently carried it to where the others waited.

"What is this place?" Andrius asked.

"Sacred," the Prophet returned, "and dangerous. You have been taught of the fires of purification, haven't you?"

Andrius didn't need to think twice. Everyone knew village history. "When Zydrunas founded this new colony to save humanity from the disease that broke out at the end of the Hausen War, he called all of his followers together and had them burn every trace of their old lives in the old world. All of their possessions, burned into the ash from which we grew," he recited.

"Good," Valdas nodded. "Only it isn't true."

"What?"

"It is true in a metaphorical sense, which is why we keep the story. After all, the First Ones did leave their old lives and the old world to find this haven against man's mortal enemy, the disease. But as to their belongings . . . well."

"You stand among them," Petras declared.

Andrius's breath caught in his throat. "You mean . . . ?"

"There was no bonfire, only a collection. Zydrunas locked all of their old things down here. Among the many strange and mysterious items in this secret room is this." The Prophet patted the giant book reverently. Dust rose from the disturbance. "Do you know what this is, Andrius?"

It couldn't be. It made no sense. And yet here it was. "One of the empty books."

"Wrong. It is the preeminent volume among them. This is *the* sacred Book of Emptiness."

"I figured you kept it upstairs somewhere."

"No!" the Prophet scoffed. "It is much too dangerous there. Something could happen to it. Zydrunas spoke of these books often, but their secrets are not known. Pages and pages but inside," he opened the book, "nothing."

Andrius looked at the book, then at the Prophet, then at the book. "It's not empty."

"Watch what you say, Andrius," Petras cautioned.

"This is hardly a typical boy, Petras. Let him speak his mind. Well, Andrius," he ran his finger along the pages. "I don't feel any words. So aren't they empty?"

Andrius couldn't help a smile as chills ran up his spine.

"They aren't the kind that you can feel. You need to sense them with your eyes."

"You . . . can read them?" Petras whispered.

Valdas held the book out closer to Andrius.

"What does it say, my son? The Prophets have long said there would come one who could read the books of emptiness."

Andrius leaned forward to study the writing. He was feeling hazy again.

"My eyes . . ." he said, and then the room was spinning.

Everything went nightish, but the noisemaker's hum continued. His face and shoulder pained him sharply just before he passed from consciousness.

ANDRIUS CAME BACK TO HIMSELF SLOWLY. HE WAS hot–burning up. He could feel the sweat beaded on his arms as he opened his eyes. He was in his bed, on top of the blankets.

In his daze, none of this made less sense than the Prophet, who was seated at the foot of his bed, listening.

"To be fair," the Prophet began, "you said that you were up for a little walk."

He smiled, and in spite of himself, Andrius chuckled. He quickly regretted it. His throat was like fire.

"Father," he wheezed. His voice was scratchy and hoarse. "Do I have the disease?"

He rose and sat beside Andrius. "No, my son. No, the disease kills very quickly. You were inoculated when you were born, besides. None here may ever fall prey to it again because of the cure."

Andrius nodded. The Prophet tilted his head.

"You do have a nasty fever, however. How are you feeling?"

"I'm not sure . . . It's like–"

"You'll feel better soon. I'm sure of it. Andrius, tell me. What did the book say?"

"The book?"

The Prophet lowered his voice.

"You know the book I speak of, my son. Before you passed out. I hate to press you like this, but it is very important."

And then Andrius remembered. He could recall its shape in his mind.

"I don't know."

"You said it wasn't empty."

"It wasn't, but . . . the writing was different. It wasn't made for fingers. I don't know what it said."

The Prophet, who had been leaning forward, now sat erect and nodded knowingly. "It was made for eyes."

Andrius coughed. It was a bad spell that lasted nearly two whole minutes. He thought that he might vomit, but there was no food for his stomach to expel.

"I'm sick, Father."

"Of course. You shall be cared for. I will send up Solveiga to attend to your needs." He stood, then fished the big skeleton key out of his sleeve. "Andrius, do you think you might be able to figure out what those books mean?"

Andrius was feeling faint. He could hardly keep his eyes open.

"Maybe."

"Maybe," the Prophet repeated, and then he laughed. He lay the skeleton key on the table beside Andrius's bed. "When you feel up to it," the Prophet said, "find out if you can. Do not allow anyone else inside the sacred chamber. It's only for the special ones, Andrius."

"Special ones?"

"People like me and you." The Prophet patted his head. "Get some rest. You must be hungry. I'll send for Solveiga."

Andrius tried to thank him, but a violent fit of coughing robbed him of words. When he was through, the Prophet was gone.

15

THE SUN WAS SILENT AND NO ONE STIRRED. IT MUST have been the middle of the night, and from the sound of it, a bad storm. Winter had arrived early this year, and it had arrived with a vengeance.

Andrius's teeth chattered as he descended the cold, marble steps. He pulled his bristling fur coat tighter, wishing that he had worn shoes.

A shaking hand felt for the lock, then inserted the Prophet's key, and just like that Andrius was inside the secret chamber again, this time fully awake and aware. He bent down to pick up his wooden pitcher, then entered the room, closing the door behind him.

He felt along the dead walls, whispering of memory and secrets. His hand touched the protrusion, and the nightishness was driven away. There was nothing hidden from Andrius's eyes.

"Where do I start?" he wondered aloud. Shelves and shelves lined the room, filled with strange objects. Some he recognized–a child's ball, some sort of six-stringed instrument, and lots of books–but most of the objects were foreign to him.

He meandered through the aisle, unable to decide where to begin. He bent down to remove an open box from a bottom shelf and was baffled by the contents.

"What is this?"

He reached inside and removed a nightish, metallic rectangle, but it wasn't metal exactly. It certainly wasn't wood.

"The whole box is filled with them . . ."

He dug through the box of small rectangles. Some were encased in a sticky material of various notes. There were markings on the front and back. He held the rectangle up to his face.

The pattern was beautiful. Seven shapes in a neat row.

"I haven't worked on my patterns since I got sick," he said to himself. He felt strange about it. He made a mental note to get back to them as he let the rectangle fall from his hand.

In all, a confusing and rather uninteresting box.

A thought stopped Andrius as he was reaching up to another shelf: the Prophet wants the book translated.

Andrius swallowed hard, feeling guilty for having been distracted. There would be plenty of time to explore. He looked toward the central pedestal, upon which the Book of Emptiness rested.

The sun, or the sacred chamber's false sun, sang particularly strong over the Book of Emptiness. It was large, ornate, primarily grassentree but bound with dirtyshoe straps of leather.

Reverently, he took a breath and touched the relic dating back to the time of Zydrunas himself. It was rough under his hands.

"I'm afraid I won't be able to read it," Andrius whispered, but suddenly the fear in his chest was gone, as if some unseen thing had swept it away.

He took a deep breath and opened the book.

It was beautiful.

Complex and flowing markings scratched onto the page, nightish patterns on a milkoud background. Andrius ran his fingers over the writing. It was mostly flat. Nothing seemed punched out or raised, and there were only occasional dots. He turned the page to find the same situation repeated, only differently. He tried to read the dots, but there were too few and they were spaced too far apart. They made no sense.

Deep in thought, Andrius raised the wooden pitcher to his lips and took a drink. He pointed defiantly at the book.

“I’m going to figure you out.”

He set down his pitcher, pulled the fur up on his neck, and got to work.

ANDRIUS’S FAILURE WAS NOT FOR LACK OF EFFORT. He stared at the scared pages for hours, trying to find any kind of a pattern. There was repetition occasionally, but he couldn’t figure out what it meant. The pages were turned first one way, then another, even upside down. It was like no writing Andrius had ever looked upon–if, in fact, it was writing at all.

Finally he retreated to his room to sleep. The sacred chamber was actually warmer than his bedroom, but he missed his covers.

Jehena brought him hot soup when he awoke, and then he returned to the sacred chamber to study again. Once more, the book made no logical sense.

He studied it intensely nonetheless. The Prophet had entrusted him with a task. He was one of the special ones. He could not fail.

Yet his fever caught up with him eventually, and racked by whole-body coughs, Andrius dragged himself wheezing back to bed, where he dreamed of his father Aleksandras, and he hoped that he was faring well through the storm.

He had other dreams too, but he did not remember them.

"... WE HAVE NO NEWS. HOW COULD WE? THE WORLD–"

"Petras, listen to me–"

"The world is covered in snow. Do *you* want to go out and take a census?"

"No one is suggesting–"

Andrius woke up suddenly, feeling groggy. He kept his eyes closed. People were arguing in hushed voices outside of his room.

"You were suggesting, just this moment, Tadas. He almost died, and you would have him do it again."

"Preparations . . ."

"We can't help that now," the voice said curtly. Andrius recognized the Regent of Stone–his Regent. Andrius opened his eyes. Petras continued. "We could not have known winter would come so soon. When the weather breaks, we will–"

"Who almost died?"

The two men stopped. Petras and Tadas, the Regent of Brick, tilted their ears when Andrius spoke. He was sitting up in bed, leaning to look out the door.

"Andrius?" Tadas asked hesitantly.

"Sorry," he said sheepishly. "I shouldn't have interrupted. I just heard that someone almost died. Who was it?"

Petras mopped his brow.

"It was you, Andrius. You almost died of cold. Even now, I am told that your fever persists."

Andrius reached up and touched his own forehead. It was hot. His hand came away with sweat.

"I don't know much about diseases . . ." Andrius replied.

"Fevers kill, Andrius," Petras said gravely. He grabbed Tadas's arm and squeezed tightly. "That's why you have to stay in bed, where it is warm and we can take care of you."

"He doesn't have to–"

"I don't think that is your decision, Tadas!" Petras said abruptly.

Andrius was confused. He felt very small.

Tadas sighed. "Yes, Petras, you're right. But you don't need to be so morbid. Andrius is . . . unique. A fever won't rob us of him. And we'll find out how much of the village is dead when the sun comes out again."

Andrius slowly laid back on his pillow and tried to shut out the noise. The two men continued to bicker softly about the winter's toll on the village and what should be done.

It had been well over a week since anyone had gone outside.

THE AIR WAS COOL ALL AROUND HIM AS ANDRIUS ran his eyes over the text of the Book of Emptiness for the thousandth time. No epiphany seemed forthcoming.

He recognized patterns, but then they would change. It made very little sense.

There was one symbol that he was fairly certain to be an "a," and another that was either an "o" or an "i" if he was doing this right, but he wasn't sure.

He thought of Milda. She would be able to help, but she would not be allowed inside the chamber. She wasn't one of the special ones.

"She's special to me," Andrius muttered. A fit of coughing took him then, and he sank to the floor. The weight of his task sat heavy on his shoulders. "How can I do this?" He shook his head. "It's impossible."

The grassentree book sat upon its stand in an impenetrable aura of mystery. It was so long and foreign; the thought of ever trying to understand it filled Andrius with despair.

He put his head in his hands. He wanted to cry, but nothing came. Not long after, the familiar cloak of sleep began to descend upon him, and he was whisked from the world.

When he woke up he was shivering, but he did not want to leave.

Andrius stood up and shook out his chilled limbs. He took a few steps, and then his eyes lighted upon the shelf of lesser books of emptiness. He gravitated toward them.

There were so many of them. He reverently removed a thick hardcover book from the second shelf. It had the same kind of markings as the Book of Emptiness and a pattern on the front. There were two men screaming on top of something in the water, like a house. A monster was emerging from the river at them, milkoud teeth matching its milkoud skin. Andrius could not stop staring at it.

"I could put people in my patterns . . ." he whispered to himself. He would work on his patterns today. He was decidedly inspired. Maybe he would even make one like the front of this book.

Andrius looked at the milkoud monster and wondered if it lived beyond the barriers of their civilization, in the Regions of Death. There was no way to know for sure.

He was moving to replace the book when a glance through the gap broke his concentration. Something rested against the wall, on the other side of the bookcase.

"Is that what I think it is?"

But it would have been too incredible.

The book went back into its slot, and Andrius made his way around the back of the line of shelves, stepping over dilapidated boxes.

He gasped.

There it was–right where Andrius had noticed it. It was kind of fuzzymum in note, but bands of skyhigh abounded in many places, and a patch of nightish and milkoud crowned the top, near the handle.

It was Daniel's backpack. Daniel from across the fence–or the crazy man named Drunas, as the Prophet had said.

"They told me he ran away . . ." Andrius bent down to touch the smooth material. Something wasn't making sense, but then he had a thought that explained everything. His face grew animated as he stood upright.

"Daniel?" he whispered, and then he listened to the silence of the sacred chamber. His smile faded as he listened. "Daniel?" he said again, louder this time. It was a large room but not that large.

"He must be away right now," Andrius said. "He's living down here."

He looked around, trying with all of his might to imagine how Daniel could have accomplished such a task. His long disappearance from the village was starting to make sense–though Andrius wondered how he got his food. Maybe he was stealing from the kitchen.

Andrius didn't care. He was excited to talk with him again, and the Prophet would be relieved to know he was found.

For the moment, however, Daniel seemed to be absent.

Andrius looked all around the chamber, but he could find no other signs of the man with eyes like his own.

He was drawn to the bookshelf again. This time he bent down to examine the bottom row. The books here looked different from the others. They were taller and skinnier and made out of a different kind of material.

Andrius selected a milkoud volume and set it on the floor, sitting down cross-legged to analyze it. It was much different from the others. It had been heavy for such a small book, and it was covered in patterns. It had the strange writing on it as well, but instead of just nightish, the markings were sudaisy, bloodnote, and skyhigh.

"Maybe you'll be easier to figure out," Andrius mumbled. He was curious, but not optimistic. He grabbed the corner of the cover and opened the book.

It was beautiful, breathtaking. Spread across both pages was such a pattern! Grass and hills and trees and a herd of sheep grazing by a fence. Underneath several parts of the pattern were the markings, but in short bursts—not like the other books of emptiness that went on and on.

On the right side of the book were boxes in a row, from the top of the page to the bottom, each bearing the face of a different kind of animal. Andrius scratched his head.

He grabbed the book by both sides and picked it up, then dropped it in terror as an unearthly voice came forth from the book.

"Sheep! Baaah!"

"Agh!"

Andrius turned and ran, accidentally ramming his knee against a large black box. He winced, then ducked behind the obstruction and peered over the top.

The book was still there, lying face down. It wasn't talking anymore.

Andrius's heart was racing and his breath came in gasps, then in a violent cough.

When it subsided, he peered over the top of his bunker again.

"Who was that?" he demanded. No reply seemed forthcoming. The book had not moved.

He looked around.

"It's mean to scare people."

The room seemed to be vacant. Andrius was its only occupant. Yet he had heard a voice.

Slowly, tentatively, and without ever taking his eyes off of the book, Andrius approached.

Nothing happened. The false suns continued to whine overhead as they sang over the room.

Andrius leaned over to touch the book, but the voice did not speak again.

Warily, he turned it upright and sat down, spreading the book over his lap. He studied it closely, looking first at the pattern, then up and down the line of animal boxes.

There was a horse, then a chicken, then a fox, a pig, a sheep, a cow, and then a man wearing a straw hat.

Andrius stared for a long time, but nothing happened. He began to calm down, eventually laughing to himself.

He grabbed the edges of the book to hold it up once more as he reassured himself.

"My fever must be worse than I thought. My imagination–"

"Sheep! Baaah!"

"Agh!"

Andrius kicked back violently at the mysterious voice,

launching himself into a metal shelf and flinging the book away. He screamed again and covered his head as a box fell from the shelf, bumping his shoulder on the way down.

He curled into a tight ball and held himself, trying to hide. He waited, trying not to focus on the pain in his head, back, and shoulder. He listened.

Silence.

"Hello?" He waited. No one was speaking.

The box blocked his eyes from the rest of the chamber, so after a while he pushed it a few inches out of the way and looked around carefully.

The book had landed across the room by the closed chamber door, still face down.

Andrius took a deep breath, closed his eyes, and then he pushed up from the ground. He crept over to the book and picked it up, not bothering to sit this time. As he held it up once more, he flinched but did not drop it.

"Sheep! Baaah!"

Andrius lifted his thumb, then coughed a few times. He let his thumb press against the book again.

"Sheep! Baaah!"

He moved his hand and saw a sheep's head in the little box he had been touching.

"Sheep," Andrius repeated, looking at the markings under the sheep, then back to the pattern inside the box. "What kind of a book is this?" He turned it over, but the back appeared unremarkable, though it had more notes than most of the other books.

He looked down the line of animal faces again, hovering his thumb over the sheep. Slowly, he pressed down.

"Sheep! Baaah!"

"I don't know how you're doing this," Andrius said quietly, "but I think I know what you're doing . . ."

Taking a deep breath, Andrius shifted his grip and held a thumb over the chicken.

"Chicken! Cluck cluck cluck!"

There were markings under the chicken, different from those under the sheep.

He turned the page and pressed down again.

"Chicken! Cluck cluck cluck!"

It was a new pattern, spreading across two pages like the other, but instead of a grassy field it showed chickens pecking at the ground in front of a huge bloodnote shack. Every object in the pattern had writing beneath it. Andrius held his breath as he turned page after magnificent page.

"Chicken! Cluck cluck cluck!"

He pressed down on the other animals and heard the unworldly voice say "Horse! Neigh!" and "Pig! Snort snort!"

The significance of the marvel clutched between his shaking hands did not escape him.

"This is the key . . ." he whispered. He finally tore his gaze from the magical book and looked over to the Book of Emptiness.

"Man! Hello!"

Andrius startled. His thumb had slipped onto one of the boxes. He looked to find a human face staring back at him.

Chills ran up Andrius's feverish skin.

16

"YOU MAY ENTER."

The doors of Valdas's sitting room burst open. Solveiga and Petras half dragged, half carried Andrius inside. He was covered in perspiration and his eyes were closed as he laughed, then jerked his head to the side and started shaking.

Valdas stood. "What's going on?"

"It's Andrius," Petras replied, turning the corner and heading for Andrius's bedroom. "One of the servants heard strange noises coming from the chamber stairs. We found him there, ranting and convulsing and covered in sweat."

"His fever is back," Solveiga said over her shoulder.

Andrius opened a tear-filled eye and noticed the Prophet following. He looked concerned.

Petras heaved and suddenly Andrius was on the bed.

"Key, key, key, key. I have it. Boxes and–boxes and in key chicken with the sheep . . ." His raving devolved into indeterminable noises then as he thrashed about, resisting Solveiga as she tried to undress him.

"He is badly overheated," she cried. "Hold him down!"

Petras hurried over and gripped Andrius's arms to immobilize him. His legs still thrashed and kicked.

"Has he lost his mind?" the Prophet asked.

"Let us hope not, Prophet," the Regent of Stone replied through gritted teeth. "He is in the throes of the fever. His ranting is nonsensical."

"I can hear that for myself, Petras."

Andrius's legs were suddenly cooler. Solveiga tossed Andrius's garment to the ground and shouted out the door.

"Jehena! Come with a bowl of cool water. Ilona, bring towels!"

"This is unfortunate timing, Petras," the Prophet said softly.

Andrius settled down suddenly, his violent spasms replaced by occasional tics. He muttered quietly as the others spoke.

"Jehena and I are going to our winter home at the end of Wood today. I hate to leave him in this condition."

"The snow has sufficiently melted for your journey?"

"Yes," the Prophet said sorrowfully. "It was a bad storm. The cost will be high."

"Tadas is taking a census," Petras said, easing his hold on Andrius, who was now semi-lucid but very confused and in much pain.

The Prophet nodded. "I know. Thanks to this one here, fewer will have died than we would normally expect. He has the village's gratitude for that."

The Prophet thought for a moment as Solveiga fussed with Andrius's bed. Jehena excused herself as she passed Petras with Solveiga's water.

Andrius felt a strange, cold sensation as a wet cloth was drawn across his bare flesh.

"I never love to be without Solveiga, as you know, Petras; she is very useful to me. Nevertheless, I will leave her with Andrius. The boy must recover or it would grieve me badly. The Prophet's own." He smiled bittersweetly.

"Should I send you word of his condition if the weather allows it?"

"No," the Prophet replied. "You know the rules, and they are sacred. I am entrusting him to you until my return. I will take another of my wives with Jehena and I to take Solveiga's place—perhaps two. Take care of him."

Andrius felt terror creep into his heart and he began to rant and thrash once again.

"Hold him down, Petras!" Solveiga screamed.

Andrius pitched and rolled violently. The only sensation he had was of beads of sweat burning as they dripped into his feverish eyes.

THE KEY TURNED SHARPLY IN THE OLD LOCK, AND Andrius stood shaking at the entrance of the secret chamber. He held his wooden pitcher in his left hand and with his right he felt along the walls until he came to the protrusion that enabled his eyes to hear. Nightishness was driven away, and Andrius could look upon everything. It was right where he had left it.

"Thank goodness," he muttered.

It had been two days since his last episode with fever, two days full of sleeping and drinking an uncomfortable amount of water. He should have still been in bed, but his curiosity would not be abated.

The talking book was on the floor. Next to it lay the sudaisy stick he had found next to the Book of Emptiness. It was an odd little stick, but he found that he could make markings in the book with it if he pressed down and dragged it across the page.

Andrius set his blanket on the ground and sat, pulling the book onto his lap and taking up the writing stick. He had begun writing dots next to the foreign markings–the raised kind he was used to.

"I hope I can match all the letters," he said, taking a sip of water. He winced. His stomach was so full of liquid already, but he knew he needed it to get better.

Andrius gripped the writing stick and stared at the page. The transcription had begun.

HE HAD FIGURED OUT THE ALPHABET. HE MADE A couple of mistakes along the way, but after transliterating the talking book all the way through, he corrected his errors. Now he stood over the Book of Emptiness with his list of letters and their dot equivalents, trying to read the sacred text.

It was much harder than he had anticipated.

The letters didn't match exactly. It seemed like the writer had used a writing stick, but in all the other books the letters were uniform–always the same shape, always the same size. The writing in this book made it hard to read.

After several minutes of staring at the title page, he determined that it read: "Fhe Records Ot All Fhings."

Andrius looked at the page frowning.

"What's a 'fhing'?"

He coughed then and felt himself getting lightheaded.

"Time to go," he said to himself.

A STORM CAME AGAIN, AND ANDRIUS SLEPT FOR nearly two days. He was still sick, and his cough persisted, but somehow he felt a change inside of himself for the better. Trips to the sacred chamber were continuous. He spent all of his time in that forbidden room, studying, agonizing over books and texts written in the strange script for which he could find no name. He left only to eat and to sleep. Water he kept with him always as was his habit.

He had moved his patterns down to the chamber so that he wouldn't have to leave when he wanted to work on them. All of this reading was giving him new ideas for a pattern that his instructor was sure to like. Perhaps he would finally be chosen to represent his age-peers during the Day of Remembrance.

He mastered the alphabet, driven by curiosity as much as by the Prophet's directive. The process of reading was slow, but he found himself getting faster over time. The only thing that eluded him was the large tome: the Book of Emptiness. The writing inside of it was not uniform, so he had decided to study some of the other books first to improve his skills.

After all, he could not risk making a mistake for the Prophet. When he looked over the first few pages of the Book of Emptiness, he knew he was not getting it all right.

So he studied the other books.

The thin, illustrated books were first. He had found a note that called them "illustrated." By looking at the patterns mixed in with the script, he learned words he had never heard of before, looked at things he had never imagined: airplanes, trains, something called a carousel. It was all so fantastical and bizarre yet wonderful.

Most of these books said that they were "for children," but Andrius didn't understand that. They were so intricate, so full of knowledge and wonder–powerful tools of learning. And they were written by people like him, people who use their eyes! People for whom the sun sings.

He slept only when he had to, when his eyes burned from use. He graduated to the books that were only text. These were much harder, but they were incredible.

Andrius walked to the familiar shelf and chose a book he had been studying. The front of the book was bloodnote–red, as the books called it–and it had no illustration, just two horizontal lines and the words "The Iliad." It was the single most magical story he had ever heard.

He had almost not read it because he didn't know what an "Iliad" was. He still didn't, but it was amazing. It retold the events of an ancient time, when the earth was covered with humans. These humans fought and killed each other in a great war, sailing in large, wooden ships across a body of water that seemed a hundred times as large as his village's river. And the ships! Andrius had never thought of such a thing until he read the children's books. He thought that perhaps he would make a ship for the river and travel along its path.

Everyone was afraid of the river, but Andrius wasn't. Everyone was afraid of running, too.

There were already a hundred new concepts that Andrius had learned from the *Iliad*. "Armor" was hard metal to protect a soldier. Birds came in different kinds and had different names. Something called "light" seemed important, and "darkness" was scary, and there was much talk of "gods." As much as Andrius could figure, these were superior beings who couldn't die, looking over the affairs of men. "Prayer" was how you reached the gods, but it seemed just like talking. He didn't know how to do it. The Prophet had never talked about prayer.

Andrius remembered that the book was in his lap, and he had no need to reminisce when he could simply read. He cracked open the dusty pages with excitement. Today he hoped to figure out what a certain word he kept coming across actually meant. He wanted to know what it meant to "see."

WEEKS PASSED, AND ALL ANDRIUS DID WAS READ and sleep. He couldn't even work on his patterns since the snow and storms outside made collecting ingredients difficult. Instead, he read and studied day after day. His rate of learning increased daily, even as his sickness began to wither and fade. He was going to make it.

After the children's books and the *Iliad*, Andrius had read two others, and now he sat with a large volume entitled *Michelangelo* propped on his knees.

His mouth was agape every time he picked it up to read.

There were illustrations, but it was not a children's book. Large, complicated patterns–pictures–covered many pages, but then came pages and pages of small writing which told about this great man Michelangelo.

He had designed all of the illustrations himself, and the book said that they were only "prints" of the originals, which were massively big. The illustrations had names, even. The Sistine Chapel was one of Andrius's favorites, and though he loved the pictures of carved rocks, he was especially drawn to the illustrations of patterns.

He was fascinated. He read the thick book in a week, then he went back to look through all the pictures, and then he decided to read it all again. There was even more magic in this book than there was in the *Iliad*.

Andrius sat in awe, wrapped in his fur, sitting with his back against the bookshelf with his trusty pitcher by his side, reading aloud in a quiet voice.

"Michelangelo amazed the world with his statues, but he will always be remembered as the complete artist, conquering such difficult subjects as sculpting, design, scientific study and innovation, mixing, drawing, and painting."

Andrius drew a deep breath and closed the book in satisfaction. His eyes hurt, but it was well worth it. He had improved his reading and had gotten to look at the works of the ancient master.

"Sculpting, design, scientific study . . ." Andrius absentmindedly repeated to himself as he reclined. He had learned mostly what all of those terms meant, that Michelangelo was an artist, placing beauty into his creations to inspire the world to believe, to view things in a new way, to remember the heroes of old and the Bible stories–although he still wasn't sure what the latter meant.

"The illustrations–paintings," Andrius corrected himself as he rested his eyes, "are still my favorite part." He always forgot to call them by their names.

He was halfway asleep, dreaming of the beautiful works of art and the new words he had acquired, when he sat up suddenly with a thought.

Panic swept over him. He threw his blanket to the side and snatched up the thick volume, clutching it to his chest as his eyes searched the room.

"Where is it?"

Andrius fought off the encroaching despair as he searched fervently through first one box and then another, teased by the seed of a thought that had been planted in his mind.

"Come on, come on! Where are they?"

He began pulling items off the shelves, forgetting his reverence for the antiquated relics in the desperation of his task.

Then, behind a large box, he laid eyes on them and he stopped.

Gingerly, still clutching the book with one hand, Andrius reached behind the box and touched a thin slab of bark, one of many he had stored there for safekeeping. It was one of his patterns–the one he had submitted to the contest this year.

Gravely, with shaking fingers, Andrius drew the pattern out into the now-cluttered hall and gently set it on the floor. He stood, staring at it desperately.

He began shaking his head and his breathing grew labored as he opened the book in his hands, to the page that showed Michelangelo's *The Creation of Adam*, and he stared. First he stared at the book and then at his pattern, back and forth, back and forth.

The book fell from his hands and Andrius slid to the floor, hunched over his trembling knees.

Then he wept, because he realized that he was a painter, and the world was blind.

17

THERE WAS RELIEF IN THE STORM ONCE AGAIN. FOR an entire day it did not snow, though the ground was thick with it. The Prophet was still away; the people still kept to their homes. Andrius passed the day in thought, looking out over the blanketed landscape from the glass window beside his bed.

Then came an unexpected stretch of warmer weather, and much of the snow melted off the roads. Andrius took to going for walks in the early afternoon sun, feeling it sing over him. It was as if he had been given new eyes.

He had vocabulary for the experience now. The *sunlight gleamed* off of the snowy *whiteness*. Colors and sight and vibrancy were all named, described, and taken for granted in the books of emptiness. Once there were people like Andrius. Once, people could see.

And now he was the only one. It was a troubling reality.

The warm spell held on, and inside Gimdymo Namai it was discussed that perhaps the villagers should return to work and lessons so long as it persisted. Andrius sat in on the meetings between the Regent of Brick and the Regent of Stone as they debated. They did not know that Andrius was there. They did not "touch four walls." He could see and they could not.

Returning to work and to lessons was dismissed from consideration, but a village gathering was agreed upon. The break in oppressive weather would allow the ill-prepared to resupply, gather the villagers for moral support, and for the collective honoring of Zydrunas. Andrius knew about these developments before he was sought out and told. He already had a course of action stirring in his mind.

"ANDRIUS! ANDRIUS!"

With a start, Andrius closed the book on his lap, turned off the light–the protrusion and its false suns–and headed up the stairs to where Solveiga was calling his name. He realized, suddenly, that she had been calling his name for a while, but his mind had been somewhere else.

"Andrius! Where are you?"

"I'm right here," he replied, pulling the heavy door shut behind him. He locked it as he always did.

"Today is the first day–"

"I know," Andrius cut her off as he hurried by. "Lessons start again today, and they'll be first thing in the morning again. I'm probably almost late."

"Age-group lessons are over already." Solveiga did not like being interrupted. "*Your* lessons, which you teach, start very soon. Hurry."

Andrius paled.

"I missed lessons?"

"You are the Prophet's own. You cannot miss your own lessons on the new sense, however. It was arranged by the Prophet specifically for you. Now go."

Andrius didn't need to be told again. He burst out from behind the heavy double doors of Gimdymo Namai and into the fragile, newborn spring. Birds sang psalms of thanks for the clear weather, and Andrius ran down the road, clutching his ornately carved pitcher to his chest as he ran, the water splashing up onto his chin and neck.

"Will people still remember me?" he wondered aloud, between gasps. "It's been months."

His question was answered when he arrived at the field where hundreds of villagers had assembled, chatting patiently as they waited for him to arrive. The story of his blizzard rescue had spread.

"Oh, good." Andrius breathed a sigh of relief. He had been worried that no one was going to show up.

"Andrius? Is that you?"

He turned, and there she was, beautiful as ever.

"Hi, Milda."

She smiled as she felt her way forward, stumbling a little now and then until she reached him. She gripped him by the elbows, then leaned up and gave him a kiss on the cheek.

"It has been a thoroughly exasperating winter. Thank you for making sure I'd get to feel the spring. I would have died in that storm."

"Is that him?" someone asked nearby.

"It's the Prophet's own!"

"He's here!"

Andrius felt a fluttering in his stomach, mostly from the kiss but also from the throngs of people around, cheering for him. They had their eyes peeled wide open, showing off milky, clouded, dead orbs that could not see.

Milda patted his arm, then took a step back and sat down.

"Do well, Andrius," she shouted above the noise.

Andrius nodded, then turned and began making his way up to the knoll where he would stand and teach his lessons. He was nervous. He had learned so much. He had so much to tell.

The applause and cheers grew in intensity as he took his place. It was unending. Shouts of acclamations and "The Prophet's own!" and "Foremost in the village!" and "Zydrunas's pride!" carried continuously on the wind. His father Aleksandras was in the front row, bursting with joy as he meekly applauded. Andrius was relieved that he had made it through the winter.

He listened, unbelieving, to the applause, then held up a hand to stop it before realizing the uselessness of such a gesture. Instead, he raised his voice.

"Thank you!"

He was drowned out by the noise. He took a deep breath and tried again.

"Thank you! I'm here! I'm ready to start!"

This time he was heard, but his announcement only garnered more cheers. Someone near the front called out, "He isn't afraid of the snow! He led me and a host of others through a blizzard. He saved our lives!"

Andrius tried repeatedly to calm the crowd, but it was several minutes before they were quiet enough for him to speak. By then, what little excitement he had turned to anxiousness.

With the crowd finally quiet and attentive, Andrius had no idea what to say.

"I wish the enlightenment of Zydrunas on you all," he greeted them automatically.

The crowd parroted the traditional response back to him:

"And on you as well, with all his wisdom."

Andrius cleared his throat, then scratched his head. Innumerable blank eyes stared at him, many with eyes closed entirely.

"The Prophet, may he be exalted, told me to do something," he began slowly. "There are books in Gimdymo Namai that you maybe have heard of. They're called the books of emptiness, and I can read them." The crowd was perplexed at first, then amazed. Andrius had to shout over the swell of applause before it died down. "They aren't empty! The books aren't empty." The crowd, thankfully, was listening again. Andrius fixed his gaze on Daumantas, who was listening respectfully.

"They were made for people like me who can hear with their eyes. It's called seeing." Andrius held back tears as he quietly repeated, "They called it seeing." He took a deep breath and shook his head. "So when we talk about this new sense from now on, it has a name: sight. Seeing. It isn't anything like hearing. That was just the best way I knew how to understand it before. Before the books.

"There's a lot of things we got wrong. I was right about notes, sort of, but as best as I can tell, they used to be called colors! And their names were different. Skyhigh is blue. Sudaisy is yellow. When you look down at the grass"–he smiled weakly–"it's green. They understood it all before, when these books were written. And now I can understand what they say."

The crowd wasn't sure how to react, but then Daumantas began clapping all alone. His response quickly spread across the crowd, followed by shouting and whistling.

The chant, "Open your eyes and look at things," took over, and Andrius closed his. He shook his head.

"Stop it," he whispered. Then, he raised his voice. "Please, listen to me!"

Unsure, the people let the chant die on their lips. Andrius fidgeted, shifting from one foot to the other.

"I don't think that's going to work for you," he said, biting his lip. "Before, when the books were written, before the disease, almost everyone could see. They took it for granted. Now I'm the only one, but it used to be backward. I'm learning a lot from these books, and I still have a long wayto go—there are at least sixty books in there. But there's one thing I can't get around." He paused, gathering his courage. "You're all blind. It isn't that you don't understand some technique or that you don't practice enough. Your eyes are broken. And . . . I don't know if I can make that okay."

Soft murmuring began stirring among the crowd. The tone was starting to change.

"I don't know why this happened to us," Andrius continued. "The disease starts by attacking the eyes, so maybe that's why you're all . . . blind. I don't know why I'm not, and I can't promise that I can teach you to see."

The murmuring now turned to grumbling. Andrius's cheeks flushed as he saw the disappointment and annoyance on the villagers' faces. He was afraid.

"I will keep you informed as I learn more about it from these books. There's one in particular that the Prophet wants me to read for him, but it's hard because of how it was written. But I'll figure it out."

"Open your eyes and look at things!" a man shouted from deep in the crowd, standing and holding his fist in the air.

It was like a knife to Andrius's heart. "I don't think that's going to help you."

The grumbling resumed.

"You're broken. Pretending you're not won't fix that."

People stood up in disgust, beginning to leave. Andrius lost control of the meeting.

"I can't promise you sight, but I'll teach you everything I know!" he shouted, but the people were already on their feet milling around, grumbling, and tapping their canes to find the way back to the road.

Andrius watched them as a knot tied tightly inside of his stomach.

"They liked me," he said to himself, sinking to the ground. "Only a few minutes ago, they liked me."

"Oh, I'm sure they'll be back."

Andrius sat up. There, standing in front of him and overflowing with pride, was the old man who had raised him as a son.

"Papa," Andrius whispered.

Aleksandras felt his way forward, then knelt down before his son, placing an affectionate hand on the back of his neck and rustling his hair.

"Hello, my boy. You're a special one, Andrius. I always said so. I always knew it."

"Daiva never thought so."

Aleksandras waved a dismissive hand.

"Oh, you know how she is. But I'm here, and I'm proud of you. Saying something unpopular is a good thing that I was never much good at. You'll grow to be a fine man, my boy." He hugged Andrius tightly. "A fine man."

Andrius appreciated the embrace. He felt Aleksandras's love, and it calmed his heart.

Aleksandras released him and stood up. "Come on, Andrius,"

he said, holding up a basket. "Have lunch with me. It's been a long, cold, Daiva-filled winter, and I want to catch up with my boy. The Prophet's own!"

Andrius wiped his face. "Okay, Papa."

"We'll sit somewhere in the grass out there," Aleksandras said, gesturing blindly. He lowered his voice. "And if I understand this 'seeing' thing correctly, I think you'd better guide us."

He laughed then, an honest-to-goodness laugh, and Andrius had to chuckle too.

"Come along, Andrius," the old man said, helping his son to his feet. "Let's go talk."

THEY WENT DEEPER INTO THE MEADOW THAN anyone typically did, but Andrius felt his father's trust, and so on they went, finally settling on the sunny side of a big tree's roots. It was like an island in a sea of grass.

Aleksandras smacked his lips as he removed the cloth from the top of the basket and began handing Andrius boiled eggs, dried fruit, cheese, and bread.

"Mm, it smells good, doesn't it, Andrius?"

"Yes, Papa."

Andrius was already peeling the shell from an egg. Aleksandras took a bite of cheese and was quick to show his satisfaction.

"Mm! I got this just this morning from Bronius down the road. It certainly tastes good."

Andrius was listening, but his eyes were on a yellow butterfly that flitted playfully through the air, riding on the breeze.

"It smells good and it tastes good," Aleksandras pronounced. "So tell me: what does it look like?"

The butterfly gracefully landed on a tall stalk of grass, opening and closing its wings.

"It looks good, Papa."

"No, my boy. I know you for a poet. Describe it to me." He held an egg in front of his face, and then slowly, painfully, he opened his eyes. "Describe it to me."

Andrius swallowed a bite, then coughed. "The shell is white. Milkoud is how I would say it before the books. You can feel its shape already. It has little brown dots all over. On the inside it's mostly white, but the center is like hidden gold. It's yellow. Sudaisy."

"Yellow . . ." Aleksandras repeated. He rotated the egg in his fingers and blinked. "You know, I'm glad for what you said today. I was beginning to think I was doing it wrong."

Andrius picked up his pitcher of water and took a drink. He would need to refill it soon.

"But there's one thing you were wrong about, Andrius," Aleksandras continued. "There is always a way. Maybe you can't teach seeing, but I'm old enough to know that there isn't a problem in the world without a solution. Maybe you have it, maybe you don't, but nothing is"–he closed his eyes as he searched for the right words–"broken beyond repair. Somehow, somewhere everything can be fixed. Sometimes you just aren't the one who can do it."

Andrius thought about what Aleksandras was saying as the butterfly caught a gust of wind and lifted off again, flitting peacefully.

"What do you . . . see right now, Andrius?"

"I see a butterfly."

"A butterfly! I've heard that word before. What is it?"

"It's a bug that flies. Two big wings, two skinny things going out from his head."

"Is it beautiful?"

"Yes," Andrius said. "It is."

Aleksandras lay back in the grass, content. "Does it have a color?"

"Papa, everything has a color."

"Oh, I understand. I wasn't sure."

"It's yellow."

The old man smiled. "Yellow."

He sat up and lifted his eyelids again, revealing white, useless eyes. The butterfly flitted right in front of his face, but he did not track the movement.

"I can almost see it."

The butterfly floated back and landed on Aleksandras's head, startling him. Andrius laughed.

"I guess almost isn't quite good enough. Is he on my head?"

"Mm-hm."

"Well, that's okay. Hello, friend! Yellow butterfly, you are welcome to sit on me any time. What should we name him, Andrius?"

Andrius giggled, and for the first time in months he remembered that he was just a boy.

"You don't name bugs, Papa."

"No?" He feigned surprise. "Maybe not, but remember: this is my butterfly. Don't confuse him with the others."

"I don't know if I've seen a yellow one before."

"No? That's because he's mine. He's special." He laughed, and the butterfly flitted away. "Oh, there you go."

Andrius looked at his father a while, then he picked himself up and sat next to where he lay.

"Maybe I will see in the next life, eh, my boy?"

"What do you mean?" Andrius was disturbed by the statement.

"Oh, you're too young to remember."

"No! No, Papa, in a book I read, the *Iliad* . . . What's an Iliad?"

"I don't know."

"Me either. But in this book the men say something about a next life with the gods above or in Hades to be punished."

Aleksandras slowly sat up.

"Of that I don't know. We really aren't supposed to talk about it. When I was a boy, a woman in the village named Tiesa-Pranasas had a dream. Someone was talking to her in this dream, telling her that what we do in the village matters, because death isn't the end. We go onto something else. Reward or punishment, I think, so maybe it's like in your book. She said the dream-talker promised to tell her more."

Andrius eagerly awaited the next part of the story, but Aleksandras had fallen silent.

"Well, what happened?"

"Valdas wasn't Prophet then. He wasn't even born yet. It was Azuolas, and he put up with it for a while. The idea spread through the village, but eventually he said that such discussion was not in keeping with the teachings of Zydrunas, so it had to be stopped."

"Did it stop?"

"At first, no, but eventually, yes."

"How?"

Aleksandras fished an egg out of the basket and began to peel it. "She wouldn't stop telling her dreams, so they killed her."

"They killed her?"

Aleksandras sighed heavily. "A severe peace must be kept severely," he quoted.

"A severe peace must be kept severely," Andrius repeated.

Aleksandras slapped him on the back. "But you! You are in good standing, my boy. The Prophet's own! I'll bet you'll be Prophet someday with the way you're going. Don't tell anyone I said so, but there's talk."

Andrius perked up. "Really?"

"That's the gossip, but you know how these things are. What I am sure about, however, is that the Prophet will be very pleased when he returns to Gimdymo Namai and you get to tell him that you can read the books of emptiness."

Andrius plucked a blade of grass. The knot in his stomach untied a bit.

"There are still a lot of books to go. I've barely even started the one he wanted me to read."

"Well, I think it's your most important job, and I know you'll do well. A mission from the Prophet, ha! That's my boy, Andrius. I always knew you were special."

Andrius blushed, unable to look at his father.

Aleksandras chuckled to himself and broke off a piece of bread to nosh as he lay back down in the grass. He let out a contented sigh.

"Now," he said, "tell me about these 'clouds.'"

18

IT SNOWED AGAIN. SPRING HAD SPRUNG AND THEN IT reverted back to its hiding place beneath a blanket of white. The villagers took refuge in their homes, hoping for a close to the winter that wouldn't end.

Andrius, confined to the reaches of Gimdymo Namai, sat near the middle of the sacred chamber in the basement, thinking. His heart hurt him from the inside, but he was not sure why. He was used to loneliness. This was a different sort of pain.

He looked up at the lights in the ceiling, singing over him, and determination filled his mind.

"I've read all the picture books and four text books," Andrius said to himself, rising. "If I can't read the big one now, I'll never be able to."

His wooden pitcher sloshed with water as he carried it toward the central stand, upon which rested the green book, the Book of Emptiness. The whole chamber seemed to point toward the spot, accenting it, lining up to it. It was the center and truest point of the secret chamber. Andrius was set on today being the day that he solved the mystery, once and for all. He knew that the writing was difficult to read, but the difference between today and his previous attempt was months of practice.

He was confident, an emotion with which he was not well acquainted.

Something caught his eye on his way to the book and he stopped, fixating on the orange and blue material. Andrius suspected now that it was called a "suitcase" or a "backpack." It belonged to Daniel, who, it was now apparent, did not live in the basement. Andrius didn't know where he was.

He felt a sudden temptation to rifle through Daniel's belongings. Something inside the backpack might tell him more about the strange man who had carried it. It was almost as if the weirdly colored pack was calling to him.

Andrius shook himself and turned toward the book once again. He had a job to do.

He set his wooden pitcher on the floor, then stared at the cover of the Book of Emptiness. It was a large book, nearly the size of his chest. Andrius measured its length with his hands; it was two spans tall, one and a half wide. It was easily the biggest book he had ever seen.

Andrius's skin crawled suddenly and he took a deep breath. His chest tightened, almost as if he was doing something wrong, but he had been asked by the Prophet. The words of the Book of Emptiness had remained unknown to the village forever. It was time to learn from its wisdom.

Perhaps it would teach them how to see again. Andrius tensed at the thought.

He reached forward hesitantly and touched the bottom corner of the rough, green material. Another deep breath and the book was open.

Andrius squinted at the title page. The handwriting was messy, but he was better at reading now. It looked like the T's were F's, but Andrius was not fooled this time. He read aloud the great book's title.

"The Record of All Things."

It was cold, but Andrius was sweating. He could feel the weight of history on his shoulders. He felt like Achilles attacking the walls of Troy. He would do battle with the handwritten pages.

The next sheet was topped with an unfamiliar word and a number: "July 10." Underneath, the book's first entry began. It took a bit of squinting to separate the strong strokes of the letters, but it became clear to Andrius as he sounded out the words.

"I, Zydrunas–"

Andrius gasped and nearly fell over.

"It can't be . . ."

He double-checked the letters. He triple-checked them. He wasn't wrong.

"I, Zydrunas."

Zydrunas, the great founder and philosopher and healer and warrior himself–*he* had written the Book of Emptiness! Andrius squealed then giggled with unsurpassable delight. This was greater than anything he had ever dared to dream for himself. The First Prophet had written a book, and Andrius would be the first to read it.

His imagination took him hostage. Perhaps the book would tell of his righteous war defending the world from the Hausen Confederacy, or it might tell how he invented the cure for the disease, or explanations of his teachings. It might explain everything.

Andrius's eyes grew wide with understanding. The Book of Emptiness was written in letters for the eyes.

Zydrunas could see.

Andrius returned to the page with renewed vigor, deciphering each word as quickly and carefully as possible. He thought of nothing else. It was time-consuming but rewarding. The first page amazed and taunted him:

I, Zydrunas, write these sacred words upon these pages of lethe. The covers are the banks of the River Styx, and forgetfulness flows between them. I wish I could drink of its waters, but I am not blessed with the gifts of the simple, the blindly ignorant, the blissfully stupid. I am Prometheus, punished eternally for my selfless gift to humanity. I die each day upon this mountain, but I am unable to pass away. Only pain exists for me now.

I write these words of my fading glory, on the eve of my descent. The Italians have taken Brussels, having long since traded sides. This does not surprise me. They were always only mindless soldiers of fortune, not to be depended on.

The Romanians are in retreat and have threatened to break their alliance–more importantly, the Russians have buckled and are beginning to fracture. The dream is at an end. My final flowers are wilting. Soon the Traditionalists will have prevailed in even the formerly strongest nations for the cause. My bedrock, my home, my precious mother Lithuania will fight until the end, but even they will fall. Vilnius is under siege. It cannot hold out much longer now.

Sudden relocation has brought me here, to this dark room recessed in the mountains with a small group of my most loyal adherents, but even they are unaware of our location for safety's sake. Upon arrival, I had to shoot the navigators. Our position is the last hope for redemption. I, nine men, and their families–whom I insisted accompany them–resist alone in this outpost, planning and awaiting news.

I am in contact remotely with eighteen spies in Europe and fourteen spread abroad. Perhaps all hope is not yet lost. The Hausen Compact will be destroyed. It must be. I come to bring light–how dare they reject my reforms. Swift vengeance is coming. The Traditionalists cannot prevail. I shall overcome. I will sweep the world under the soles of my feet.

I am Zydrunas, and my name will echo into the ages.

Andrius let go of the sides of the book and took a sip of water, but he couldn't stop reading for long.

August 30:

One spy remains; the others are silent. Perhaps they are dead, perhaps biding their time, but my heart tells me they have failed.

Vilnius has fallen to the enemy.

August 31:

My last man in the field, the sole surviving spy, is asking to join us. He is a German of mixed descent, predominantly Latin, I think, and his name is Paul Morales. I cannot fall prey to this ruse. They have captured him and turned his loyalties.

The Hausen filth shall not learn of my location. Still, he pleads that they will find him soon, they will kill him, he must come to us. I do not believe his weeping. He is a traitor to the glorious struggle. Utopia had been within reach, and now it is lost.

Even if his desperate pleas are sincere, his death is only fitting as a sacrifice of mourning. I mourn him. They say that I do not, but I mourn him. All of them.

September 3:

I wish paper could properly contain my laughter. I am told that the victorious Neanderthals–the Hausen Confederacy and their Traditionalists–have declared me a war criminal, as if the war was already finished! They compare me with the monsters of history.

With my mirth is sadness. It is a perverse and unjust world.

September 4:

The war is over. The Hausens used spy communication to reach me. Morales has been no doubt martyred for the cause. They seek to lure me with promises of clemency, as if clemency was the thing which I sought.

I reiterated my purpose. I seek not clemency but a new world order. I seek hegemony. I seek perfection. I seek the obliteration of my detractors and those who resisted my programs of social harmony.

They speak of their God and justice, and my stomach churns with revulsion. Their small minds will never understand.

Man is god. I am preeminent among men. I will destroy them.

I cut the lines before they could infect my men with their lies. Their promises taste like gravel in my mouth.

Clemency.

September 6:

I am in agony. My soul is tortured. Greatness is a curse. Brilliance, a cruel punishment.

September 7:

They look at me. I cannot leave my quarters, but that they look *at me with their simple, ignorant eyes—and these, the best men in all the world.*

The whole earth has been infected with a disease, and I alone am the cure. My ideas would save them, but foolishness reigns, and the cause has failed. My followers look on me pleading for direction.

I am irked by their beady, prying eyes.

September 25:

Our outpost has begun to function more like a country village than a military outpost.

September 28:

How can they forget? And these, the best men in all the world. Before they were faced with the greatest war of liberation and conquest in all of man's storied history. Now, so soon after defeat, they are instead preoccupied with questions of crops and hunting and firewood collection.

The river that runs through this place is the River Styx, and I am in Hell.

October 19:

My weeks and hours of meditation and planning have come to fruition. I have declared myself, in scorn and mockery of the world's idiotic, deistic superstitions, the First Prophet, and I've declared that another Prophet will come after me. Despite their weaknesses, these last nine men follow me without question, as do their families. They have seen what I am capable of and what caliber of being I am.

The world would not have me, though I am a builder of empire. The diseased world, the soul-sick fools, have spurned my brilliance, so I will build something here instead, secluded in these remote mountains. It will be glorious, crying out to the stars and moon and sky forever–but I will not build an empire. I will build a mausoleum.

I instructed Bronislovas and Titas to begin constructing huts. Our village will be divided into three sectors: the stony area, the wooded area, and the place where we may use the clay for bricks. Stanislovas, Valdemaras, and Nojus are building roads which will head here, to the headquarters, but really, the center of birthing for this enterprise. All roads lead to me.

The vision has settled in my mind, and I am reinvigorated with terrible and tremendous purpose.

November 1:

The work is finished. I no longer concern myself with the outside world now. They are dead to me– worse, they are diseased, and their sick minds have rejected my inspiration, a thing that will surely lead to their deaths. But this is not sufficient. As Hercules visited Tartarus and pulled himself out of its grip to once more return to the living, so I will defeat the forgetfulness of this place with a living memorial, an epitaph written in blood for the ages to read and lament.

Mourning is an art ill-lost. Ancient peoples once clothed themselves in sackcloth and ashes so that the rough fibers would give them rashes to remember the pain. The Egyptians shaved their eyebrows in mourning. Viking wives would sacrifice their lives in the immolation of the mythical ship-burnings, death itself called upon to seal the bands of mourning. We, as a planet, have forgotten these pagan rites in our insipidness. We must remember the greatness of the earth's error.

The Greeks, as with many things, excelled in mourning, surpassing all others. Antigone went into exile for the sake of remembrance. Hecabe killed for the sake of her mourning. And Oediupus, when the sorrow of the world's perversity and darkness overcame him, put out his eyes. In his blindness, he saw better than all of the gods collectively. Pain was his understanding. Mortification was his salvation.

Man has always left record of his deeds. Now in words, but before writing, scars recorded the past.

Who has suffered more greatly than I? The world was offered my gifts, my brilliance, and they could not see the vision. Their blindness will not be forgotten in the Stygian fields where I am now exiled. I shall do as Oedipus would have done, had he retained the poise necessary for such a revolutionary task.

The world will remember its blindness. May the Hausens be cursed forever for their backwardness.

Tonight, my great and terrible purpose will be accomplished among my followers who have never wavered. I have one more trial through which they must pass.

Andrius closed his eyes, then opened them. His eyes burned intensely, but he had to keep reading. A brown stain was smeared across the next page in places. Andrius puzzled over it a moment, then quickly returned to the text.

November 2:

I have done it.

November 3:

I am in pain, but records must be kept. It is the compulsion of man, and in this I am no exception.

Two nights ago, I accomplished my purpose. I assembled my nine and appointed three as overseers of our new colony. One for the region of Stone, one for Wood, and one for Brick. I then collected their belongings, all reminders of the old world order, and had them lock it all away here, in the room in which I write. Then, surrounded by our idolatries, our symbols of past oppressions, I explained what we must do.

The world was blind, and so we will be a people of blindness, punishing ourselves and our children with the revoking of that precious sense as a living memorial, requiem of a dream defeated.

As the nine men watched, gathered around the fire I had laid in this dark room, I must have smiled as I held my pair of scissors for all to see. Leadership leads by example, I told them. This was for our great losses and our unforgiveable sorrows, I told them. I showed no fear as I plunged the blades into my eye, opening and closing the twin knives again and again to ensure my blindness. Titas, Nojus, and Ramunas were sick on the floor, but I commanded them to rise. I pressed against my wound and held out my scissors, vowing to keep my right eye until all had done as I, so we could be certain that each had kept his vow.

They were not as zealous as I, but to their merit, each performed the deed in turn. Then, I sent them to their wives and children to complete the sacrifice, the forgotten rites of mourning.

Six of the children died, and two of the women. In all, a good rate of success for such grisly work.

My eye pains me. I will retire and return to this book soon. I do not relish the screams that are imprinted between my ears, but neither do I spurn them. The entire world should scream in such a way. My philosophy was rejected, wars fought to suppress and contain me.

Our blindness and our children's and our children's children's blindness shall preserve this tragedy as it ought to be preserved. I will stroke the pain and stoke the bitterness. Oh, how I hate the Hausens with an inhuman rage!

My training in botany will serve us well for future generations of mourners who shall gather on days of remembrance to sing of my greatness and the folly of the world. There is a plant that grows in these hills, giant hogweed, that will provide me with a cure to the world's failings. My people shall be a nation forever in darkness; I alone preserving sight unbeknownst to them in my right eye.

"In the land of the blind, the one-eyed man is king." These words are Prophetic now, surpassing the intention of their author.

All these words I inscribe and mark upon this paper of a book that will be honored and upheld as sacred forever. A thrill runs through me at the thought. Sight shall be forgotten, and this book shall be revered eternally by a people who cannot read it–a book of emptiness from a shadowed past.

I am man. I am Zydrunas, and I will rule this people forever, a one-eyed king in the land of the blind.

Andrius blinked. The writing ceased. He flipped a page, then another, and then another, frantically now. The rest of the book was blank. He had read the final entry.

19

CLOUDS BLOCKED THE SUN. THE AIR WAS LIFELESS and cold as Andrius trudged down Stone Road in the direction of the hill where he taught his seeing lessons.

He had skipped his age-group lessons today—an unthinkable thing, but he had done it three days in a row now. No consequence had yet revealed itself. He had skipped his teaching as well, until today. He was not sure if anyone would come, but he had to try.

He took a sip of water and muttered to himself. "I wouldn't come."

He had a bad habit of talking to himself aloud.

"Wider! Wider, Tomas. That's it!"

Andrius lowered the pitcher from his lips and turned in the direction of the sound. It was Bronius, the baker, and a group of fifteen others seated in a circle on the damp ground. Their white, ghostly eyes were pried open with their hands.

"What do your eyes hear, Steponas?" Bronius demanded.

Andrius approached incredulously as Steponas smiled.

"My eyes hear the ground . . . and it is skyhigh."

"Good," Bronius nodded knowingly.

Another spoke up. "My eyes hear love in front of us. I am looking at the love . . . and its note is fuzzymum."

"Good," Bronius repeated. "Open your eyes and look at things!" he declared.

The others shouted back in unison. “Open your eyes and look at things!”

Andrius was nearly inside of their circle now, unable to speak for his disbelief.

“Good, men, good,” Bronius said, quieter. “It is only by ‘opening our eyes and looking at things’ that we may attain a new sense: the hearing of the eyes which saved our Prophet, and which our Prophet has.”

“Excuse me?” Andrius said, and sixteen pairs of ears perked up.

Tomas turned his head–the wrong way.

“The hill we meet on is farther down,” Andrius said.

It was silent. Andrius felt a knot forming in his stomach. “It’s Andrius. The Prophet’s own?”

“All of us belong to the Prophet, Andrius,” Bronius said.

“We know that your meeting is held down the road,” Tomas chimed in.

“Oh,” Andrius replied, looking down. He scratched his head, then examined the group. “Then what are you doing out here?”

“We started our own group, Andrius. Your teachings have begun to stray from the truth.”

“What do you mean? I’m the one who even told you about sight.”

Bronius held up a hand.

“Eye-hearing.”

“*Sight!*” Andrius insisted. “What do you mean I’ve ‘strayed from the truth’?”

“We liked the ‘open your eyes and look at things’ bit and the ‘get a new sense’ bit, but lately we don’t like what you’re saying, so we have our own group now.”

Andrius tried to speak, but he could only breathe faster and faster as he looked at the dead eyes around him.

"But you're blind!" he finally shouted.

Steponas raised his finger. "See? That. That is part of what we don't like. We don't need you now."

Bronius nodded solemnly. "We study the ancient art of eye-hearing on our own now. Each day we grow closer to a new sense. I am their guide."

"It's called seeing," Andrius protested. "And how can you guide them if *you're* blind?"

Bronius smiled and raised his arms haughtily.

"I have attained it. I can see."

Andrius burned with anger. He saw a rock on the ground, picked it up, and tossed it at Bronius's chest. The baker startled badly as the rock struck him, and he yelled in surprise, falling backward over his heels.

"Agh! What was that? What is happening? Help me up! Help me!"

Andrius took a step back. Each of Bronius's fifteen acolytes scrambled to their feet and hunched over with arms outstretched, grasping and groping around the field for their "guide." Mykolas found him at one point, but he first grabbed Bronius's foot instead of his hand. After harsh correction, he grabbed his hand and began pulling him up when another bumped into them, knocking the trio over and sending them tumbling down a small hill.

"You're all blind," Andrius whispered, shaking his head. "It won't work!" he shouted. "Come to my lessons. I'll tell you what I've learned."

"Snow and blizzard take your lessons," Bronius cursed. "We don't need them. Be gone from our peaceful meeting, troublemaker."

Andrius stood there a moment, then turned on his heel and walked away, onward toward his hill down the road. His stomach hurt and he felt like the most foolish person in the world, but he was also enraged.

"How could they be so . . . so stupid?" he muttered through gritted teeth. "And I taught them that. 'Open your eyes and look at things . . .' I didn't know any better, but they should."

When Andrius arrived at his teaching hill, there was a crowd, but it was much diminished. Fifty men, women, and children chatted as they sat patiently waiting for the lessons to start.

Fear began to jab at the edges of Andrius's mind. He was afraid, and he was tired of feeling nervous all the time.

He saw Milda on the edge of the crowd and unconsciously made his way toward her. He could not enjoy her beauty in that moment. He was growing more and more afraid.

"Milda?" he said.

Milda quickly rose to her feet, turning her ears and not her eyes at Andrius. "Andrius! We didn't know if you would come. Are you all right? Did the fever return?"

Andrius shook his head. "Nothing is like it seems, Milda."

Her smile turned to a frown. "What?"

Andrius mumbled softly.

"What?" Milda asked louder. "Andrius, I can't hear you when you speak so quiet."

"I said can I have a hug?"

Andrius looked up at her, breathing hard, blinking through red and swollen eyes that she could not see.

She hesitated. "A hug?"

He nodded. "I need one. Before I go talk. I'm scared."

Milda looked simply confused. She hesitated, then stiffly raised her arms. "Okay . . ."

Andrius rushed into the embrace and held her tightly. He was shaking.

"Andrius!" she chided sharply, embarrassed. "What are you doing?"

She pushed him away, and he wiped his nose, staring at the ground.

"Thank you," he said.

"What in the–? Books of Emptiness, Andrius, why are you acting so weird? Andrius?"

He pretended that he didn't hear her as he walked to the front. So much weighed on his mind that he almost didn't have to pretend.

He felt a little better when he saw Aleksandras in the front row, but seeing Petras, Tadas, and Lukas, the newly appointed Regent of Wood, worried him. All three of the Regents sat together, all in the front.

"It's probably nothing," he muttered.

Andrius looked over the greatly diminished crowd and wiped a bead of sweat from his forehead. He wasn't sure how to feel. His nerves seemed to be the only part of him paying attention.

He raised his chin, clenched his fists, and spoke.

"Hello! I'm here now."

The crowd began settling down then, amid scattered applause that was less enthusiastic than it had been previously.

"I've told you that I would keep you updated," Andrius began with a wavering voice, "on what I read in the empty books and with whatever I learned about this new sense: sight. Seeing."

He took a breath. His insides were knotted so badly that he had to hunch forward to lessen the pain.

"I've figured out how to read the big one, the Book of Emptiness. It was written by Zydrunas."

The people gasped and suddenly the hillside was alive with chatter. Andrius struggled for a full minute to get it under control, in which the pointed shushing of several crowd members aided him.

"Zydrunas could see. He wrote with the letters of seeing people, and I read it."

The crowd was excited–anxious, even. The Regents sat up straighter, and everyone inclined an ear.

"Then," Andrius said, blinking rapidly, "I found another journal. Two others that he wrote. And I was surprised." His stomach was in agony. It was like there was a tiger inside, scraping at it. His words came out soft and full of fear.

"He killed–" Andrius's words caught in his throat. He had to turn his head to the side and compose himself. Petras wore a wary look on his face as he slowly rose to his feet. Hot tears began flowing from Andrius's eyes as he continued.

"He killed people. Sometimes his friends. The first book was vague, but the others . . ." He let the sentence trail off.

Petras leaned forward. "Andrius," he hissed, but Andrius didn't hear him. It was like he was alone.

"What an honor," Andrius continued, "to read the First Prophet's words, but he says he made up the title, that there really–"

"Andrius," Petras said louder now, taking a step toward the boy who would not stop talking.

"–really is no Prophet because he made it up. And he made everybody blind–"

"Andrius," Petras said sternly. The other Regents were on their feet now. "Stop this." He turned to the crowd. "Andrius is recovering from a fever. He doesn't know what he's saying. He must return to–"

Andrius would not be silenced. He was worked up, weeping now as his voice grew louder. "I don't know why we're still blind, how that passes on, but he did it. Stabbed their eyes out–"

"Andrius, be quiet!" Petras shouted, groping until he had the boy's arm in a strong grip. He whispered in his ear. "I like you, boy, but I can't save you if you won't shut your lips. Stop this."

Andrius was too sorrowful to care. "Zydrunas maybe wasn't even a good person . . . There was this one time, after the war, when–"

"Andrius!"

Petras shook the boy.

"He had his followers lead him to a–"

"Andrius! Silence now!"

"–secret place so that–"

Whack!

Andrius reeled backward, pain exploding in his jaw. He landed face-first in the damp grass. He rolled over, terrified of the powerful, barrel-chested Regent of Stone standing over him, still clenching his fist.

"How dare you speak of the Prophet and the First Ones with accusations? You will choose to be silent or you shall be silenced!"

Aleksandras stood, stumbling forward as the crowd began murmuring and rising to leave. Andrius saw it before it happened.

"Andrius? What are you doing to my boy?"

“Papa, no!”

The Regent of Wood shoved the old man, sending him to the ground groaning. Andrius screamed.

“Take him to Gimdymo Namai,” Petras ordered the other Regents. “Take him to the Prophet and lock the doors.”

“Zydrunas might not have been who we think!” Andrius shouted. “I’ve read his books! He was more like–”

Andrius saw only darkness then, having been silenced by another blow to the head.

He came back to consciousness a few moments later, disoriented and unsure how much time had passed. He found himself being carried hand and foot by the Regents of Brick and Wood. Everything hurt, and he was frozen with terror the likes of which he had never known.

The porter at Gimdymo Namai greeted them cheerfully, then quickly shut his mouth upon hearing the Regent’s harsh tone.

“Get him upstairs,” Petras ordered the other two. He was boiling with quiet rage as he led them, feeling his way up the stairs.

Andrius noticed one of the light switches on the wall of the stairwell. He wondered bitterly if it had ever been used. He almost said something, but he thought better of it.

He had gotten off from disrupting lessons, reaching over the fence, and skipping lessons. He would not get off now, no matter how many people he’d saved.

He swallowed the lump in his throat.

“A severe peace,” he mumbled to himself.

Then the door opened and there was light once again. The windows illuminated the red and yellow rug in the center of the ornate room, the leather seats, the oak bookcase. Standing there at the far end of the chamber was Valdas, the Prophet himself.

"Has someone come to welcome me back from my journey?" the Prophet asked in his buttery, rich baritone.

"Welcome, Prophet," Petras said solemnly. "I'm afraid we have a situation."

The Regents of Wood and Brick roughly placed Andrius on his feet, but they still held onto his arms tightly as Petras whispered to Valdas.

"Ow!" Andrius gasped, looking at his throbbing arms. They were turning purple around the new Regent's grip. "That hurts," he whispered.

"Shut up," Tadas replied curtly, and tightened his grip.

Across the room, Valdas nodded and shook his fine robes out as he turned around. Andrius forgot the pain in his body. This was worse.

"Andrius," the Prophet began slowly, "what was my charge to you?"

"You told me to read the books," he returned quickly. "And I did! I figured them out, Father."

Valdas rubbed his chestnut-colored beard.

"And did I instruct you to tell the whole village what they said?"

"No, but–"

The Prophet spoke coolly, calmly. It was like being held by his words with nowhere to go.

"Andrius, Andrius," he chided. "Don't you think there might be a difference between what I know and what I relate to the village? Isn't there?"

Andrius looked down.

"But the books . . ."

"They said horrible things, I know. Petras told me. Didn't you consider that I, the Prophet, may have had some knowledge to let us judge their truth?"

Andrius hesitated. "I didn't think of that."

"They aren't true, Andrius," he said with a sigh, sitting in his luxurious chair. "Now calm down. I know you have a fiery spirit. That's good! So do I. In a way it's good to hear it in you, beneath your quietness and shy demeanor. It's going to be all right. Do you need anything?"

Andrius was very confused, but he felt the pressure on his arms relax. The Prophet's presence was warm and reassuring.

"I'd like my water back," he said meekly.

Valdas spoke to Petras. "His pitcher?"

"He was carrying this, Prophet," Petras replied, handing the wooden vessel over to Valdas, who felt its grooves with his hands.

"I keep water in it," Andrius offered, sweating and unsure how to feel. "I made it."

"It's very good," he said. "Petras, give it back to him."

With great relief, Andrius rushed over and took his pitcher and a drink. He realized suddenly how attached he was to it. He carried it with him at all times, mostly because he got thirsty, but also because he had worked hard on it, years ago.

"Now," the Prophet began gently, "can we have a reasonable discussion? Take me to the chamber and read for me, and I will tell you why what you have repeated is lies."

Andrius looked around, still breathing heavily. Everyone's eyes were closed. He was about to ask a question, when an urgent rapping at the door cut him off.

"Enter!" the Prophet ordered.

The doors swung open and an exasperated porter leaned against the jamb. "We have another one, Prophet."

"Already?" He immediately rose to his feet. "Migle just had her baby this morning."

"They will be in the birthing room. It's Zydra."

The Prophet took up his gaudy metal cane and hurried past them to the stairs. "Andrius, Regents, come with me. We will discuss this on the way."

Andrius was deep in thought. It was only the nudging of one of the Regents that reminded him to follow. He quickly caught up to the Prophet as they sped to deliver the village's newest member from the womb and from the disease.

"Father," Andrius asked earnestly. "Can I ask a question?"

"Quickly, yes."

They reached the bottom of the stairs and felt their way forward.

"Everyone is blind except me. If the books are lies, if Zydrunas never really cut out people's eyes, why can't we all see?"

They were in the room now. A brunette, short-legged woman lay out on the table screaming and breathing rapidly. The Prophet felt his way to her. Solveiga was already in position. They had done this for every child born since the last Prophet's death.

"Hello, Zydra," the Prophet said in an urgent but mollifying tone. "I'm going to get you through this. Now you need to push, Zydra. You need to keep pushing."

She grimaced as she struggled to breathe deeply.

"Andrius, it's simple," the Prophet projected over the

noise. "There was an old man in the village named Kazimieras. You are too young to remember. He was deaf. He couldn't hear at all; it was tragic. Push, Zydra, push! You can do it!"

He began getting his hands in position. She was screaming with greater frequency now.

"He had a son," the Prophet continued, "named Daumantas. Do you know him?"

Andrius nodded. "Yes."

Zydra was really screaming now. Andrius couldn't help watching. It was a bizarre sight, but the Prophet kept talking.

"Daumantas can hear, can't he? That sort of thing does not pass on from father to son. Here he comes!" Valdas declared, and Andrius watched transfixed as a blood-covered infant came forth. But his mind was in another place, considering what the Prophet was saying.

"Daumantas can hear . . ." he muttered to himself.

The birthing was not yet over, and Solveiga wasted no time. She tied off the cord, and Valdas hurried the newborn child to the anointing table.

Andrius was deep in thought. "Father! How is everyone blind then?"

"The disease," the Prophet said in a low voice as he readied for the ceremonial ewer, the pitcher filled with thick, black liquid. The cure. "The disease enters through the eyes. You must have received the cure first," he said as he steadied the crying baby with one hand while he held the cure with the other. Solveiga pried the infant's eyes open as he kicked and screamed, tossing violently.

Behind them the mother was moaning loudly.

It all made sense what they were saying, but something still unsettled Andrius. A sick, wrong feeling pervaded him, and then he got a glimpse of the newborn baby's eyes.

They were blue, and they were open. They were eyes like his.

"Zydrunas was a botanist, originally," Valdas said as the viscous cure began to drip out of the pitcher and onto the child's eyes. "He discovered the cure using cartwheel flower–or the ancients used to call it 'giant hogweed.' Isn't that a trite name?" He smiled as more of the goop fell on the child's screaming face. As he began rubbing the substance into his eyes, Andrius's heart rose up inside of him all at once.

"No!" he screamed. He lunged forward, knocking the Regent of Wood in the chest with his water, scrambling toward the anointing of the cure. "Stop that! That's what makes us blind! The cure's not a cure!" He bumped into a tray of tools, sending them all clattering to the ground. "The cure's not a cure!"

He reached out a hand to take the child, but his momentum came to a sudden halt as Petras's formidable hands came crashing down onto his shoulders. Andrius strained, but he could not reach. He was hysterical.

"Zydrunas poisoned us! The cure is poison! The disease is made up! The cure is the disease! Stop it! His eyes are different–stop it!"

He hit the ground then, still clutching his pitcher. Water sloshed over his face and he gasped. A large hand clamped over his mouth, and blinking away the water, he saw the

Prophet angry for the first time in his life.

"First you question Zydrunas, and now you would let the infants die to satisfy your childish theories? Stupid boy! You putrescent, stupid boy, be silent!"

Andrius bit the hand over his mouth, and the man howled, pulling it away.

"The baby has eyes like me!" he protested, trying to scramble to his feet. "Eyes like Daniel had! We have to find him! He'll have the answers–I don't think he's crazy. We just need to find him and–"

"We killed him, Andrius!" the Prophet shouted.

The commotion of the room came to an instantaneous halt. Zydra sat up on the table.

Valdas continued in a quieter voice, but just as enraged. "He was a threat to the village, claiming to be from beyond. He made no sense, Andrius. Would you have had others clambering after him into the Regions of Death? I had him killed for everyone's good. A severe peace must be kept severely."

Andrius's heart sank. He couldn't believe it.

"I have been lenient with you," the Prophet said indictingly. "But you go too far, boy."

"Should I take him around back, Valdas?" Petras asked.

"No!" Andrius shouted. "That's where you took Herkus to kill him. No! Please! I want to help! Please, no!"

He kicked and thrashed, but he was held fast.

"Silence!" the Prophet thundered, and everyone, even Andrius, obeyed. "Throw him in the basement to calm down. Lock him in."

Andrius wanted to continue shouting, but he was afraid. He might already have gotten himself killed.

"We are having a gathering," the Prophet said to the Regent of Brick. "Tonight. Call the whole village to Stone Gathering. These lies must be corrected and the truth of Zydrunas reaffirmed."

The Regent dipped his head. "Yes, Prophet."

"Pick him up," the Prophet ordered. "I don't want to hear this boy until tomorrow. Don't give him food. Don't give him furs or blankets. Let him sit in the cold and think on his foolishness."

Andrius shook badly as he struggled to stand. They half led, half dragged him out of the birthing room.

Upon reaching the hall, what he saw stole the breath from his lungs and he stumbled, held up only by the strong arms that caught him and continued ushering him toward his cell.

Zydra was holding her new baby, who cried fiercely. When he opened his eyes, they were gray and clouded. The blue was gone. The baby would be blind.

ANDRIUS HIT THE FLOOR HARD, A SENSATION WITH which he was far too familiar. The doors slammed shut and he heard the lock turn. Footsteps echoed from the stairs, growing fainter and fainter. He lay there a long time, thinking, dreading, worrying.

His shaking hands reached into his pocket and retrieved a small piece of metal.

"You gave me a key, remember?" he said aloud, shaking his head. He didn't use it, however. He didn't know what he would do if he left. Andrius slipped the key back into his pocket and sat up, wiping his eyes.

"Everything's a lie," he said softly, holding his head in his hands. "Everything I've ever been taught . . ." He paused. It was too difficult to think about. "I'm the only one . . . I'm the only one who can tell them, and I'm only twelve years old. No one even likes me. And I'm scared! Blizzards and snow, I'm so afraid." He pulled his knees into his chest and breathed harshly. "Why wasn't someone else born with sight? Someone convincing!" He slammed his hand onto the stone floor, immediately regretting the outburst. His hand stung all over. He blew on it and shook it out, but it still stung.

Devoid of hope, Andrius let himself fall to the side, laying his ear on the cold, hard ground. He clenched his eyes shut, blocking out the artificial light coming from the holes in the ceiling. The generator hummed monotonously as he lay there for a long time, his body tense with despair.

When he opened his eyes, he saw something that made him sit up and crawl forward. Previously he would have called it fuzzymum, but now he knew it was orange. Daniel's backpack poked out from behind a shelf.

Andrius had never opened it, out of respect, but now he knew that Daniel was dead. It seemed like the right time. Something told him to stop crawling, to turn off the lights and weep, but he kept moving until the backpack was in his hands. A strange numbness covered his pain. An insatiable curiosity overtook him. He had to know what was inside.

"He wasn't born in the village," Andrius told himself. "There is no disease. He came from somewhere else."

Andrius had never seen a pack like this one. Metal teeth clenched to hold it shut, but after some trial and error, he got the largest section open.

He drew his head back sharply at the odor. It smelled like sweat and a piece of rotten fruit.

Bravely turning back to the bag, he picked out unfamiliar garments and tossed them to the side after a short examination. Digging deeper, he found a cylindrical piece of metal with writing on it. He held it up and sounded out the words.

"Pro . . . pane gas tank. Portable stove loader."

There was a lot more writing, but it didn't make much sense. Andrius set it to the side.

The bag was full of strange and useless items: a three-pronged piece of metal, a pink rectangle with liquid inside, a tube with clear glass on one end . . . But it was at the very bottom of the bag that Andrius found something to give him pause.

It was clothing–blue, plain clothes–but there was a card attached at the chest with a small image of Daniel's head, and it had writing on it. It said:

Daniel Petrov, Asst. Surgeon. ID# 548195
Markov Eye Institute

Andrius read it six times. It said "eye." He excitedly turned the clothes over and inside out, and then as he shook them, a piece of paper fell to the floor.

Andrius gasped. It was like no paper he had ever seen, in the first place. The illustration could have come out of the Michelangelo book, it was so beautiful and clear, though he did not recognize what it was a picture of. It was the words on the front that took his breath away.

Markov Eye Institute: Giving sight to the blind
for over forty years.

The paper was folded perfectly in thirds over itself, each fold like a new page. Andrius forgot all of his pain and fear as he opened the colorful paper with eyes wide.

There were pictures of people, blind people, and then pictures of other people in white coats putting the blind people next to machines, then a dark room with bright lights on a blind woman's eye as the people in white coats stood over her, working. The last picture filled Andrius with indescribable joy.

The blind people were in the last picture, smiling, and their eyes had color. They could see again. They were fixed.

Andrius turned the paper over and over in his hands, reading it again and again to make sure that he had gotten it right. Some of the wording was confusing, but the meaning was clear. Somewhere, beyond the barrier, out in the Regions of Death, there were not only other people, but there was a place where the blind could receive sight. There was a place for them to be healed.

Andrius felt dizzy. It was almost too much to take in. This changed everything.

He stood suddenly, nearly tripping. "The gathering! The whole village will be there!"

Fear seized him, then, but with great determination he shoved the paper in his pocket and removed the key.

"They have to know," he said to himself. "Don't be a coward, Andrius! Be brave one more time. They'll be so happy!" He smiled. He could just see the village bursting into applause at his announcement. This was world-altering, life-changing.

With a deep breath, Andrius turned his key and hugged his pitcher against his chest. The door opened, and then he ran. He ran as hard as he could.

His laughter rode on the wind's hopeful wings.

The sun sang only faintly now, and soon it would be silent. Andrius didn't care. He had a song in his heart.

"I WISH THE ENLIGHTENMENT OF ZYDRUNAS UPON YOU all," the Prophet declared to the crowd.

"Gladly do we receive it and live it with our lives," they replied in unison. The whole village was there. Stone Gathering was built to accommodate many people, but the entire village numbered almost a thousand. A full third of the attendees stood for lack of places to sit.

They had not bothered with a fire. The moon hid its face. Andrius followed the sounds of speech instead of his eyes.

“We have passed yet another winter,” the Prophet continued. “Through hard work and community spirit, only a few have passed on, and many survived and thrive.”

They broke into enthusiastic applause.

“I have called this meeting,” Valdas declared, “to reaffirm our basic tenets of life and history. Some ill-gotten rumors are about, and it breaks my heart to hear ignorance turn into accidental slander. So we return to the truth and repeat it!”

More applause. Valdas was well loved. Andrius stuck to the outside edges of the group, but he was almost to the front now. The Prophet’s speech was disarming and convincing as always.

“There has never been a man like Zydrunas. A man of science, first, he studied the ways of nature and mastered them. A thinking man, he studied philosophy and mastered it. He was not a violent man, offering freely his gifts of peace and progress to the world, but the small-minded, the backward, and the ignorant banded together to make war on him. This led to the conflict that ended the old world, the Hausen War, and it created the disease that spread to all humanity, leaving us alone to carry on.”

“It’s not true!”

The Prophet closed his mouth. The people murmured amongst themselves. No one would dare interrupt the Prophet, but that was precisely what Andrius had done. He was too excited to contain himself.

It was with a tremendous smile that Andrius joined Valdas at the head of the amphitheater. The Prophet did not seem amused.

“Who speaks when the Prophet teaches?”

Andrius’s stomach tied in a knot. He realized the stupidity of his impatience all at once, as well as its danger.

“I spoke, Father. It’s Andrius. I meant to think it, but I said it instead.”

“Shouted it, more accurately,” Tadas interjected.

Valdas chuckled, but there was no love in the sound. He was displeased. "Andrius, you make me sound like a liar. That cannot be what you meant."

"No," Andrius replied, releasing much of the built-up tension as a thousand people listened intently. "But what I said is true. There is no disease."

"What?"

"There's no disease!" Andrius shouted gleefully.

It was sonic pandemonium. Valdas let the crowd holler and murmur and bicker and shout for an entire minute before he hushed them with a word. Their silence was immediate.

Andrius looked all around. It was pitch-black out. He could hardly see a thing.

"Do you want to do this here?" Valdas said to Andrius. "You force my hand. I am increasingly less amused by your antics." He raised his hands and his voice. "Andrius has made a wild claim, my people! Shall we examine it?"

The crowd roared that they should.

"It is a wild claim," the Prophet repeated, then slyly added, "but the truth always comes out, doesn't it?" The Prophet tapped his cane and took a step toward Andrius.

"So tell me, Andrius. Why is the disease, that horrible malady which wiped out mankind, not real?"

"Because it isn't. There are people out there. Humanity lives beyond the barrier in the Regions of Death."

"*Living* in the Regions of *Death* seems to be an oxymoron, child."

The crowd was riveted. No one knew what was happening. No one had ever heard anyone question the Prophet before.

"But it isn't. Maybe they don't call it the Regions of Death."

"But we do," Valdas cut in. "And it has been known by this name for a hundred years. So tell me, Andrius. Were your elders wrong for a hundred years?"

The knot in Andrius's stomach came back. His voice faltered.

"Well, no. I don't know. But I found a cure. That's why I came here tonight, to tell you I found a cure!"

Valdas laughed. His hand groped in the darkness for Andrius's face and he shook his chin. "We already have a cure."

"Our cure makes people blind! Otherwise they would see, I think. Zydrunas taught us to poison ourselves, but there's–"

"Easy," Valdas interrupted. "When you speak of the First Prophet, do so with reverence."

The knot in Andrius's stomach twisted harder, making him stumble backward, but he gathered the strength to reply.

"There is a real cure. A place called 'Markov' where they fix people's eyes. I've seen pictures."

"Pictures?" Valdas interrupted.

"Yes!" Andrius replied excitedly. "Yes, they're – well, they're like carvings for your eyes, or a window to someplace you're not. But in a book."

"A window to someplace you're not," the Prophet repeated skeptically.

Andrius was frustrated with himself.

"It's hard to describe. You just need to be able to see to understand, but that's my point! We have to go down the mountain and find this 'Markov' and the people who can give sight to the blind. We can cross the barrier tonight and try to find them. We have to!"

"The penalty for crossing the barrier is death, Andrius. You know this."

"Yes, but that's because we made the rule! We have to cross over and go down the mountain. It's the only way you'll ever see. If you want the extra sense that I have, we have to go!"

"Andrius," the Prophet sighed. "I didn't want to do this to you. None of us did."

Andrius waited, suddenly afraid.

"We would have preferred to let you go on with your delusion and keep living life, but this is becoming reckless."

"Delusion?" Andrius whispered.

The Prophet chuckled, as he often did. The sound repulsed Andrius, and being repulsed at the Prophet tightened the knot inside even more.

"We've indulged you, Andrius, but everyone knows your extra sense isn't real."

It was like being hit in the head. Andrius's mind reeled.

"What do you mean?"

"'Colors,' 'sight,' the 'sun singing.' We all know it is made up, Andrius. I mean, really. It's all in your mind."

"It is not!" he screamed. The crowd gasped at his defiance.

The Prophet sighed. "What evidence do you have, Andrius?"

Andrius opened his mouth and closed it. He was having trouble thinking straight. "I'm the best at the rock game."

"You have excellent hearing, but that is not another sense."

"I see colors!" Andrius exclaimed.

"Ah, yes. Colors. Tell me, what color is my robe?"

Andrius squinted in the darkness. "I can't tell."

"You can't tell?" the Prophet returned, a hint of mockery now in his voice.

"It doesn't work at night."

"It doesn't work at night? Well, that's suspicious."

"The sun has to be singing, shining, for it to work. Or sometimes, close to a fire—"

"Andrius, Andrius, Andrius," the Prophet interrupted. "Do you hear how ridiculous you sound?"

Only the crickets chirping filled the silent void. Andrius was beginning to doubt it himself.

"What do you 'see' right now, Andrius? Anything? Or do you lack the energy to invent abstract projections?"

Andrius hunched over. His stomach ached worse than it ever had before, and he was beginning to panic. Nothing was clear on this black night.

"I don't know, I–" He stopped, having looked up. A rare wave of peace washed over him. "I see the stars!" he cried out.

"Andrius, you try our patience. What in the world are 'stars'?"

"You've never seen them," he explained, "but they are beautiful. Like guardians in the night, they watch over us from above. Someone named God put them there, I think. They sing too, like the sun, but softly so we can sleep. I wish you could see them. Oh, hail and snow, I wish you could." The panic was returning now as Andrius's words grew solemn. "That's why we have to go over the barricade and down the mountain. Only then can you have your eyes opened. We have to go into the Regions of Death, where Daniel came from."

"Daniel came from this village, Andrius." The Prophet's voice was calm, condescending. "He was insane. The Regents and I interviewed him. He was born here and he'd been living in the meadow close by. His insanity must be catching."

"But–"

"And 'stars,' please. I find it very convenient that the only thing you can see is something none of us has ever heard of before. Your game is over, and it has become disrespectful. I am ending it now."

Andrius was about to reply when the crowd started to applaud, chant, and whistle. He heard nasty things shouted about him.

Several people were yelling, "Kill him! Kill the liar!" But suddenly a voice rose above the crowd in a shrill, piercing tone that could only belong to one person.

Daiva.

"My husband is gone! He left this sacred gathering! Go after him and punish him!"

"Silence!" Valdas spoke over the crowd. He tapped his way to where Daiva was. "Who has left? Why?"

"It's Andrius." Daiva spat the words. "He always manipulated my husband, Aleksandras. He said that we should leave and do what Andrius was saying. I thought he was joking, but he's gone. I don't know how long since he's left, but he'll be heading for the barricade."

"After him!" Valdas shouted.

Andrius took a step back, but he bumped into the new Regent of Wood.

"Andrius?" he asked, grabbing him. "I think I have Andrius!"

"Bring him," the Prophet ordered. "My people, stay here until we have left. I will restore order to this peaceful village. It is all of humanity that still remains on this earth, and it will be civil and orderly. Regents! Petras! Tadas! Lukas! Daumantas! Bronius! Stephinius! Jonas! Gvidas! Darijus! Come with me. He'll have crossed the road. Do not let him escape!"

"Leave him alone!" Andrius cried as he was lifted off of his feet and thrown over the Regent's shoulder. He couldn't imagine his father doing such a reckless, brave thing. It was wonderful, but he would need Andrius to guide him, and if the Prophet found him, he would face severe judgment. Andrius's stomach twisted with fear.

Maybe he would only lose his ears and his hands.

"He has to escape," Andrius whispered to himself as they moved. "He has to."

"Quiet up there!" Lukas barked as they moved into the meadow's tall grasses. "We're listening for his trail."

"Faster!" Petras shouted, and they redoubled their pace, sending Andrius bouncing up and down on the Regent of Wood's shoulder.

Then, after they had traversed most of the distance to the barricade, and Andrius had just begun to hope that they would not find his father, the moon finally showed its face over the rim of the crown of mountains surrounding them, and Andrius could see dimly in its lullaby.

He had to stop himself from gasping. He saw his father right in front of them, holding very still and trembling, laying on just the other side of the barricade. He looked terrified, but he was silent.

The Prophet reached out his hand and grasped the wooden rail. He now knew that they had reached the edge.

"Aleksandras . . ." the Prophet chided. "Are you near, my child? Faithful servant of the village, come out and speak with me, your Prophet."

Andrius had to bite his tongue. Aleksandras was shifting his position, and the grass rustled as he moved ever so slightly. Andrius turned his head to look at Tadas, the Regent of Brick. He carried a melon-sized stone in his hand.

The Prophet continued following along the railing.

"Aleksandras, come now. Tell us where you are so we can discuss this. 'Seeing' isn't real. You know this. Why should you go to the Regions of Death to die? Stay here."

"I hear something," the Regent carrying Andrius declared. "He's here. He is close to us."

"Aleksandras," the Prophet cooed. "Reveal yourself. Speak up." The Prophet turned around and was now drawing closer and closer to the old man, who seemed to debate with himself.

"Don't do it, Papa," Andrius pleaded in a whisper. "Don't tell them where you are."

"Aleksandras, do you think I do not know where you are hiding? I am your Prophet. I know all things. You have always been an honorable man, so I'm giving you a chance to speak up for yourself. It's only fair."

The Prophet was almost on top of Aleksandras now. Andrius closed his eyes. He couldn't watch.

"Your boy doesn't know anything, Aleksandras. Come out and we will forgive this."

"My boy is special."

Andrius's eyes flew open wide. "No!"

The Prophet grinned wickedly. The old man rose to his feet and backed away, but the Regents were too fast. He was nearly beyond their grip when Tadas stretched over the barrier and snagged the old man by the collar.

"No!" Andrius shouted again, beating on Lukas's back. "Run, Papa! Get out of here! Run!"

It was to no avail. The Regent jerked him back to the fence, and the old man did not possess the strength to resist him. He only had the power to speak in a quivering voice.

"My boy is not ignorant. He is special. He was sent to us by that thing that woman dreamed of so many years ago. If he says the way is across the ancient barrier, then that's where I'd like to go. Oof!"

He moaned as they threw him to the ground, now on the proper side of the railings. His hands were quickly bound.

"Leave him alone!" Andrius yelled. "That's my Papa! That's my Papa! Stop it!"

No one was listening.

"Aleksandras," the Prophet softly intoned. "A severe peace must be kept severely. What if others followed you?"

"I am an old man," he replied. "Let me go and find out if Andrius is right, if there are other humans, if my eyes can be healed. And if I am wrong, what is it that I die?"

"What is it that you die indeed. Regents, men. Stone him."

A look of surprise came over Aleksandras's innocent face, and Andrius watched in horror under the moonlight. Tadas raised his stone and brought it down hard on Aleksandras's neck. Petras followed with a blow to the chest, crashing down with a massive rock each time. Andrius shrieked and screamed, but the world was deaf as well as blind.

Aleksandras took blow after blow until finally a stone came down upon his head and his body went limp. They continued to strike him several times more.

"Papa!"

Andrius grabbed his captor's ear and bit down hard. Lukas cried out and threw Andrius to the ground. He rolled away as the Regent reached to grab for him again.

"What's going on?" Petras demanded.

"The boy bit me. He ran into the wind."

"Get him!" Petras ordered, and they stumbled into the wind, pursuing nothing, for Andrius waited for them to pass, weeping silent, hot tears. When the sounds of their steps faded, he crawled back toward Aleksandras, his father.

"Papa?" he asked softly, gently nudging the broken man. "Papa, are you alive?"

The old man's hand began to shake, then it went to Andrius's knee.

"Andrius," he whispered, hiding the pain as best as he was able. A great smile spread across his lips. "Is that you?"

"Yes, Papa, it's me. We have to go. Can you walk, Papa?"

Aleksandras was covered in blood. Andrius had heard his bones breaking. He knew the answer, knew that his father was dying, but he had to hope.

Aleksandras ignored his question. "I almost had it, Andrius. I believe in you. I want to go down the mountain to Markov. Sometimes—" A strange, hollow rattle choked his lungs before he spoke again. "Sometimes I almost felt like I could see."

Andrius bit his lip, reaching forward to stroke the old man's bloodstained hair. "Papa, that's impossible."

"I know. But I feel like the trees were there," he pointed, "that my blood was red, that the moon—" He raised a shaking finger toward the sky, in the direction of the moon. "That the moon was right there."

Andrius shook his head. "Don't go. Don't leave me, Papa."

"I love you, Andrius," he whispered, now moaning softly.

"Papa, no. Stay here."

"Remember the . . . what was it? The yellow butterfly." The broken old man flashed a bittersweet smile. "The yellow butterfly was mine. I can see one now. Hundreds of them, coming for me—oh!" He started to try to sit up.

"Papa, no!"

"Oh . . ." Aleksandras said. "Is this . . . I see a—I think the sun is singing, Andrius."

He fell back down hard. Andrius tried to soften his fall, but he was fading fast.

"I think the sun sings for me."

"Papa," Andrius said sternly, getting to his feet. "We have to go now. Right now."

"Hello, yellow butterfly. You are unimaginably beautiful."

Then a large stone smashed into Aleksandras's face, and he was dead.

"No!" Andrius screamed. "Why did you do that?"

The Regents and the Prophet's men had returned without him noticing. Petras had delivered the final blow.

"Why did you do that?" Andrius shrieked again.

"Hold him down," the Prophet calmly ordered.

"No! Let me go! Stop it! No!"

Andrius was wrestled to the ground easily, being so much smaller and so greatly outnumbered. Each limb was pinned down, and his protests were of no consequence. He could hardly breathe; he could hardly think. He lay beside Aleksandras, now dead.

The Prophet came and stood over Andrius, blocking out the moon.

"Let me explain a few things to you, Andrius," he said in his rich, alluring voice. Andrius hated the sound. "You need your commitment to be renewed. You've lost your way." The Prophet held out a hand to one of his men. "Give it to me."

"What is that?" Andrius demanded. "What are you doing?"

"When young men want to renew their dedication to Zydrunas, they go into the field."

Andrius suddenly knew what was in the Prophet's hand. Fear gripped him as he tried to twist away, but thick hands held his head, then his eyes, and the Prophet's hand came closer.

"They gather some of this, Andrius. cartwheel flower. And they crush it up."

"No." Andrius was weeping. It seemed as though he had cried all of his tears, and yet he found more. "No, please. Anything but that."

The Prophet raised his voice.

"And they rub it in their eyes, Andrius! They do it to remember the disease and Zydrunas and their village, which is the whole world. So you will remember too."

"I never had the cure," Andrius protested. "I don't need it. It's why I can see! My mother Janina ran when I–"

The Prophet's lips came to Andrius's ear without warning, whispering harshly.

"I know about Janina, boy. I'm the one who impregnated her. Why do you think you haven't been killed yet? Several times you should be dead. You should have been dead by the time you were seven, but of all the women I've planted my seed in, only Janina gave me a son. And you will learn to follow the village's way. I will *make* you. That old man was not your father."

He drew back and spat to the side. Then, to Andrius's horror, he brought the fistful of crushed cartwheel flower to his face and began rubbing the toxic substance into Andrius's eyes.

"I am," Valdas declared.

Andrius screamed. His eyes burned, his heart pounded, and the last vestige of hope in him died as panic took him under the cold, dark sky to perish.

21

ANDRIUS BEGAN THE DAY LIKE HE BEGAN EVERY DAY. He opened his eyes. The habit had stayed with him, though it was now a useless gesture. The sun sang, but he could not hear it. He was blind like the rest of the village.

It had been almost a year since the cartwheel flower was forced on him, and Andrius had hardly spoken a word. He felt around haltingly on his bed of straw until he touched his cane, then his pitcher of water, which he was never without. He was no longer allowed to live in Gimdymo Namai, but he had to find his way there every day. It was harder without being able to see the road.

Andrius sighed and got out of his barnyard bed, feeling his way to the shack where Daiva had already eaten all of the breakfast food. The door still squeaked, the chickens still laid, and Daiva still hated him with an intensity he'd never understood.

Valdas welcomed him warmly as he entered Gimdymo Namai. Andrius remained silent. A woman shrieked, there was much commotion, and Andrius was numb, only performing the duties that had been forced upon him.

Whenever a baby was delivered, he was set on the table and Andrius poured the cure over its eyes.

He felt nothing. Neither joy nor pain, mirth nor regret. He felt nothing. Day after day the Prophet preached Zydrunas's philosophy to Andrius and made him work in the birthing room.

There were always a lot of babies born this time of year.

His stomach turned a little every time he picked up the ceremonial ewer and poured it over a child's face, but this was the closest thing to emotion that he felt.

Breathing was an inconvenience, eating, a necessary evil. Sleep was his only comfort. Every day in the blackness that surrounded him always, he groped his way home through the cold.

"This is your life now," the Prophet told him. "Do it well, and who knows? You may be Prophet yourself one day."

Valdas's disposition toward Andrius had improved significantly. He was the only one who would willingly speak to Andrius for some months, but that was starting to change little by little.

Still, Andrius held his tongue. He had nothing to say.

THE DAY BEGAN AND ANDRIUS REMEMBERED NOT TO open his eyes. It was meaningless now. For the first time he remembered early enough to forsake his longtime reflex.

His chores finished, he managed to forage a bowl of swelled grain from the kitchen. Daiva thundered in, shaking the house as he tried to eat in peace.

"It was just like Aleksandras to leave me alone like this," Daiva complained. "And they still haven't matched me with another husband? It's unbelievable!" She belched, and the smell offended Andrius's nostrils. He rose and opened the squeaky door to leave.

"Andrius, is that you?" Daiva asked suddenly. "Don't forget your cane."

It was already in his hand. He never forgot it these days. Andrius took a long drink of water from his pitcher and then he began tapping his cane back and forth, back and forth, occasionally colliding with a roadstone so he knew how far he had gone.

The porter at Gimdymo Namai let him in without questioning. He knew Andrius's footstep now, as well as what time he arrived each day.

The days ran together for Andrius. Standing beside his table in the birthing room, it was as if the morning had never happened at all.

Valdas greeted him cheerfully. A screaming woman was carried in, and Valdas encouraged her to push. He and Solveiga still delivered every child, and Andrius poured the cure over the new villagers for Valdas and Solveiga to rub into their new eyes.

Andrius's eyes itched today. It was a strange and unpleasant sensation. He felt the breeze coming into the room. The shutters must have been opened. He heard the sounds of a mother giving birth, but he never paid attention to that. But his eyes really itched.

He set down his water to scratch them, but it didn't help. It was like they itched inside, but that would hurt too much to scratch. It was aggravating.

"He's out!" Valdas declared. "Solveiga, tie him off. He's wonderful. Quickly now, get him to Andrius."

Andrius heard them move the child to his table. He reached for the ewer that held the cure, but his eyes itched fiercely. He rubbed at them vigorously.

"Andrius, we have no time to lose. The disease enters through the eyes. You know this."

He had to move, but his eyes seized in horrible itchiness once again as he reached for the ewer. Finally, intent on scratching them directly, he opened his eyes.

And he saw.

It wasn't like he used to see. It was like the first lilt of the sun on a cloudy morning, though it was full day. But he saw dim shapes, outlines, shafts of light.

And then, a tiny yellow butterfly flapped by, floating on the breeze.

"Andrius," the Prophet warned. "What are you doing? We only have so much time."

He looked around. His eyes hurt, and everything was dim and fuzzy.

"Now!"

He automatically went to reach for the cure, stored in the ceremonial ewer. But something stopped him once more.

His pitcher sat next to the ewer. They were the same size, almost the same shape.

"Andrius! Do you want this child to die?"

"Sorry."

Andrius grabbed the container and held it high, and then, with his heart beating fast, he poured out the contents like he had done so many times before.

The Prophet sighed with relief as he began rubbing the cure into the baby's eyes.

"Thank goodness. You took a while, Andrius."

"I apologize," he said numbly.

The Prophet continued to massage the substance into the child's eyes as it screamed.

"You've really come along, my son. Your fever made you act unruly and strange last winter, but now . . . now you have an important role and you are dedicated to it."

The liquid made a squishing noise as he worked it into the baby's eyes. Andrius hated the sound.

“I’m glad that you’ve fallen in line,” the Prophet said. Pride was evident in his voice. The liquid continued squishing until he was done, and Andrius stood silently.

“Here you go,” Valdas declared as he handed the baby back to its mother. “The philosophy and science of Zydrunas has saved your child.”

“Thank you,” the mother returned as she cradled her newborn son. She kissed him again and again.

“I could do this every time,” Andrius said.

“What?” Valdas perked his ears up. “What do you mean?”

The impossible happened then. Andrius smiled.

“Nothing. I have a bad habit of talking to myself.”

Andrius set his pitcher of water back on the counter next to the cure.

ACKNOWLEDGMENTS

IT TOOK ME A LONG TIME TO WRITE THIS BOOK. I didn't feel worthy of it, some of the time. Finding the right tone took a while as well, but the picture of what it was supposed to be was always clear: It's a story of hope in a dark place. A story that deals with the painful reality of what a breakthrough costs. It's a story that I've always wanted to tell, and I have many people to thank for their encouragement and help along the way.

First, I have to thank my beautiful wife Rita, who always saw the value of this particular book and encouraged me to finish it well. Rita, I'm thankful for your grace, your insight, your humility, and your love.

Thank you to Bill Farrell, a wonderful writer and a mentor to me. If not for you, this book wouldn't have seen the light of day—at least not for a long time. Thank you for your friendship, your advice, and for talking me down when the pressures of writing seem overwhelming. You and Pam have been such a blessing to my family.

Kevin Miller—you already know. Among the very long list of things I have to thank you for, thanks for being one of the first to read this book, and for keeping the secret before it got signed.

David and Mark Hoffman, thank you for your wisdom, for believing in this work I have to do, and for giving me a platform to experiment and hone my skills.

Mike Van Meter, thank you for being an advocate. And, you know, for officiating my wedding.

Mom, Dad, Jeff, Emily, Trevor, and all the little guys—thank you for your prayers and support. Dad, you once told me that "Everything has a cost in life, and it gets more expensive as you get older. If there's something you really need to do in your life, start it now." It's why I became a writer right out of school. I can't thank you enough.

Zac Hays, Chris Alley, and Isaiah Leper—you guys need to write a book so we can call ourselves the Inklings. Thankful for your friendship and regular times of musing, praying, and hearing each other out.

Rita and Robert Cartwright, Monica Hunter, Maggy Wong, Jim Cantos, Mark Thomas, Dan and Michele Franklin, Ben and Alyssa Gordon, and Micah Scott—you know.

Thanks to Kristen Fogle and everyone at San Diego Writers, Ink for giving me a place to teach and share excitement about writing.

Thanks to David Esselstrom, Ph.D., Professor Emeritus of English at a university I didn't even attend—your experience and insight have been invaluable to me. Every time we talk and debate, I spend a long time mulling over what you've said. You've helped me see the *ars gratia Deus* inside of *ars gratia artis*.

I have a great debt of gratitude to someone named Tommy Edison who posted a long series of videos online about what it's like to live everyday life as someone blind from birth ("The Tommy Edison Experience" on YouTube).

I'm grateful to the mentors I've never met: David Mamet, Aaron Sorkin, Michell Ivers, Donald Maass, William Goldman, and others who have been munificent enough to share their thoughts and experiences with crafting the written word.

Thanks to USC—fight on.

Thanks to Foothills—fight on.

And thanks to my late grandpa Earl, who taught me to write.

Steve, you're an awesome agent and I'm glad to be in business with you. Thanks for all of your hard work on this.

And finally, I would be remiss if I did not thank the God who put the stars in the night sky and gave me eyes to see them.

— W. A.